THE DRINKER

HANS FALLADA

THE DRINKER

TRANSLATED BY
Charlotte and A. L. Lloyd

INTRODUCTION BY
John Willett

THE MARLBORO PRESS

Originally published in German as
Der Trinker
© Rowohlt Verlag, Hamburg, 1950

This translation first published by Putnam & Co., 1952

This new edition first published by The Marlboro Press, 1990
by arrangement with Libris, London

Introduction © John Willett, 1990

Translation © The Marlboro Press, 1990

The publication of the present volume is made possible by
a grant from the National Endowment for the Arts

Manufactured in the United States of America

Library of Congress Catalog Card Number 89-63598

ISBN 0-910395-56-X

The Marlboro Press
Marlboro, Vermont

CONTENTS

IN 'The Goose Girl', subject of one of George Cruikshank's most charming illustrations, the brothers Grimm tell the story of a lovely young princess riding with her personal maid to the city where she is to marry a royal prince. The maid threatens to kill her, usurps her clothes and her horse 'Falada', and successfully impersonates her in the royal apartments; the princess is sent off with the boy Curdken to mind the royal geese. Frightened that the horse may tell what has happened, the imposter has it beheaded. But 'when the true princess heard of it she wept',

> and begged the man to nail up Falada's head against a large dark gate in the city through which she had to pass every morning and evening, that she might still see him sometimes. Then the slaughterer said he would do as she wished, cut off the head, and nailed it fast under the dark gate.

Each time she goes through the gate, the princess holds brief but significant conversations with the truncated head. These come to the ears of the old king, who arranges a banquet at which both girls are present and the maid is trapped into condemning herself to

> nothing better than that she should be thrown into a cask stuck round with sharp nails, and that two white horses should be put to it, and should drag it from street to street till she is dead.

This, the reader infers, is arranged and a satisfactory royal wedding then takes place, after which the happy couple rule 'in peace and happiness all their lives'.

It was from this characteristically bloody and imaginative 'German Popular Story' that the author of *The Drinker* took his lifelong pseudonym, marking it as his own by inserting a second 'l' and wryly adopting the forename of that other Grimm unfortunate, the simpleton who is swindled again and again and convinces himself each time that he is 'Hans in Luck'. But the name Fallada also recalls a poem by a slightly younger writer from the opposite end of Germany, Bertolt Brecht. For he too made use of it just after the First World War for his description of a dying carthorse whose still live body is carved up by hungry Berliners, naming his powerful poem 'Falada, Falada, there thou art hanging'. Twelve years later, at another moment of desperate crisis in Germany, when the Weimar Republic was about to fall into the lap of Adolf Hitler, Brecht turned the same poem into a revue sketch with a reporter interviewing the horse under the heading 'A HORSE ACCUSES'. This is not to say that there was any tangible link between the great political poet and the outwardly unpolitical novelist Rudolf Ditzen who took the name Fallada. We do not even know if they knew one another's works. But Hans Fallada was at once the probing reporter and the bleeding, accusing dying horse.

Psychologically disturbed from an early age, he had felt the need to cloak his own identity after writing his first, Expressionist-style novel of a disturbed and self-destructive adolescence, whose publication in 1920 not only shocked and hurt but might also, he feared, disgrace the name of his father, a strict and upright north German judge. Yet he developed slowly, and it was not until the publication of *The Drinker* that his rare combination of objective curiosity and extreme personal despair became plain for all to read.

All my life long I have fed on people. I have stored them in my mind along with their ways of moving, speaking, feeling, and now I have them there, ready for instant use. Nothing has ever interested me so much as the realization why people behave as they do. My otherwise hopeless memory is excellent for each detail, the most trivial facts that I learn about the habits of my fellow men.

By then he had shed the egocentric mannerisms of his two earliest books, emerging at the end of the nineteen twenties as a compelling story-teller, a writer without frills whose interest in the lower levels of society made him one of the most successful authors of the coolly critical movement known as 'new matter-of-factness' or 'Die Neue Sachlichkeit'. Of the sixteen books which he published from 1931 to 1943, his most productive years, seven were more or less instantly translated into English; their German sales by now run into millions. Yet they remain very remote from what German criticism slightingly terms 'Trivialliteratur', and with the writing of *The Drinker* at the end of that time Fallada showed the deeply pessimistic basis of his readability. Indeed he can be seen as a paradigm of his country's moods between the establishment of the Weimar Republic and the end of Hitler's Third Reich: its moments of rational, systematic illumination and its terrifying plunges into the dark. How, we may wonder, could a writer come to unify such extremes?

Just twenty-one when the Great War broke out in August 1914, Fallada was already determined on a literary career. His father, the future Supreme Court judge, would have liked him to grow up with the same strict concepts of duty, justice and precision as he himself tried to exemplify; his much younger mother, daughter of a protestant pastor, seems always to have been a subordinate figure. Their son however was incorrigibly awkward and accident-prone, and although the family circle was apparently a close-knit, cultivated one, he did badly at school, was more than once dangerously ill, suffered from masturbation guilt, and had a penchant for self-destructive

ix

adventures which led his despairing parents to seek medical help before he was eighteen. All this culminated in an unprovoked and irrational duel with one of his few friends, which ended with him killing the friend under still obscure circumstances and then trying to shoot himself. At the same time he had become an obsessive reader, starting with that great adventure story of solitude, *Robinson Crusoe*, but soon turning to those more adult books which he had secretly discovered in his father's library: the works of Flaubert, Daudet and Zola (before he was twelve, he later claimed), Dickens, Dostoevsky and other great nineteenth-century writers. These were not at all the sort of literature that Judge Ditzen wished him to read, yet on the other hand he was formally denied the synthetic Westerns of Karl May so beloved of his more frivolous contemporaries. It was indeed a belated act of revolt when Fallada celebrated his eventual success as a writer by buying the whole set of May's works and reading all sixty-five of them, in some cases more than once.

His own literary ambitions seem to have been encouraged in the first place by his aunt Adelaide Ditzen, a gifted spinster then living in Rome as a medical secretary, who came to the rescue after the tragic duel and offered to look after him in the Leipzig criminal lunatic asylum to which he was consigned. She started teaching him English, French and Italian, and introduced him to the work of Romain Rolland, to whom he then wrote offering his services as a translator. Though it seems that Rolland knew the aunt (who had an interesting circle of literary acquaintances that included Nietzsche and Malwida von Meysenbug), the only result at first was a series of rejections from leading German publishers. Then, on his release from the asylum, less than a year before the war, he was sent, once again at the aunt's suggestion, to learn farming and estate management with a neighbouring landowner in the hope that the country life would further his recovery. This did not proceed entirely smoothly, partly because the story of the duel caught up with him, and partly because on his volunteering for the army in August 1914 he was rapidly discharged as mentally unfit. But it did determine his primary profession for the next fifteen years, and undoubtedly it also served the further purpose suggested to him by his aunt: providing him with a wide range of human and social material to observe and note.

What she had not foreseen was the vicissitudes through which his experiences of German (and very largely Prussian) rural economy would take him. First came his work as a specialist in the potato business, which brought him to Berlin in the crucial war years 1916–17, where he was introduced to fashionable Expressionist circles and the use of morphine; this was when he wrote *Der junge Goedeschal*, the work for which he changed his name, an unsuccessful and (for him) untypical ego-novel about his school miseries and fiascos. Then came short spells on various estates, interrupted by periods of treatment in clinics. Then, with the apparent abandonment – or at least postponement – of his writing ambitions, his addictions led him to start fiddling his employers' accounts, with the result that he was twice sent to prison, the first time for two months in the north German university town of Greifswald, where he had been born; the second for a term of two and a half years in the big prison at Neumünster near Kiel. Morphine, alcohol and cigarettes (between 120 and 200 a day, according to his biographer Tom Crepon) had together come to provide what he called his 'little death', that combination of oblivion and elevation which would seduce him off and on throughout the rest of his life.

At first it looked as if his second term of imprisonment might have cured him of this, and he wrote hoping to renew his links with Ernst Rowohlt, the publisher of *Goedeschal*, who had by now rejected Expressionism and become a leading promoter of Die Neue Sachlichkeit. There was no answer. Meanwhile he started trying to make a living addressing envelopes in Hamburg, where he came into contact with the socialist movement through the Issels, a working-class family whose storekeeper daughter became his wife and principal moral support right up to the events outlined in *The Drinker*. Late in 1928, even before the engagement had been announced, his parents helped him to buy himself into local journalism back in Neumünster, and, after a difficult time spent canvassing for advertisements, he got rid of his publisher/employer by denouncing him to the local Socialist mayor for misuse of election funds. As the new editor of the Neumünster 'Advertiser' Fallada was a close observer of the prolonged dispute between the Schleswig-Holstein farmers and the Socialist-led administration, one of the key conflicts of that critical time, and in the summer of 1929 he and his wife went to the North Sea island of Sylt on a facility trip which accidentally brought them face to face in the dunes with Ernst Rowohlt.

These events at last established Fallada as a writer. For Rowohlt suggested that he should come to Berlin at the beginning of the new year to take a part-time job in his publishing firm, and this in turn allowed Fallada to revise and complete the novel which he had begun writing about the farmers' campaign. The result was the publication in spring 1931 of *Bauern, Bonzen und Bomben* (a title that can be loosely rendered as 'Farmers, Functionaries and Fireworks'), the first of what we now see as his characteristic books. Unlike its three immediate successors this was not translated into English, but the BBC transmission of Egon Monk's film version in the nineteen seventies will not have been forgotten by those who saw it, while in Germany the book stood out in a year remarkable for the publication of Erich Kästner's *Fabian*, the premières of Zuckmayer's *Captain of Köpenick* and Pabst's film of *The Threepenny Opera*, as well as the closing on economic grounds of Klemperer's radical Kroll Opera. It sold well (though Fallada's royalty payments were held up when the Rowohlt firm had to go into temporary liquidation during the 1931 bank closures), was serialized in the *Kölner Illustrierte* before publication, and was soon regarded along with

Kästner's poems and Egon Erwin Kisch's reportages as typical of literary Neue Sachlichkeit.

It was another Rowohlt writer of this trend, the satirical journalist and cabaret poet Kurt Tucholsky, whose long review in the *Weltbühne* best analysed what seemed so exceptional about this regenerated novelist's talents.

> The technique is straightforward; it is good old Naturalism, slightly short on imagination, but then the author is not claiming to have written a great work of imaginative literature . . . This is no artistic masterpiece. But it is genuine, so uncannily genuine that it gives you the shivers . . . It is written by someone who knows that particular world like the back of his hand, yet can keep exactly the right distance needed to depict it . . : close, but not too close.

For all his critical acumen Tucholsky underrated Fallada's artistry and his respect for the great nineteenth-century novelists, with their skill in communicating 'slices of life . . . real life'. But he rightly commented on his refusal to fake, to regurgitate political slogans or invent spurious dialogue; and in particular his sharp but not hostile eye for the inadequacies of the provincial SPD, the still numerically powerful German Social Democratic Party. 'It seems highly significant,' he continued in the same review,

> that we have no comparable novels about doctors, or stockbrokers, or the big city; it's as though the members of those lofty strata of the bourgeoisie have no eyes in their heads to see what is going on around them. No doubt they take it too much for granted. Fallada has seen.

Farmers, Functionaries and Fireworks is indeed an excellent book, and not least because it so captures the climate and characters of provincial life at a moment when this was developing in a very different direction from the still comparatively progressive and anti-Nazi Berlin. Its particular importance from our present point of view however is that it at last got its psychologically handicapped author doing what he was best at. His painfully acquired insights into some of the less agreeable aspects of German life at a time of change now came into harmony with his narrative talent and stylistic directness, and an underlying urgency in the writing began to sweep the reader along. Quite clearly this is to be associated with the relative stability of his personal life following the fresh start which he was able to make in 1928; and his wife Anna (or 'Suse' as he called her) was central to it. 'All those who had known me when I was young and full of hope,' he wrote later,

> and then been concerned to observe my decline, but kept a glimmer of belief in my star none the less – there weren't many of them, alas, but they welcomed Suse with pleasure and affection, as if she had always belonged with them.

His rehabilitation was evidently not total, at least where drink was concerned, and at least for the two or three years when the couple were living in the area of Berlin; but the drug problem appeared to have been mastered, and once they had moved to the country following the Reichstag Fire he enjoyed a long and generally productive period of tranquillity, right up to the events that preceded *The Drinker*. Only a few weeks before their marriage he had written to warn her that

> I hope you realize that your prospect is one of financial insecurity, that I am in bad health, that I can and must give you no children, that I have been rejected by my social class.

But their son was born in Berlin a year later, and a daughter and another son would follow.

Yet Fallada's working life after his initial success was far from being as relaxed as its outward circumstances might suggest. For he worked at high speed and with a concentrated intensity that reminded him and others of the 'little death' that he had previously sought in drink and drugs: a spell of utter seclusion from his normal surroundings, when he turned back to his store of experiences and encounters, and the story and the characters took over. It became another form of self-suppression, verging almost on the old self-destruction, but conducted according to timetable, with all the pedantic exactness that his father had brought to the practice of law. Meals had to be punctual, a set quota of pages per day completed, his working hours kept clear of family interruptions. 'From the minute I sit down,' he wrote in his extremely popular *Heute bei uns zu Haus* (Our Home Life Now),

> and write the first line, I am lost, a compelling force is in command. That force dictates just how and how much I must write, whether I want to or not, even if it makes me ill. Good resolutions, the most sincere promises, go by the board – I must write . . . A hundred times I have wondered what it is that drives me so.

Not money, he concludes (for this was after more than ten years as a successful author), nor any fear that he might lose the thread of his inspiration; there is no risk of its breaking, and he is simply forced to follow it to its end. Often it turns out to be a lot longer than expected, then suddenly,

> in the middle of my writing I start realizing that I'm almost through. Suddenly the material is exhausted. Everything I was still planning, scenes I had imagined, turn out not to be needed, the novel has rounded itself off. It is finished.

With great reluctance and many delays, he sets himself to revise and type his longhand manuscript, then to correct it once more with the aid of his wife. Once published he only wants to forget it. Review articles are destroyed before he can see them, and 'never', he claims, 'have I been able to bring myself to reread a single line in any book of mine once it has appeared'.

So he worked in the period between *Farmers, Functionaries and Fireworks* and *The Drinker*, the greater part of which was spent in the lake-strewn north German countryside at Carwitz near Feldberg, halfway between Greifswald and Berlin. Here he lived the life of a beekeeper and small landowner, interrupted by occasional newspaper contributions and, once or twice each year, the blindly compulsive writing of a novel. Certain features of the books would recur: the mistrustful, often devious country-people; the generous yet worldlywise girls of the urban working class; the escape from the city to the land; the untrustworthy gentry; the policemen and criminal types whom he had known in prison; the sometimes appalling bourgeois mothers and widows. The particular tilt or balance could not be foreseen; it varied from book to book. And if we include his two wartime instalments of gently fictionalized autobiography, he wrote eighteen of his twenty-five books in those ten years. Then came the break which resulted in the present work.

Before leaving Berlin, at the height of his country's economic and political crisis, he had written the most famous of all his books, the story of a young shop assistant who becomes forced into poverty with his pregnant working-class wife. The employers are Jewish, the wife's father an old Social Democrat, her brother a Communist, a fellow-employee a Nazi; the ground seems to have been prepared for a social, if not actually political novel of the last days of the Weimar Republic. But if this was the intention it got modified in the course of the writing, for as soon as the scene shifts from the provinces to Berlin the wife's family drops out, new eccentric characters appear – drawn with something of the same affectionate understanding as Christopher Isherwood's Mr Norris three years later – and although the precariousness of the couple's life is shown in convincing monetary detail, the solutions offered are limited to a combination of lucky windfalls (of more or less fishy origin) and mutual love. Even the presentation of the book is ambiguous, for while its original cloth covers bore two characteristic (if irrelevant) drawings by George Grosz, the title, thought up in a session dominated by the publisher, was the trivializing question *Kleiner Mann – was nun?*: *Little Man, What Now?*

It was a worldwide success, an American Book of the Month Club choice in 1933, a film directed by Fritz Wendhausen the same year, the first paperbook published by Rowohlt after the Second World War; it was praised by Thomas Mann, Carl Zuckmayer, Jakob Wassermann, Hermann Hesse and others; and it incidentally set the Rowohlt firm afloat once more after the crisis of 1931. And much of its success was due to the tender portrayal of the wife 'Lämmchen' – clearly based on the personality of Suse Issel – and to that combination of humour, sentiment and a certain self-pitying resignation which lies in the popular German notion of 'the little man'. Naturally the pressure was on Fallada to repeat it, and he decided to base its successor *Wer einmal aus dem Blechnapf frißt* (*Who Once Eats out of the Tin Bowl*) on his prison experiences. Before he could get properly started however, Adolf Hitler came to power, and the subsequent burning of the Reichstag on 27 February 1933 marked the end of parliamentary government, the suppression of all opposition to Hitler's National Socialist (or 'Nazi') party, and the inauguration of the aggressive dicatorship known as the Third Reich.

Briefly Fallada was arrested, on the more or less instinctive suspicions of his neighbours in the commuter belt east of Berlin where he and his wife had hoped to buy a house. This was no great setback, for during the twelve days which he spent in the local gaol he wrote systematically, and Rowohlt quickly secured his release. But his wife was nearing the end of her second, more difficult pregnancy; the Grosz drawings had to be removed from *Little Man, What Now?* in favour of a feeble drawing of a smiling young couple with their child (by one Walter Müller); and a move right into the country seemed advisable. For any reputable writer the climate and the working conditions had plainly changed.

There were still six years to go before Hitler led his country into war, and five more till the final bursting of Fallada's self-constriction with the writing of *The Drinker*. He never wished to emigrate, and appeared critical of those who did. He continued producing his books with much the same fitful fluency as he had shown in the last years of the republic. But when he completed the prison novel at the end of November 1933 he thought it prudent to damp down some of the details and add an apologetic foreword just in case the new regime took exception. And he almost instantly felt driven to start another long novel – some 540 pages in the German original – reflecting the loss of one of the twin girls that his wife had meanwhile borne, but at the same time giving the portrait of an egocentric male-chauvinist north German farmer deeply rooted in his ancestral soil. This took a mere three weeks to write and seemed to the author a great step forward in his work. Yet the odd thing was that, whereas *Who Once Eats out of the Tin Bowl*, for all his fears, was at first well received, the new book *Wir hatten mal ein Kind* (*Once We Had a Child*), with its tear-jerking title and its ideologically timely mixture of masculine dominance and blood-and-soil ruralism, was the subject of a campaign to demolish his reputation by the party purists. It seemed then that it was useless for him to make concessions, whether deliberate or unconscious, to the Nazi New Order: for, as the official *Völkischer Beobachter* put it, 'He was never one of ours.' Early in 1935 he again took to drinking. In August he had to show his 'Ahnenpass' (the disgusting booklet that revealed whether one had racially pure ancestors or not); in September the Propaganda Ministry declared him 'unacceptable' and forbade him to publish abroad; and although this was rescinded, that winter he more than once had to go into a sanatorium.

None the less his narrative power and his ability to create characters had not left him, and he had a large readership and a supportive publisher. So he decided to set his sights lower, but to stay put and continue writing – stories, articles, light novels like *Altes Herz geht auf die Reise* (*Old Heart Goes on a Journey*, which became an Ufa film), and endearing but essentially cosy

xviii

works like his two warm-hearted books of reminiscence. In the second half of the decade, too, he translated two successful and eminently compatible light works from America, Clarence Day's *Life With Father* and *Life With Mother*. It was proposed by Rowohlt and the popular film director Willy Fritsch, with the backing of Goebbels and his Propaganda Ministry, that he should write a film story for the actor Emil Jannings, but the film was stopped, allegedly because Alfred Rosenberg and his ideological purists found Fallada's involvement unacceptable, while the novel version *Der eiserne Gustav* (*Iron Gustav*) was doctored to give it a Nazi ending. And yet it was during these years of self-censorship and official mistrust that he managed to write and publish, seemingly without official interference, the two-volume novel *Wolf unter Wölfen* (*Wolf Among Wolves*) which he wrote in two bursts of intense creativity covering ten months of 1936/37. This is a large scale, pitiless portrayal of the state of the German countryside in the early years of the Weimar Republic, with vivid pictures of those Nationalist, anti-Communist groups and individuals who were paving the way for fascism during the great inflation of 1922/23. Published in Septembr 1937 at the height of the Nazi campaign against degenerate art, perhaps only a political innocent could have ventured to write it – or else an extraordinarily sensitive political subconscious. One friendly speaker on Berlin Radio even compared it with Dante's *Inferno* and Balzac's *La Comédie humaine*, adding that it could be seen as more impressive than either, since 'it deals with an Inferno which we have all been through'. Though it finally lapses into a trusting optimism, it is not merely Fallada's finest achievement but perhaps the one great novel to have appeared under Hitler's Third Reich.

If *Wolf Among Wolves* was an exceptional product of his relatively stable forties, *The Drinker* represents a total rejection of that stability, beginning with his marriage, which was dissolved by mutual agreement just before his fifty-first birthday in the summer of 1944. Not long before he had prefixed one of his books of reminiscence with a public tribute to his wife Suse, the 'Lämmchen' of *Little Man, What Now?*, who

> first made me what I have become, she taught an aimless man how to work, a desperate man how to hope. It was thanks to her faith, her loyalty, her patience that we managed to build up what we now possess, what we rejoice in every day. And it all came about without much talk, or fuss, or finger-wagging, but simply by her being there and sticking to me through good times and bad.

Now however he had turned against her influence and wrote, apparently in secret, this relentless first-person story (the only one among all his main novels) about a provincial provision dealer who falls out with the capable wife on whom everybody thinks he depends, starts obsessively drinking, becomes besotted with the waitress whom he calls his *reine d'alcool*, and from that point starts dropping irrevocably, through a richly squalid series of subsidiary tales and episodes, to the horrible bottom of his society. How much of this is hallucination, how much imagination – the reader thinks of Kafka's *In the Penal Colony* – how much reality? What is its basis in the author's own experience, what in the life of his country in the last year of the war?

Not published till after the Nazi surrender – in the Federal Republic in 1950, in the GDR three years later – it was written in the autumn of 1944, and it marks the catastrophic ending of Fallada's most fruitful period. The war was then nearing its end, with the Russians advancing through Poland and Romania, and the Western Allies in France and Belgium. The Propaganda Ministry had listed him as undesirable; Rowohlt had been expelled from the official Chamber of Culture and gone into the army: during 1943 he was discharged as 'politically unreliable' and his firm, already 'gleichgeschaltet' (or incorporated in the officially-approved system), finally

closed down. Though the Labour Service briefly commiss-
ioned Fallada to come and report on their activities in
occupied France and Czechoslovakia, he was now once again
drinking himself stupid and seems to have written nothing,
possibly because he did not much like what he saw. What was
much worse for him was that just at this juncture a smart,
seemingly unattached Berlin woman arrived in Feldberg who
not only reminded him of his chief Berlin attachment at the end
of the earlier war, but was also an alcoholic and a morphine
addict. Already in matrimonial trouble because of an affair
with his family's au pair girl, he now became hopelessly
involved with this Ulla or 'Uschi', with the immediate result
that he and his wife divorced by mutual agreement. Then on
his first visit home there was a quarrel during which he loosed
off two shots from a half-forgotten gun, and was carried away
to a closely guarded criminal asylum in the neighbouring city
of AltStrelitz on a charge of attempted murder. It was there
that, under the pretence of writing a propaganda novel, he
wrote *The Drinker*, not in code as has sometimes been
suggested, but in fine criss-crossed lines to economize paper.
Dates in the margin of the original show that it took him a
fortnight.

Critics of this book have complained that he wrote it
without any final literary polish; that the style is too
straightforward to qualify as high art. If so it is because of the
immediacy with which he wrote, without (so it is said) any
kind of revision either then or later. And yet it is not set down
like a diary, for it has a plan and a shape like a Gadarene slope,
as the whole of the narrator's life is seen hurtling to its
self-motivated perdition. Magda is Fallada's wife Suse; *la reine
d'alcool* a lower-class stand-in for Uschi the Berliner; Else the
maid has features of the au pair; the setting is the area of his
Carwitz home, and the asylum the one in which he was
writing. What is above all very genuine is the self-destructive-
ness and the desire to hurt the wife who is in many ways so
evidently his better half. The pain of this terrible paradox is

stated at the beginning of the third chapter, leading to the reflective words

> But man gets used to anything, and I am afraid that perhaps he gets used quickest of all to living in a state of degradation.

Nothing specifically suggests that such a state was also the state of Germany in the days of the Final Solution; for there is no direct reference either to National Socialism or to its organizations, merely to the officials of the asylum and the courts, who would not have been all that different under the Republic. All the same, it is difficult to read the book without also reflecting on the huge degradation of a great European country, as well as the lesser degradations which National Socialism inflicted on the writer himself: the false triviality of some of his lesser books, for instance, the fiasco of the Jannings film, or the commissions to report on labour in the occupied countries and to write an anti-Jewish novel about Kutisker und Barmat, a bank that went under in the nineteen twenties. Fallada was after all an artist with an acute interest in individual lives, and if it is true, as Georg Lukács has said, that

> in the oppressive atmosphere of fascism, Fallada lost that inner confidence in his feelings which – for all his lack of firmly pondered and held views – characterized his initial critique of society.

then he surely will have felt a sense of shame as well as resentment.

How we take *The Drinker* today, then, depends in some measure on our view of its author's attitude to the Third Reich. Personally uncommunicative, at least in his stable moods, he gave no evidence of courage but had a complex kind of obstinacy none the less. He was never pro-Nazi; he was unwilling to leave Germany; he would not risk any form of resistance. Tom Crepon, whose mildly fictionalized East German biography of 1978 was written with Suse Ditzen's aid and approval, reports a visit of May 1934 by the younger

xxii

Rowohlt with Martha Dodd and Mildred Harnack, the American who joined the 'Red Orchestra' group with her husband Arvid and Harro Schultz-Boysen, and was beheaded in 1943. She asked Fallada if it was still possible to write as one wished, and when he said yes, if you were prepared to compromise on unimportant points, she turned away, remarking 'What is important, what is not?'. Martha Dodd's conclusion was that Fallada had resigned himself, and was content in his new isolation. Yet clearly this contentment had worn through by the middle of the Second World War, and if the deterioration of his marriage was a major factor so was his plain incompatibility with the system. These two elements in his decline seem to have aggravated one another, to judge from the timing of his lapses. Thus it appears to have been a particularly severe blow when the Rowohlt firm was finally closed down, not least because its offence had been to publish such 'undesirable' authors as the cabaret poet Joachim Ringelnatz (who had died in 1934) and Fallada himself. It was this that led to the (unfulfilled) commission from another publisher to write the antisemitic 'Kutisker' book.

That the picture of the asylum given in *The Drinker* stands for more than the bare events of the author's own incarceration is clear, since it helped that he was imagined to be at work on the 'Kutisker' job, and he was in fact released after less than four months. Unexpectedly, in view of his announced intention to return to his wife, he then married the disastrous Uschi, with whom he would spend his last two years. These saw the breakdown of all his resolutions as they shared the 'little death' of their renewed addictions, first in her Feldberg house near his own and then in her flat in the ruins of Berlin; and the incoherence of their life together from then on seems reflected in the incoherence of his first, largely autobiographical postwar novel *Der Alpdruck* (*The Nightmare*), which actually appeared before *The Drinker* and proved much harder to write. It was the first time since the nineteen twenties that Fallada had lost his grip on the reader. Yet in its scrappy way the book gives a convincing impression of the arrival of the Red Army in Feldberg and the moral collapse of the inhabitants, and describes with a certain irony the circumstances that led to its author – who would never have accepted, nor perhaps been offered, public office under Hitler – being installed as mayor of Feldberg for four months till his strength gave out. Thereafter he looked for literary and journalistic contacts in Berlin, and found them again among the Soviet occupiers and their helpers, notably the poet Johannes R. Becher who had returned from emigration in Moscow to head the Kulturbund (or League of Culture) which the Russians sponsored, initially in all four sectors of the city.

Becher knew Fallada's work from before 1933, and happened to have come from a curiously similar background: a stiff-collared lawyer father, a suicide pact where only the other partner died, a period of Expressionist excess (including a morphine addiction) and a sobering-up process, governed in Becher's case by a political discipline. He now sought out Fallada, helped him to find occasional work with the Soviet German-language Berlin daily *Täglicher Rundschau*, got him preferential rations and housing and, at a Christmas party in 1945, introduced him to the Soviet writer Konstantin Fedin and the chairman of the German Communist Party, Wilhelm Pieck. By the former's account Fallada was still maintaining his isolation, for he disagreed with Pieck about his party's optimistic expectations of the German workers and the probable impact on them of the Nuremberg War Crimes trials, saying finally that 'the business of the politician is to obey reality; the business of the artist, to portray that reality as it is'. A month or two earlier Becher had passed him a collection of documents taken from the Berlin Gestapo and the People's Court, providing details of the case against an obscure working-class couple who from 1940 to 1942 had conducted their own private propaganda campaign against Hitler, then been caught and executed. His objective all along, it seems, was to reactivate the narrative writer whom his Moscow colleague Georg Lukács had judged 'one of the greatest hopes of German literature', and see if Fallada could not produce that major novel of the Third Reich for which the country – and indeed the world – were waiting.

It is not clear whether Becher was aware of *The Drinker* until after Fallada's death at the beginning of 1947, but when it finally appeared in the Federal Republic he was appalled: 'a wholly unnecessary book', he noted in his diary, 'harmful and repellent, with no new human insights, no literary appeal. A pity.'

At least he cannot fully have realized what a break it had meant in its author's approach to writing. And, to start with, Fallada was evidently doubtful how much he could make of the frightening real-life dossier which he had been given. He understood the responsibility which it imposed on him, writing a preliminary article for the Kulturbund's magazine which concluded:

> I, the author of a novel which has yet to be written, hope that their struggle, their suffering, their death were not entirely in vain.

But as he came to plan that novel he became doubtful, first estimating its length as a 'paltry three hundred pages', then abandoning it on the ground that the material could only justify an essay of twenty typed pages and anyway 'who still wants to read about that kind of thing?' In the end he signed a contract for the film version with the East German state film company, DEFA, and with Uschi absent again in hospital wrote the 540-page *Jeder stirbt für sich allein* (*Everyone dies for himself alone*) in a mere twenty-four days, an achievement to match those of his great period. The result was not only more than Becher could have hoped for; it is one of Fallada's best novels, with a great gallery of well-observed characters, both men and women, ranging from the old civil servant to the smart young SA-men and the shabbiest Gestapo informers. Who would have thought that either the resigned and untalkative Fallada of 1934 or the shattered personality of *The Drinker* could so sensitively penetrate under the skin of the police state?

Right-thinking German literary criticism is still uncertain where to shelve Hans Fallada: Expressionism or Entertainment, Nazi or anti-Nazi, GDR or Federal Republic? – like so many of the most interesting writers he cannot be placed under an exact label. Yet he has his position in modern literary history alongside Kästner and Anna Seghers, Tucholsky and Plievier, Renn and Remarque, as part of the new sobriety of the later nineteen twenties, and counterpart to equivalents such as Rudolf Schlichter and Paul Hindemith in the other arts. Like Feuchtwanger's *Success*, moreover, and Döblin's *Berlin Alexanderplatz*, a number of his novels can be read as adjuncts to history proper, clues to the changing society of their particular place and time. Thus *Farmers, Functionaries and Fireworks* and *Wolf Among Wolves* bring life to the generally neglected story of Hitler's rise to power in the provinces; *Who Once Eats out of the Tin Bowl* has been called the best novel of prison life under the Weimar Republic; *Little Man, What Now?* joins *Fabian* and the Isherwood Berlin stories as pictures of the Republic's last months; while the final novel is a perceptive account of oppression and a feeling tribute to the old-style individualism of the Berlin working class. And *The Drinker*? It springs like a blow in the midriff from the bombast, false folksiness and anodyne classicism of National Socialist culture, and it is hard not to take its steady descent into the pit as a parable – less specific than the big novels but all the more shocking – of Germany's march into the depths.

If there is an English analogy here it is with Evelyn Waugh, whose opinions and actions are by no means progressive or universally admired, yet who wrote a handful of books that share much the same conflicting qualities as Fallada's. Thus whatever the nature of Waugh's professed view of English society and of the issues for which it was fighting in the nineteen forties, it did not stop him from producing the extraordinarily revealing trilogy about the Second World War for which he will long be read. And similarly, in *Wolf Among Wolves* and *Jeder stirbt für sich allein* the awkward misfit Fallada achieved something that an admirable, humane, intelligent, constructively-disposed, much less anguished-looking 'inner emigrant' like Erich Kästner never, so far as is known, even attempted: a large-scale critique of the reality around him. But the obvious comparison to be made with Waugh relates to that author's *The Ordeal of Gilbert Pinfold*, the critically observed, largely satirical account of a middle-aged man's fantasies which reads as a brilliant work of the imagination. Like *The Drinker* it is not quite that, for, as Francis Donaldson showed us in her *Portrait of a Country Neighbour*, it closely reflects a very strange period in Waugh's life when he was haunted simultaneously by the 'black box' of fringe medicine and by a team of BBC interviewers, and began drugging himself with soporifics. *Pinfold* in other words was rooted in a peculiar kind of reality outside normal experience, just as Fallada's hallucinatory novel is rooted in his breakdown of 1944. Both books can be read without any knowledge of their background in the real world of their authors' lives, both are set down objectively without a preconceived display of moral, religious or political prejudices and principles; if anything they are likely to extend, if not actually conflict with the reader's prior ideas about the writer in question. For both imply a lot about their country, and both are relevant to the remainder of their author's writing. Is it then illuminating to know the true biographical and psychological setting? Is it a help to the reader? Does it matter?

Despite what Tucholsky and others said about Fallada's failure to write an 'artistic masterpiece', one of the main lessons of Neue Sachlichkeit is that there is nothing inartistic about authenticity; the artistry lies not in the style but in the way that authenticity is structured and handled. Moreover there is not much – at least in Western societies – that does more damage to our contemporary arts than the assumption that a work cannot be serious if it is clearly, even simply expressed, reflects reality and holds the attention of its audience. What distinguishes the writings of artists like Waugh and Fallada, then, from those trivial entertainers whom, in sales terms, they may be thought to rival is their ability to select, however unconsciously, from the real world round them and treat their material imaginatively but honestly, without distortion. The shape, the play of continuity and contrast, the element of timing involved in exciting narrative or masterly poetry, these are what needs to be brought to bear on the writer's experience if it is to appeal to the reader's imagination, and not just to his or her appetite for random facts.

The artist who can bring this off is worth study, for the secret of his success has to be looked for in some particular relationship between his gifts, the breadth of his experience and his individual development as a person. Admirable as they are, niceness and morality are not what determines this; we are struck in the first place by the artistic success, which we may sense quite naively, then feel that its deeper reasons must need exploring, and go on to find a new sympathy with the actual personality together with all its weaknesses and faults. Indeed we may even think we hate or despise a writer, yet wish very much to know them better because we see that beyond this superficial reaction there is a unity between the individual and his or her achievement that demands to be understood. Nowhere is this more the case than when an extraordinary work is created out of extraordinary suffering, particularly when the means seem so ordinary and direct as those which Fallada uses. We are back to the goose girl of German popular tradition. The writer is beheaded, the writer reports. Bleeding reality becomes material for the imagination. There are not two heads for the passer-by to look at but one.

JOHN WILLETT

THE DRINKER

I

OF COURSE I have not always been a drunkard. Indeed it is not
very long since I first took to drink. Formerly I was repelled
by alcohol; I might take a glass of beer, but wine tasted sour
to me, and the smell of schnaps made me ill. But then the time
came when things began to go wrong with me. My business
affairs did not proceed as they should, and in my dealings with
people I met with all kinds of setbacks. I always have been a
sensitive man, needing the sympathy and encouragement of
those around me, though of course I did not show this and
liked to appear rather sure and self-possessed. Worst of all,
the feeling gradually grew on me that even my wife was
turning away from me. At first the signs were almost unnotice-
able, little things that anyone else would have overlooked.
For instance, at a birthday party in our house, she forgot to
offer me cake. I never eat cake, but hitherto, despite that, she
had always offered it me. And once, for three days there was
a cobweb in my room, above the stove. I went through all the
rooms in the house, but there was not a cobweb in any of
them, only in mine. I meant to wait and see how long she intended to annoy me with this, but on the fourth day I could
hold out no longer, and I was obliged to tell her of it. Then
the cobweb was removed. Naturally I spoke to her very firmly.
At all costs I wanted to avoid showing how much I suffered
through these insults and my growing isolation.

But it did not end there. Soon came the affair of the door-mat. I had had trouble at the bank that day; for the first time they had refused to cash a cheque for me. I suppose word had got round that I had had certain losses. The bank manager, a Herr Alf, pretended to be very amiable, and even offered to ring up the head office about an overdraft. Of course I refused. I had been smiling and self-confident as usual, but I noticed that this time he had not offered me a cigar as he generally did. Doubtless this customer was no longer worth it. I went home very depressed, through a heavy fall of autumn rain. I was not in any real difficulties yet; my affairs were merely going through a period of stagnation which could certainly have been overcome, at this stage, by the exercise of a little initiative. But I just couldn't summon up that initiative. I was too depressed by all the mute dislike of myself which I encountered at every twist and turn.

When I got home (we live a little way out of town, in our own house, and the road is not properly made up yet) I wanted to clean my muddy shoes outside the door, but today the mat, of course, was missing. Angrily I unlocked the door and called into the house for my wife. It was getting dark, but I could see no light anywhere, and Magda did not come either. I called again and again but nothing happened. I found myself in a most critical situation: I stood in the rain outside the door of my own house, and could not go indoors without making the porch and hall quite unnecessarily muddy, all because my wife had forgotten to put the mat out, and moreover had failed to be present at a time when she knew full well I should be coming home from work. Finally I had to master my feelings: I tiptoed carefully into the house. As I sat on a chair in the hall to take my shoes off, having switched on the light, I found that all my precautions had been in vain: there were most ugly marks on the pale green hall-carpet. I had always told Magda that such a delicate green was not suitable for the hall, but she was of the opinion that both of us were old enough to be a bit careful, and in any case, our maid Else used the back-door and generally went about the house in slippers. Angrily I took off my shoes, and just as I was pulling the second one off, I saw Magda, coming through the door at the head of the cellar steps. The shoe slipped from me and fell noisily on to the carpet, making a disgusting mark.

"Do be more careful, Erwin," cried Magda angrily. "What a sight this carpet is again! Can't you get used to wiping your feet properly?"

The obvious injustice of this reproach took my breath away, but I restrained myself.

"Where in the world have you been?" I asked, glaring at her. "I called you at least ten times!"

"I was seeing to the central heating in the cellar," said Magda coolly, "but what's that got to do with my carpet?"

"It's just as much my carpet as yours," I answered heatedly. "I didn't dirty it for fun. But when there's no mat outside the door . . . "

"No mat outside the door? Of course there's a mat outside the door!"

"There isn't," I shouted. "Kindly go and see for yourself!"

But of course she would not dream of looking outside the door.

"Even if Else has forgotten to put it out, you could very well have taken off your shoes in the porch. In any case, there was no need to throw that shoe down on the carpet with such a thump."

I looked at her, speechless with rage.

"Yes," she said, "you've nothing to say. When you're told off, you've nothing to say. But you're always telling me off . . . "

I did not see any proper sense in her words, but I said: "When have I told you off?"

3

"Just now," she answered quickly, "first because I didn't come when you called, and I had to see to the heating because this is Else's afternoon off. And then because the mat wasn't outside the door. With all the work I have to do, I can't possibly look after every little detail of Else's work as well!"

I controlled myself. In my heart I found Magda wrong on every point. But aloud I said: "Don't let's quarrel, Magda. Please believe me, I didn't make the marks on purpose."

"And you believe me," she said, still rather sharply, "I didn't intend that you should have to shout all over the house after me."

I kept silent. By dinner-time, we both had ourselves quite well in hand again, and even managed a fairly sensible conversation, and suddenly I had the idea of fetching a bottle of red wine which someone had given me, and which had been in the cellar for years. I really do not know why this idea occurred to me. Perhaps the sense of our reconciliation had put me in mind of something festive, of a wedding or a baptism. Magda was quite surprised, too, but she smiled approvingly. I drank only a glass and a half, though this evening the wine did not taste sour to me. I got into quite a cheerful mood and managed to tell Magda a few things about those business affairs of mine, which were causing me so much trouble. Naturally I did not refer to them as troubles, on the contrary I presented my misfortunes as successes. Magda listened to me with more interest than she had shown for a long time past. I had the feeling that the estrangement between us had completely disappeared, and in my joy I gave Magda a hundred marks to buy herself something nice; a dress or a ring or whatever she had set her heart on.

2

SINCE then, I have often wondered whether I wasn't completely drunk that evening. Of course, I wasn't; Magda as well as I would have noticed it. And yet, that evening I must have been intoxicated for the first time in my life. I didn't sway, my speech wasn't thick. That glass-and-a-half of musty red wine could not have had such an effect on a sober man like me; and yet, the alcohol transformed the whole world for me. It made me believe there had been no estrangement, no quarrel between Magda and myself; it changed my business troubles into successes, into such successes that I even had a hundred marks to give away, not a considerable sum of course, but in my position, no sum was quite inconsiderable. Only when I awoke next morning and all these events, from the forgotten door-mat to the present of the hundred-mark note, passed before my mind's eye—only then was it clear to me how disgracefully I had treated Magda. Not only had I deceived her about the state of my business affairs, but I had fortified this deceit by a gift of money, so as to make it more credible, with something that would legally be called "intent to defraud". But the legal side was quite unimportant. Only the human aspect was important, and in this case the human aspect was simply horrible. For the first time in our married life I had deliberately deceived Magda—and why? In Heaven's name, why? I could very well have continued to keep quiet about the whole thing, just as I had kept quiet up till then. Nobody forced me to speak. Nobody? Ah yes, alcohol had made me do it. When once I had understood, when once I had realised to the full, what a liar alcohol is, and what liars it makes of honest men, I swore never to touch another drop and even to give up my occasional glass of beer.

But what are resolutions, what are plans? On this sober morning I promised myself at least to take advantage of the warmer mood which had arisen between Magda and me last night, and not to let things drift again into friction and estrangement. And yet before many days had passed, we were quarrelling again. It really was absolutely incomprehensible—fourteen years of our married life had gone by almost without a quarrel, and now, in the fifteenth, it appeared that we simply couldn't live without bickering. Often it seemed positively ridiculous to me, the kind of things we found to quarrel about. It was as if we had to quarrel at certain times, no matter why. Quarrelling seemed like a poison, which quickly became a habit and without which we could scarcely go on living. At first, of course, we scrupulously kept up appearances, we tried as far as possible to keep to the point of the quarrel, and to avoid personal insults. Also the presence of our little maid Else restrained us. We knew that she was inquisitive, and that she passed on everything she heard. At that time it would have been unspeakably horrible to me if anyone in town had got to hear of my troubles and our quarrelling: but not much later it was to become completely immaterial what people said or thought of me; and what was worse, I was to lose all sense of self-respect.

I have said that Magda and I had become accustomed to quarrelling almost daily. In point of fact we were really only bickering about nothing at all, just for something to relieve the ever-growing tension between us. That we did so was really a miracle, though not a pleasant one: for many years

6

Magda and I had led a remarkably happy life together. We had married for love, while we were both very minor employees, and with an attaché case each we had started our career together. Oh, those wonderful penniless years of our early married life—when I look back on them now! Magda was a real artist in housekeeping. Some weeks we managed on ten marks and it seemed to us we were living like lords. Then came that brave time, a time of ceaseless struggle, when I made myself independent, and when with Magda's help I built up my own business. It succeeded—good God, how lucky we were with everything in those days! We had only to touch something, to turn our hand and mind to it, and it succeeded, it blossomed like a well-tended flower, it bore fruit for us. We were denied children, however much we longed for them. Magda had a miscarriage once; from then on all hope of children was gone. But we loved each other nonetheless. For many years of our married life we fell newly in love with each other, over and again. I never desired any other woman but Magda. She made me completely happy, and I presumed she felt the same about me.

When the business was running smoothly, when it had grown as much as the size of our town and our district allowed, our interest began to flag somewhat. Then, in compensation, came the purchase of our own plot of land just out of town, the building of our house, the laying-out of our garden, the furniture which was to be with us for the rest of our life—all things which bound us closely together again and prevented us from noticing that our relationship was beginning to cool off. If we no longer loved each other as much as before, if we no longer desired each other so often and so warmly, we did not regard this as a loss, but took it as a matter of course. We had simply become a long-married couple: what had happened to us, happened to everyone; it was a natural thing. And as I have said, the comradeship of planning, building, choosing furniture, completely made up for it. From being lovers we had become comrades, and we felt no sense of loss.

At that time Magda had already ceased to be an active partner in my business, a step which we both regarded as inevitable. She had a larger household of her own; the garden and our few fowls also demanded some care; and the extent of the business easily allowed the employment of new staff. Later, it was to become apparent how fatal was Magda's withdrawal from my business. Not only because we thereby lost a great part of our mutual interests, but also it became obvious that her help was irreplaceable. She was far more active than I, more enterprising, also much cleverer than I in dealing with people, and in an easy jocular way she managed to get them where she wanted them. I was the cautious element in our partnership, the brake, as it were, that checked any too-rash move and made the going safe. In actual business dealings, I was inclined to hold back as much as possible, not to force myself on anybody, and never to ask for anything. So it was inevitable, after Magda's withdrawal, that our business went on in the old way at first, nothing new came in, and then gradually, slowly, year by year, it fell away. Of course, all this only became clear to me much later, too late, when there was nothing left to salvage. At the time of Magda's withdrawal I felt rather relieved, even: a man who runs his own firm demands more respect from people than one whose wife is able to have a say in everything.

3

ONLY when we started quarrelling did I notice how estranged Magda and I had become during those years when she had been looking after her household and I had been managing the business. The first few times I still felt quite ashamed of our lack of restraint, and when I noticed that I had grieved Magda, that she was even going about with tear-stained eyes, it hurt me almost as much as it hurt her, and I swore that I would be better. But man gets used to anything, and I am afraid that perhaps he gets used quickest of all to living in a state of degradation. The day came when, at the sight of Magda's red-rimmed eyes, I no longer swore to behave better. Instead with mingled satisfaction and surprise, I said to myself: "I gave it to you properly that time! You're not going to get the upper hand of me always with that sharp tongue of yours!" It seemed horrible to feel that way, and yet it seemed right, it satisfied me to feel so, however paradoxical that may seem. From there, it was only a short step to the point where I consciously sought to hurt her.

At that most critical moment in our relationship, the grocery contract for the prison came up for tender, as happened every three years. In our town (not exactly to the delight of its inhabitants) we have the central prison of the province, which always has some fifteen hundred prisoners within its walls. We had had the contract for nine years. Magda had worked very hard to get it originally. On the two previous occasions when it had come up for tender, Magda had only to pay the prison governor a brief courtesy visit and the contract was ours without further ado. I had always taken this contract so much for granted as a part of my business, that this time I hardly bothered about it, I had the previous tender—whose price-list had been satisfactory for nine years—copied out and sent in. I also contemplated a visit to the official concerned; but everything would go its usual way, I didn't want to seem importunate, I knew the man was overburdened with work—in short I had at least ten good reasons for abandoning the visit.

Consequently, it came as a thunderbolt out of a clear sky, when a letter from the prison administration informed me in a few bare words that my tender was refused, that the contract had been given to another firm. My first thought was: above all, Magda mustn't hear of this! Then I took my hat and hurried off to the governor, to pay the visit now, that would have had some point three weeks ago. I was received politely but coolly. The governor regretted that our long-standing business connection was now severed. However he had not been able to act otherwise, since part of the price-list I quoted had long ago been superseded, in some cases by higher prices, in other cases by lower. On the whole, it would probably just about balance out, but my tender had—if I would pardon his frankness—merely made a bad impression on the responsible officials, as if it was all the same to my firm whether we got the contract or not. I learned moreover that a quite new firm, eager to get on at any price, and one which had already given me trouble several times before, had once again come out on top. Finally, in all politeness the governor expressed the hope in three years' time, they might again be able to resume their previous business connection with my firm, and I was dismissed.

I knew that in the prison governor's office I had not shown any of the consternation, the desperation even, that I felt at this stroke of bad luck; I had disguised my inquiry under the cloak of politeness and of curiosity about the name of the lucky winner. When I stood outside the heavy iron gates of the prison again, when the last bolt had clashed to behind me, I looked into the bright sunshine of that lovely spring day like someone who has just awakened from a heavy dream, and doesn't yet know whether he is really awake or is still sighing under the weight of the nightmare. I *was* still sighing under it. In vain the iron gate had dismissed me to freedom; I remained the prisoner of my own troubles and failures.

Now it was impossible for me to go back into town to my office, above all I had to pull myself together before I saw Magda—I went away from the town and from people, I walked over the fields and meadows, further and further, as if I could run away from my troubles. That day I saw nothing of the fresh emerald green of the young crops, I did not hear the gurgling of the brooks, nor the drum-roll of the larks in the blue-golden air: I was utterly alone with myself and my misfortune.

It was quite clear to me that this was no small mishap for my business, to be taken with a shrug of regret; the delivery of groceries for fifteen hundred people, even at a modest profit, was such an important item of my turnover, that it could not be given up without drastically altering my whole prospects. Compensation for this loss was not to be thought of, other such possibilities did not exist in our modest town. By a supreme effort, it might have been possible to increase the number of retail firms by a few dozen, but apart from the fact that this would by no means be any substitute for my loss, I felt incapable of making any such effort at the moment. For some reason I had been feeling rather low for nearly a year now. I was more and more inclined to let things go their own way and not excite myself too much. I was in need of rest—why, I do not know. Perhaps I was getting prematurely old. It was clear to me that I would have to dismiss at least two of my staff, but even that did not disturb me unduly, though I knew how it would be talked about. It wasn't the business that worried me at the moment, but Magda. Again and again my main thought, my main worry was: it's got to be kept from Magda! I told myself that in the long run I wouldn't be able to conceal from her the dismissal of two of my staff and the loss of the contract. But I pretended that everything depended on her not finding out just yet, that perhaps in a few weeks I would get some substitute or other. Then I had a bright moment again. I stopped, kicked hard against a stone in the dusty road, and said to myself: "Since Magda is bound to find out, it's better she should hear about it from me than from other people, and moreover it's better she should hear about it today than some other time. Every day it's postponed will make confession more difficult. After all, I'm not guilty of a crime, only of neglect." I kicked the stone again. "I'll simply ask Magda to help me with the business again. That will reconcile her to my failure, and I and my business can only gain by it. I really am rather under the weather and could well do with some help. . . ."

But that bright moment quickly passed. The respect of other people, and particularly of Magda, had always been so important to me. I had always carefully seen to it that I was looked up to as the head of the firm. Now, especially now, I couldn't bring myself to forego a single iota of my dignity, or to humiliate myself before Magda. No, I resolved, come what may, to master the affair myself. Also I didn't want the help of a woman with whom I quarrelled almost daily. It was easy to foresee that the bickering would go on in the very office—she would insist on having her way, I would oppose her, she would throw my failures in my face—oh no, impossible!

I stamped my foot in the dust of the road. I had no idea where my feet had been taking me, I had been so absorbed in my troubles. I was standing in a village not far from my home town, a favourite spot for springtime excursions on account of its charming birch woods and its lake. But on this week-day morning there were no trippers. People were too busy at home. I was standing just outside the inn, and I was conscious of feeling thirsty. I went into the low, wide, rather dark bar-room. Previously, I had always seen it full of townsfolk, the bright spring frocks of the women making the room brighter and giving it, despite its low ceiling, an airy appearance. For when the townspeople were here, the windows had been open, coloured cloths lay on the tables, and everywhere bright sprays of birch stood in tall vases. Now the room was dark, brownish-yellow American cloth covered the tables, it smelt stuffy, the windows were shut tight. Behind the bar stood a young girl with unkempt hair and a dirty apron, whispering busily to a young fellow who seemed to be a bricklayer, by his lime-spattered clothes. My first impulse was to turn back. But my thirst, and particularly the fear of being left at the mercy of my troubles again, made me approach the bar instead.

"Give me something to drink, anything to quench a thirst," I said.

Without looking up, the girl ran some beer into a glass, and I watched the froth drip over the edge. The girl turned off the tap, waited a moment till the froth had settled, and then let another spurt of beer run in, then, still without a word, she pushed the glass towards me across the tarnished zinc. She resumed her whispering with the young bricklayer. So far she had not given me a glance.

I lifted the glass to my mouth and emptied it thoughtfully, gulp by gulp, without once setting it down. It tasted fresh, fizzy, slightly bitter, and it seemed to leave in my mouth a feeling of airy brightness that had not been there before.

"Give me another of the same," I was about to say, but I changed my mind. I had seen a short squat bright glass before

13

the young man, the kind called a noggin, in which schnaps is usually served.

"I'll have a noggin of that," I suddenly said. Why I did so, who had never drunk schnaps in my life, who had a deep aversion to the very smell of it, I really don't know. At that very moment all my lifelong habits were changing, I was at the mercy of mysterious influences, and the strength to resist them had been taken from me.

Now for the first time the girl looked at me. Slowly she lifted her rather coarse-grained eyelids and turned her bright knowing eyes on me.

"Schnaps?" she asked.

"Schnaps," I said, the girl took down a bottle, and I wondered if a female had ever looked at me before in such a shamelessly knowing way. Her glance seemed to penetrate right to the root of my manhood, as if seeking to find out how much of a man I was; it seemed positively physical, something painfully, sweetly insolent, as if I were stripped naked before her eyes.

The glass was filled, it was pushed towards me across the zinc, the eyelids lowered again, the girl turned to the young man: the verdict had been reached. I raised the glass, hesitated—and with a sudden resolve I tipped its contents into my mouth. It burned, it took my breath away, I choked, but managed to force the liquor down my throat, I felt it going down, burning and acrid—and suddenly a feeling of warmth spread in my stomach, an agreeable and genial warmth. Then I shuddered all over. Half aloud, the bricklayer said, "The ones that shake like that are the worst," and the girl gave a short laugh. I put a one-mark note down on the bar and left the inn without another word.

The spring day greeted me with its sunny warmth and its gentle breeze as fine as silk, but I came back into it a changed man. A lightness had mounted to my head from the warmth in my stomach and my heart beat free and strong. Now I could see the emerald green of the young shoots, now I could hear the trilling of the larks in the blue sky. My cares had fallen away from me. "Everything will come right in the end," I cheerfully assured myself, and started for home. "Why worry about it now?" Before I reached town, I had turned into two other inns, and in each of them I drank another noggin to repeat and strengthen the quickly-fading effect of the schnaps. With a slight but not unpleasant sensation of numbness, I reached home just in time for lunch.

4

IT WAS clear to me that now I had to conceal from my wife not only the loss of the grocery contract, but also my drinking. But I felt so much on top of the world at the moment, that I was sure this would present no difficulty at all. I stayed longer in the bathroom than usual, and not only washed with particular care, but also thoroughly brushed my teeth in order to get rid of any smell of alcohol. I did not know yet what attitude I was going to adopt with Magda, but a slight feeling of unease warned me not to be too talkative—to which I felt a strong inclination. Perhaps a serious, calm and collected pose would be best. The soup was on the table already when I came in, and Magda was waiting for me. I lightly gave her my hand and made a few remarks about the lovely spring weather. She agreed, and told me of a number of things that needed doing in the garden, and asked me to bring her from town that evening certain vegetable seeds which she had just noticed were missing. I promised to do so immediately, and so we got through the soup without a hitch. I was well aware that, every now and then, Magda surreptitiously eyed me up and down, with an unspoken question, but confident that nothing about me was noticeable, and that all was going well, I paid no attention to her glances. I recall that I ate that soup with particular relish.

Else cleared the table, and as she did so she whispered some domestic question to my wife, which caused Magda to get up and follow Else into the kitchen, probably to cut up or taste something. I was left alone in the dining-room, waiting for the meat course. I was thinking of nothing in particular; I was filled with a pleasant contentment; I was enjoying life. I had no warning of what I was about to do next. Suddenly, to my own surprise, I got up, tiptoed over to the sideboard, opened the lower door, and there, sure enough, was the bottle of red wine which we had started on that fateful November evening when our quarrels had begun. I held it up to the light. As I expected, it was still half-full. There was no time to lose, Magda might return at any moment. The cork was driven rather deep into the neck of the bottle, but I pulled it out with my nails, put the bottle to my mouth, and drank and drank like an old toper. (But what else could I do? There was no time to get a glass, quite apart from the fact that a used glass would have given me away.) I took three or four long pulls, held the bottle up to the light again, and saw that only a miserable drop was left. I finished that off as well, replaced the cork in the bottle, shut the sideboard door, and tiptoed back to my place. My stomach heaved, upset by the sudden flood of alcohol; it was convulsed as if by cramp, a fiery mist rose before my eyes, and my forehead and hands were damp with sweat. I had a hard job to pull myself together before Magda returned. Then I sat down at table again, feeling pleasantly abandoned to my drunkenness, and only the necessity of at least going through the form of eating, presented any difficulty. My stomach seemed a very delicate thing, ready to revolt at any moment. Each single bite had to be fed to it with the greatest care, and I regretted that the food which I had to swallow for appearances' sake was going to disturb the drunkenness which was quietly making itself felt.

It never occurred to me that it might be a good thing to exchange a few words with Magda. Instead, my mind was busy with another problem, which presented grave difficulties.

The wine-bottle was in the sideboard all right, but with the scrupulous way in which Magda ran her household, she was bound to notice within a short time that it was empty. I couldn't possibly allow that to happen. I must take precautions in time. But how incredibly difficult it was! The best solution would be to buy another bottle of red wine this very afternoon, pour about half of it away, and put it in place of the empty one. But when was I to do it, how could I get to the sideboard when I had to be at the office all the afternoon, and Magda and I always spent the evening together, she with some needlework and I with my newspaper? When? and what was I to do with the empty bottle? Would I be able to buy some wine of the same brand? Did Magda remember what sort it was, what kind of label it had? Best would be to get up secretly at midnight, carefully take the label off the old bottle and stick it on the new one. But supposing Magda were to surprise me at it! And moreover, had we any glue in the house? I would have to smuggle some from the office in my brief-case. The more I thought about it, the more complicated the whole affair became. Already it was absolutely insoluble. It had been easy enough to empty the bottle, but I should have thought before, how difficult it was going to be to restore it to its former condition. Supposing I just broke the bottle, and pretended that I had knocked it over while looking for something? But there was no wine left to spill. Or dare I simply half-fill it with water, and put off filling it with wine until some later time?

My head was more and more muddled. While I cast around in my mind, I had quite forgotten not only the meal but Magda as well. So I started, when she asked me with genuine apprehension in her voice: "What's the matter, Erwin? Are you ill? Have you got a temperature? You look so red."

I eagerly seized on this pretext, and said calmly: "Yes, I

really don't feel quite well. I think I'd better lie down for a moment. My . . . my head's throbbing."

"Yes, do, Erwin. Go to bed immediately. Shall I ring Dr Mansfeld?"

"Oh, nonsense," I cried angrily, "I'll just lie down on the sofa for a quarter of an hour, and I'll be all right. Then I must get back to the office."

She led me to the sofa like an invalid, helped me to lie down and spread a rug over me. "Have you had trouble at the office?" she asked anxiously. "Tell me what's worrying you, Erwin. You're quite changed."

"Nothing, nothing," I said, suddenly angry. "I don't know what's the matter with you. A little attack of giddiness or blood pressure and immediately there's something wrong at the office. Business is fine, just fine!"

She sighed softly. "All right, then, sleep well, Erwin," she said. "Shall I wake you?"

"No, no, not necessary. I'll wake up of my own accord—in a quarter of an hour or so. . . . "

Then I was alone at last: I let my head fall back, and now the alcohol flooded right through me in an unrestrained free-running wave. With a velvet wing it covered all my sorrows and afflictions, it washed away even the little new worry over my unnecessary lie about business being fine. I slept. . . . Slept? No, I was extinguished, I no longer existed.

5

IT IS already beginning to get dark when I wake up. I throw a startled glance at the clock: it is between seven and eight in the evening. I listen for any noises in the house. Nothing stirs. I call, softly at first, then louder: "Magda!" But she doesn't come. I get up stiffly. My whole body feels battered, my head is hollow, my mouth dry and thick. I glance into the dining-room next door: no supper table is laid, though this is our usual supper-time. What is the matter? What has happened while I slept? Where is Magda?

After some reflection, I grope my way to the kitchen. Walking is not easy, it is as if all my limbs are stiff and bent, they move with difficulty in their joints.

I half expected to find the kitchen empty too, and almost dark, but the light is on, and Else is standing by the table, busy with some ironing. As I come in she looks up with a start, and the expression on her face is no more reassured when she sees who it is. I can well imagine that I look a bit wild. Suddenly I feel as if I am dirty all over. I should have gone into the bath-room first.

"Where is my wife, Else?" I ask.

"Madam has gone to town," replies Else, with a quick, almost fearful glance at me.

"But it's supper-time, Else!" I say reproachfully, though I have not the slightest inclination to eat any supper.

Else shrugs her shoulders, and then says, with another quick glance, "There was a telephone call from your office. I think your wife has gone to the office."

I swallow with difficulty; I am conscious how dry my mouth has become.

"To the office?" I murmur. "Good God! What's my wife doing at the office, Else?"

She shrugs her shoulders again. "How should I know, Herr Sommer," she says. "Madam didn't tell me anything." She reflects for a moment, then goes on. "They rang up shortly after three, and your wife has been gone ever since." So for more than four hours already Magda has been at the office. I am lost. Why I am lost I cannot say, but I know that I am. My knees grow weak, I stumble forward a few steps and slump heavily into a chair. I let my head fall on the kitchen table.

"It's all up, Else," I groan. "I'm lost. Oh, Else. . . . " I hear her set down the iron with a startled crash, then she comes over to me and puts her hand on my shoulder. "What is it, Herr Sommer? Don't you feel well?" I don't see her. I don't lift my face from the shelter of my arms. In the presence of this young girl I am ashamed of my gushing tears. It's all over, all lost, my firm, my marriage, Magda—oh, if only I hadn't drunk that wine this lunch-time, that's what made everything go wrong; without that, Magda would never have gone to the office (a fleeting thought: I've still got to settle that affair of the empty wine bottle, too!). Else gently shakes my shoulder. "Herr Sommer," she says "don't give way like that. Lie down again for a bit, and I'll quickly make you some supper in the meantime." I shake my head. "I don't want any supper, Else. My wife ought to be here by now, it's high time . . . "

"Or," says Else persuasively, "would you like to eat a little something here in the kitchen with me, Herr Sommer?" Adding rather doubtfully. "As your wife is out. . . . " By its very novelty, there is something seductive about this quite unheard-of proposal. To eat in the kitchen with Else? Whatever would Magda say? I raise my head and look at Else properly for the first time. I have never looked at her like that before: for me, she was always merely a dark shadow of my wife in the remoter regions of the house. Now I see that Else is quite a pleasant dark-haired girl of about seventeen, of a somewhat robust beauty. Under a light blouse she has full breasts, and at the thought of how young those breasts are I feel a hot wave run over me.

But then I come to my senses. It's all so impossible. Already this business of letting myself go before Else just now is utterly impossible.

"No, Else," I say, and get up. "It is very nice of you to try to cheer me up a bit, but I had better get over to the office as well. If I should miss my wife, please tell her that I have gone to the office." I turn to go. Suddenly it is hard for me to leave the kitchen and this friendly girl. I notice how pale her face is, and how well her high-arching eyebrows suit it.

"I have many worries, Else," I say abruptly, "and I have nobody to stand by me." Emphatically, I repeat, "Nobody, Else. Do you understand?"

"Yes, Herr Sommer," she answers softly.

"Thank you, Else, for being so nice to me," I add. And I go. Only as I am getting ready in the bathroom does it occur to me that I have just betrayed Magda. Betrayed and deceived. Deceived and defrauded. But at once I shrug my shoulders: that's right! Lower and lower. Deeper and deeper into it. Now there's no holding back!

6

I MADE my way cautiously to the office, cautiously, because at all costs I wanted to avoid meeting Magda in the street. I stood on the other side of the street in the shadow of a doorway, and looked across at my firm's five ground-floor windows. Two of them belonging to my main office, were lit up, and occasionally through the ground glass I saw the silhouettes of two figures: that of Magda and of my book-keeper, Hinzpeter. "They're going through the books!" I said to myself with a deep sense of shock, and yet this shock was mingled with a feeling of relief, for now I knew that the conduct of the business was in Magda's capable hands. That was just like her, immediately on hearing the bad news, to give herself a clear picture of the situation by going through the books. With a deep sigh I turned away and walked right through the town and out of it, but not towards my home. What should I do in the office, what should I do at home? Invite the reproaches that were bound to be made? Try to justify what was utterly unjustifiable? Not at all. And while I walked out again into the countryside, which was slowly growing darker and darker, it became painfully clear to me that I was played out. I had nothing left to live for, I had lost my footing in society, and I felt I had not the strength to look for a new one, nor to fight to regain the old. What was I to do now? I went on, I walked away from office, wife, home town, I left everything behind—but I would have to go home again eventually, wouldn't I? I would have to face Magda, listen to her reproaches, hear myself rightly called a liar and a cheat, have to admit that I was a failure, a failure of the most disgraceful and cowardly kind. The thought was unbearable, and I began to play with the idea of not returning home at all, but of going out into the world, of submerging myself in the darkness somewhere, in some darkness where a man might disappear without trace, without a final cry. And while I was outlining this to myself, with some feeling of self-pity, I knew that I was deceiving myself, that I would never have the courage to live without the security of hearth and home. I would never be able to give up the soft bed I was used to, the tidiness of home, the punctual, nourishing meals. I would go home to Magda, in spite of all my fears, I would go back to my own bed this very night—never mind about living in the darkness, never mind about a life and death in the gutter.

"But," I asked myself again, and I quickened my hasty steps, "but what's the matter with me? I used to be a fairly energetic and enterprising man. I always was a little weak but I knew so well how to conceal that, that up to now even Magda probably hadn't noticed it. Where does all this weariness come from that has been growing on me for the last year, paralysing my limbs and brain, and making me, till now a fairly honest man, into a deceiver of my wife, and the kind of character who looks lustingly at a servant-girl's breasts? It can't be the alcohol. I never drank schnaps before today, and this lassitude has been hanging over me for such a long time now. Whatever can it be?" I tried this theory and that. I reflected that I was just over forty. I had heard talk of the change of life in men, but I knew no man of my acquaintance who, on passing forty, had changed as much as I. Then I recalled my loveless existence. I had always longed for love and appreciation, secretly of course, and I had had it in full measure, from Magda as well as from my fellow-citizens. Then gradually I had lost it. I didn't know how it had all happened. Had I lost love and

24

appreciation because I had grown so bad, or had I grown so bad because I had lost its encouragement? I found no answer to these questions: I was not accustomed to thinking about myself. I walked faster still. I wanted to get to the place where I would find rest from all these torturing problems. At last I stood before my goal, before that same country inn I had visited this fatal morning. I looked through the bar-room window for the girl with the pale eyes, who had passed such a contemptuous judgment on my manhood after one insolent glance. I saw her sitting under the dim light of a single little bulb, busy with some needlework. I looked at her for a long time, I hesitated, and with a painful and voluptuous sense of self-abasement, I asked myself just why I had come to her. And I found no answer to this question, either.

But I was tired of all these problems. I almost ran up the paved path to the inn, groped in the dark passage for the door-handle, entered quickly, and with a pretence of cheerfulness I cried: "Here I am, my pretty one!" and sat down in a wicker chair beside her.

All that I had just done resembled so little my usual be-haviour, was so different from my former sedateness, that I watched myself with unconcealed astonishment, almost with anxious embarrassment as if watching an actor who has taken on too daring a rôle, and who is unsure whether he will be able to play it convincingly to the end.

The girl looked up from her sewing, for a moment the pale eyes were turned on me, the tip of her tongue appeared briefly at the corner of her mouth. "Oh, it's you," was all she said, and these three words conveyed once more her judgment of myself.

"Yes, it's me, my beauty," I said quickly, with the glibness and arrogance that came so strangely to me, "and I would like one or two or maybe half a dozen glasses of that excellent schnaps of yours, and if you like, you can drink with me."

"I never drink schnaps," countered the girl coolly, but she got up, went to the bar, got a little glass and a bottle, and poured out a drink by the table. She sat down and put the bottle on the floor beside her.

"Anyway," she added, taking up her sewing again, "we're closing in a quarter of an hour."

"Then I'll have to drink all the quicker," I said, put the glass to my lips and emptied it. "But if you won't drink schnaps," I continued, "I'd gladly buy you a bottle of wine or champagne even, if there is such a thing here. Regardless of cost."

In the meantime she had re-filled my glass, and I emptied it again in one go. I had already forgotten all that had happened and all that lay ahead, I lived only for the moment, for this reserved yet knowing girl who treated me with such obvious contempt.

"We've got champagne all right," she said, "and I like to drink it, too. But I'll have you know that I don't intend to get drunk, nor go to bed with you just for a bottle of champagne."

Now she looked at me again, accompanying her immodest words with a bold insolent look. I had to go on playing my part. "Whoever would think of such a thing, my sweet," I said lightly. "Go and get your champagne. You'll be allowed to drink it quite unmolested. To me," I added, more firmly after I had had another drink, "you're like an angel from another planet, a bad angel whom fate has set in my path. It's enough for me just to look at you."

"It costs nothing to look," she said with a short evil-sounding laugh. "You're a pretty queer saint, but before the night's out I think I'm going to find out what you're so excited about."

With that, she poured me another drink, and got up to

fetch the champagne. This time she was away longer. She drew the curtains, then went outside, and I heard her close the shutters, and lock the door. As she went through the barroom again, she said "I've locked up, nobody else will be coming. The landlady's in bed already." She said this in passing, then stopped, and added in an ironic tone, "But don't build your hopes on that." Before I could answer, she had gone again. I used her absence to pour myself out two or three drinks straight off. Then she came back with a gold-topped bottle in her hand.

She put a champagne glass on the table before her, skilfully unbent the wire and twisted the cork out of the bottle without letting it pop. The white foam rushed up. She poured, waited a moment, poured again, and lifted the glass to her mouth.

"I'm not going to drink your health," she said, "because you would want to drink with me, and for the time being, you've had enough."

I didn't contradict her. My whole body was so full of drunkenness, it seemed to hum like a swarm of bees. She put down her glass, looked at me with narrowed eyes and asked mockingly, "Now then, how many schnapses did you have while I was away? Five? Six?"

"Only three," I answered, laughing. It never occurred to me to feel ashamed. With this girl, all such feelings disappeared completely.

"Incidentally, what's your name?"

"Do you intend to come here often?" she countered.

"Perhaps," I answered, rather confused. "Why?"

"Why do you want to know my name? For the half hour we sit here, 'my sweet' or whatever else you like to call me, will do."

"All right, don't tell me your name," I said, suddenly irritable. "I don't care."

I took the bottle and poured another drink. Already it was quite clear to me that I was completely drunk and that I should not take any more. Even so, the urge to go on drinking was stronger. The coloured web in my brain enticed me, the dark untrodden jungles of my inner self tempted me; from afar, a soft seductive voice was calling.

"I don't know whether I shall often come here," I said rapidly. "I can't stand you, I hate you, and yet I've come back to you this evening. This morning I drank the first schnaps in my life. You poured it out for me, you stole into my blood with it, you've poisoned me. You're like the spirit of schnaps: hovering, intoxicating, cheap and. . . ."

I looked at her, breathless, myself the more astonished at these words which hurtled out of me, goodness knows where from. She sat opposite me. She had not taken up her sewing again. She had crossed her stockingless legs and had pushed her skirt back a little from her knees. Her legs were rather sturdy, but long, and fine-ankled. On her right calf I saw a birthmark nearly the size of a farthing—it seemed beautiful to me. She held a cigarette in her hand; she blew the smoke in a broad stream through her nearly closed lips; she stared at me without blinking.

"Go on, pop," she said, "you're getting on fine, go on. . . ."

I tried to think. What had I been talking about just now? The impulse to touch her, to take her in my arms, became almost overwhelming. But I leaned back firmly in my wicker chair, I clung to its arms. Suddenly I heard myself speak again. I spoke quite slowly and very distinctly, and yet I was breathless with excitement. "I'm a wholesale merchant," I said, "I had quite a good business, but now I'm faced with bankruptcy. They'll all laugh at me, all of them, especially my wife. . . . I've made a lot of mistakes, and Magda will throw them all in my face. Magda's my wife, you know. . . ."

She looked at me steadily, with that very white face of hers, that had about it something almost bloated. Above her nearly colourless eyes, stood her dark high-arching brows.

"But I can still draw money out of the business, a few thousand marks. I'd do it anyway, just to annoy Magda. Magda wants to save the business. Does she think she's better than I am? I could sell the business. I know already to whom, it's quite a new firm. He would give me ten, perhaps twelve thousand marks for it, we could go travelling. . . . Have you ever been to Paris?"

She looked at me. Neither affirmation nor dissent were to be read in her face. I went on talking, quicker, more breathlessly. "I've not been there either," I continued, "but I've read about it. It's a town of tree-lined boulevards, wide squares, leafy parks. . . . When I was a boy I learned a bit of French, but I left school too soon, my parents hadn't enough money. Do you know what this means: *Donnez-moi un baiser, mademoiselle?*"

Not a sign from her, neither yes or no.

"It means, 'give me a kiss, mademoiselle.' But one would have to say to you, *Donnez-moi un baiser, ma reine! Reine* means queen. You're the queen of my heart. You're the queen of the poison they cork up in bottles. Give me your hand, Elsabe—I'm going to call you Elsabe, my queen—I mean to kiss your hand. . . . "

She filled my glass.

"There, drink this up, then you're going home. It's enough —you've had enough to drink, and I've had enough of you. You can take that bottle of brandy with you. You'll have to pay for the whole bottle, saloon price. It's no swindle. Don't you come in here tomorrow saying I swindled you. You poured I don't know how many out for yourself."

"Don't say that, Elsabe," I said, half-blustering, half-whining. "I'd never do such a thing! What do I care about money——!"

"Don't teach me about men! When they're drunk and randy it's all 'What do I care about money!' and next morning they turn up with the police, shouting about being swindled. The brandy, and the champagne, and my cigarettes . . . that comes to. . . . "

She named a sum.

"Is that all?" I said boastfully and pulled out my wallet. "Here you are!"

I put down the money.

"And here . . . ," I took out a hundred-mark note and laid it beside the other. "This is for you because I hate you and because you're ruining me. Take it, take it. I don't want anything from you, anything at all! Go away! I've got you in my blood already, I couldn't possess you more than I do. You're very likely dull and boring. You're not from hereabouts, you're from some city, of course, where you left everything behind—this is just the remains!"

We stood facing each other, the money lay on the table, the light was gloomy. I swayed gently on my feet. I was holding the half-empty brandy bottle by the neck. She looked at me.

"Put your money away," she whispered. "Take your money off the table. I don't want your money . . . you'd better go!"

"You can't force me to take the money back. I'm leaving it here . . . I present you with it, my queen of bright brandy called Elsabe. I'm going. . . . "

Laboriously I made my way to the door. The key was on the inside and I struggled to turn it in the lock.

"Hey, you," she said behind me. "You. . . . "

I turned round. Her voice had become low but full and soft. All the impudence had gone out of it.

"You . . . " she repeated, and now in her eyes there was colour and light. "You—do you want to?"

Now it was I who looked at her silently.

"Take your shoes off, be quiet on the stairs, the landlady mustn't hear you. Come on, be quick...."

Silently, I did as she told me. I don't know why I did. I didn't desire her now. I didn't desire her in that way, at all.

"Give me your hand."

She switched off the light and led me by the hand. In the other hand I still held the brandy bottle. It was completely dark in the bar-room. I crept after her. Moonlight through a little dusty window fell on the narrow angular staircase. I swayed, I was very tired. I thought of my own bed, of Magda, of my long way home.

It was all too much for me. The only consolation was the bottle of brandy in my hand, that would give me strength. I would have preferred to stop already and take a pull out of the bottle, I was so tired. The stairs creaked, the bedroom door groaned softly as it was opened. There was moonlight in the room, too. A rumpled bed, an iron wash-stand, a chair, a row of hangers on the wall....

"Get undressed," I said softly, "I'll be with you in a moment." And more to myself, "Are there any stars here?"

I went to the window, which looked out over an orchard. I opened it a little; the spring air with its soft breeze and its perfumes entered, mild as a tender caress. Under the window lay the sloping tar-papered roof of a shed.

"That's good," I said, softly again, "That sloping roof is very good."

I couldn't see the moon, it was behind the house-roof above my head. But its glow filled the sky with a whitish light; only the brightest stars were to be seen, and even they looked dim. I was uneasy and irritable.

"Come on," she cried angrily from the bed. "Hurry up! Do you think I don't need any sleep?"

I turned, and bent over the bed. She lay on her back, covered to the chin. I stripped the cover back and laid my face for a

31

moment against her naked breast. Cool and firm. Breathing gently. It smelt good—of hair and flesh.

"Hurry up!" she whispered impatiently. "Get undressed—stop that nonsense. You're not a schoolboy any more!"

I straightened up with a deep sigh. I went to the window, took the bottle and swung myself out on to the shed roof. I heard a furious cry behind me, but I was already letting myself drop into the garden.

"Drunken old fool!" she called from above, and then the window banged.

I stood among bushes. I smelt the scent of lilac. The spring night was perfect in its purity. I put the bottle to my mouth and drank deeply.

7

I WALK and walk. I walk along, singing to myself one of those *wanderlieder* that I used to sing when hiking with Magda. Then for long stretches I limp on aching feet. I have stubbed my toe against a stone, it is bad going for my shoeless feet. My socks have long since been torn to ribbons. I come to a stream, clamber down the bank, sit on a stone and put my feet in the water, which shocks me for a moment with its icy coldness. Then it feels good, and sitting on the stone I fall asleep. I wake up shivering, icy. I have fallen from my seat, I walk on. The faster I walk, the longer the road seems to become. The fruit trees along the roadside positively fly past me, yet I seem to be no further on. I don't know where I am, only that I'm a long way from home. I don't know what time it is, only that it's still night. The moon is some two handsbreadths above the horizon. And I walk on. I walk through a sleeping village. Not a light anywhere, everyone asleep, I am the only one abroad. Erwin Sommer, proprietor of a wholesale market produce business. Not now, not now, that was before. The one who is walking through this moonlit night, who is he? Once he was someone—long ago he was. Down and out now, finished, almost forgotten. . . . At my shuffling step, a dog wakes up in his kennel and starts to bark. Other dogs awaken and now the whole village is barking and I shuffle through it on sore feet, a tramp, and yesterday I was still . . . oh, shut up! And I stop in the shadow of the wooden church spire and raise the bottle to my mouth again and drink. That stills the questions, soothes the pain, that is a whip for the next half hour on

33

the road. But there is not much left in the bottle. I'll have to go easy with the precious stuff. I'll swallow the last mouthful —and it must be a big one—on my own doorstep, before I face Magda. But Magda is asleep. I shall lie down very quietly on the sofa, there won't be any argument tonight. And tomorrow? Tomorrow is a long way off. By tomorrow I shall have had a deep, deep sleep, I shall have forgotten everything that happened today, I shall be the head of the firm again, who had committed a small blunder, it's true, but who is perfectly capable of making amends. . . .

I have hidden the empty bottle in the garden bushes, and now, very quietly, on my bare feet, I mount the steps to the front door. I manage to unlock the door without a sound. I am not a bit drunk now, though I have only just taken one or two long swigs of brandy—there was more left in the bottle than I had thought. So much the better. I am all the more clear-headed and certain. I shan't make any mistake, I shan't wake anyone up. How cunning I am. I am tempted to go into the bathroom to bathe my sore feet, but my clear head reminds me that the noise of the taps would awaken Magda, so I sneak into the kitchen. I can wash in the kitchen. Only little Else sleeps next to the kitchen. She's good to me, she comforted me, she's not hard and efficient like Magda. I switch on the light, I look round the kitchen. I choose a large enamel basin, and I think to look into the boiler by the stove, to see if there is any warm water. The water is actually luke-warm still. I am proud of my cleverness. I get the washing soap, the hand-towel, kitchen cloths, a brush. I sit on a chair and put my feet into the water. Oh, how good it feels, how soothing that gentle caress is! I lean back, I close my eyes—if only I had something to drink now, I would be absolutely happy.

There's always something lacking for human happiness, we can never be perfectly content. I've drunk all the red wine, and there's nothing else to drink in the house. Tomorrow I must start a wine-cellar, and there must be a few bottles of schnaps in it, too. Schnaps is a very good thing—a pity I've wasted so many years of my life when I might have been drinking schnaps—in all moderation of course. I lean back still further, enjoying the bath, feeling the burning pain recede ... and suddenly I jump up! The water slops out of the basin and floods over the tiled floor. But I take no notice of that. I have had a revelation. Of course we have something to drink in the house! Didn't Magda get some Madeira for certain kinds of soup, ox-tail for instance? And doesn't she use rum for her preserves? I know that from her housekeeping accounts. And I run on my bare feet into the larder, I search, I sniff at bottles, I smell vinegar and oil—and here, here it is: "Fine old Sherry," and here's port wine, no less, the bottle three-parts-full, and rum, half-full—oh, how beautiful life is! Intoxication, forgetfulness, to float along on the stream of forgetfulness, into the twilight, deep into the darkness where there is neither failure nor regret ... good alcohol, I salute you. *La reine* Elsabe, I have rested on your naked breast, I have breathed the scent of your hair and your flesh!

I have filled the basin again, I have set the three uncorked bottles before me, I have taken a long pull from the rum bottle. At first it repels me after the gentler, purer taste of the brandy. The rum tastes sharper, more burning, it is adulterated and all the more fiery on that account. I feel it spreading in my blood like dark-red clouds, it stimulates my imagination, it makes me more wide-awake, more watchful, more cunning. ... I know I must tidy up the kitchen properly, wipe the flood off the floor, carefully cork the bottles and put them away again. Nobody must notice anything, not even Else. Good little Else, she's fast asleep, she's young still, she sleeps the sleep of youth, but I, her master, I sit here in the kitchen and watch over her sleep. If a burglar were to come now . . . but where did I leave the corks? I don't see them anywhere, I haven't got them in my pockets either—perhaps they're still in the larder? I must go and look, I must put the bottles away properly corked. But the water is so gentle to my feet, and I am getting so tired, I would like to sleep, just for a brief moment, then I'll tidy up, I'll put everything in perfect order, and I'll find the corks too. . . .

Who's coming? Who is disturbing me again? Oh, it's only Magda, efficient Magda. In the middle of the night, no, rather towards morning, there she stands in the kitchen door-way looking spick-and-span, fully dressed anyway, and stares silently at me with a pale startled face. I half straighten up, make a gesture of greeting, nod to her and say cheerfully: "Here I am again, Magda! I just made a little trip, a little excursion into the springtime. Have you heard the larks sing yet this year? Tomorrow we'll go together. You'll see how lovely and green the birches are, and you can make the acquaintance of the Queen of Schnaps, *la reine d'alcool*, I've christened her Elsabe. . . . You're so clever, Magda, I saw you at the books with Hinzpeter, in the office. You've been through the books, you've a clear view of things now. I've always been afraid of that clear view! I drink to you, Magda, and again and again! I know it's your rum, but I'll replace it, I'll replace everything. We've still got money. I can sell the business. It belongs to me, I'm the boss, I can do what I like! Or have you got something to say against it?"

She said nothing. She looked silently at me, then at my bleeding feet. She was very pale. Two tears welled up in her eyes and ran slowly down her pale cheeks. She didn't wipe them away. Intently I followed their course with my eyes, until they fell on her dress. Those tears didn't upset me; on the contrary it pleased me that she wept, it was a sweet feeling to me, that she could still suffer on my account.

36

I drank again.

"You're so mercilessly efficient. Yes, I didn't get the prison contract, but you'll put that right somehow. I've always lived in your shadow; you never let me feel your superiority, but I could never reach as high as you, and now I'm right down. But one can live below the surface as well. I met a curious girl who is right down, too, but she can feel pain and happiness. One can feel joy and sorrow down below, Magda, it's just like being up above, it's all the same whether you live up or down. Perhaps the most beautiful thing is to let yourself fall, to shut your eyes and plunge into nothingness, deeper and deeper into nothingness. One can go on falling endlessly Magda. I haven't reached the end, I haven't touched bottom yet. All my limbs are still intact."

"Erwin," she pleaded, "Erwin, don't say any more. Stop drinking now. You're ill, Erwin. Come, go to bed. I'll bandage your feet. They look terrible. I'll bandage your feet."

"You see," I cried, and drank again, "you begrudge me even these few mouthfuls. They're your bottles, of course, but I'll pay for them. I'll pay you in cash or kind. That's fair dealing, you can't say anything against that. You ask about my feet. I've been on a trip in the country, while the efficient mistress is at work, surely the master can have some relaxation, once in a while. I walked barefoot, walking barefoot is supposed to be healthy. . . ."

She let me go on talking. She had quickly left the kitchen and returned with a large sponge, a jar of ointment, and some bandages. She knelt beside me, and while I went on talking over her head, more and more thickly and incoherently, she washed my feet, washed the dirt of the road out of my wounds, wiped them gently, applied the ointment, and bandaged them up.

"Good, good," I said, "you're really good to me, Magda. If only you weren't so damned efficient!"

8

I WAKE up, I am lying in bed, the windows are open, the curtains move gently in the breeze. Outside, the sun is shining. It
must be rather late, the bed beside me is made already. There
is no one in the bedroom but myself. I feel very sick. There
is a burning dryness in my stomach. Only slowly can I bring
myself to think. I become aware of pain in my feet. I turn back
the covers and see the bandages. And like a thunderclap everything comes to me again: the way I watched the shadows on
the glass from outside my office, all that vulgar boozing in the
bar-room, the shameful scene in that common barmaid's room,
my drunken shoeless walk home, and worst of all, the scene in
the kitchen with Magda! How I degraded myself, oh, how I
degraded myself! A burning wave of remorse sweeps over me.
The shame of it, the torturing shame of it! I hide my face in
my hands, I shut my eyes tight. . . . I don't want to see, I don't
want to hear, I don't want to think any more. I set my jaw,
I grind my teeth. I groan: "It can't be true! It isn't true! It
can't have been me! I've dreamed it all! I must forget all about
it. Straight away, I must forget all about it. None of it must
be true!"

I tremble as if with a cramp, and then come the tears, tears
for all that I have so wantonly thrown away. Endless, bitter,
and eventually comforting tears.

And when I have finished crying, the sun is still outside my
window, the cool fragrant curtains sway in the gentle breeze.

Life is still here, young and smiling. You can begin again at any time, it only depends on you. A little table is standing by my bed, with a breakfast tray upon it. The coffee is keeping warm under a cosy, and now I begin to have breakfast. I bite into a roll. Ineffectively I chew over and over on the first tough mouthful; but the coffee has been made extra strong, gradually my appetite returns, and I enjoy all the little delicacies which Magda has considerately laid out on the tray: sharp anchovies, lovely fat liver sausage, and wonderful Cheshire cheese. Rarely have I eaten with such relish. I feel like a convalescent. Thankfully I greet the neat familiar objects which surround me, greet them like faithful old friends whom I have missed for a long time. Now I find a note from Magda on the bedside table. She tells me that she has just gone to the office for a few hours, she asks me to stay in bed, or at least in the house, till her return; the bath-water has been heated for me.

Half an hour later I left the house. Although walking was very painful on account of my sore feet, I did not intend to remain inactive any longer. I had cleaned myself up from top to toe, put on fresh linen, my best suit—and now I was going to take my old place in the world again.

No hesitation this time; no peering out of door-ways after shadows; I went straight in. I gave a friendly greeting to my staff in the two outer offices, and entered my private office. Magda jumped up from my desk-chair. Formerly she had never sat at it; she had a place at a side table. It hurt me rather that she had already struck me off the list of active partners; she blushed deeply.

"Erwin!" she cried. "I thought. . . . " And she looked first at me, then at Herr Hinzpeter.

"Good morning, good morning, Herr Hinzpeter," I said amiably, "Yes, you thought . . . but I found I felt much better this morning, except for my feet . . . of course, my feet . . . but never mind that. Now tell me what you've found out, and what you've already decided on. Can we make up for the loss of that prison contract?" I sat down in my desk-chair. I looked at them amiably, quite the boss, ready to listen to the suggestions of his staff before making his decision. Barely an hour ago I had been crying out that I wanted to forget, that I must forget. . . . And now here I sat. I couldn't forget, for Magda's pallor and my aching feet in their tight shoes reminded me: but I wanted them to forget. Another five minutes and it would seem like a bad dream to Magda, that not twelve hours before, she had seen me sitting at the kitchen table, three bottles in front of me, my dirty feet in a bowl, the tiled floor swimming with water—just a bad dream! She must forget! She must forget! (I quite realised that it was absolutely disgraceful of me, just to pass events over without a word, to wipe them off the slate, to allow no allusion to them: it was utterly and absolutely disgraceful!) Anyhow, it transpired that not for nothing had I counted on Magda's energy.

Early in the morning she had already paid a visit to our friend the prison governor, to find out whether there wasn't perhaps something to be salvaged. And lo and behold, the good fellow had in fact given her a tip, a very valuable tip. . . . One section of the prisoners, at the beginning of their sentence, were put on to picking oakum—old used or frayed rope was pulled to pieces, reduced to strands, and then, with the tow so gained, new rope was made. There was always a large demand for this old rope, and at the moment the prison administration's supplies were almost at an end. The governor had suggested to Magda that she might go to Hamburg and buy up old cordage, two or maybe three truckloads. He said there was quite good business to be done in this way, provided one knew the right places to go to, and furthermore, he dropped a hint or two as to where those places were.

As I have said, I listened benevolently to all this. Of course it was only a small casual undertaking that, even with the most advantageous buying, could not nearly replace a three years' grocery contract for almost fifteen hundred men, but it was something we could take in our stride, even if it didn't really fit into the framework of my business.

"And who do you think should go, Magda?" I asked. "Perhaps you yourself . . . ?"

"No, much as I'd like to," she replied hesitatingly. "I don't think I can go just now. Particularly now . . . " she broke off and looked at me rather helplessly, yet with meaning. This was one of those looks that I was not going to put up with in any circumstances. So I said, "You're quite right, Magda. You can hardly be spared at the moment. And besides, there's the household. Else is still rather young (dear comforting Else!) I think it's best if I go. I feel quite well again, and as for my feet, well, I can arrange something about that . . . I can always take taxis . . . "

Magda hastily interrupted me. "You can't go, in any case, Erwin. You know you're not well." She looked firmly at me, not maliciously, rather sadly and affectionately, but firmly. This time I lowered my glance.

"No," she continued, "the best thing would be to send Herr Hinzpeter. He could leave this evening, already, and perhaps be back the morning after tomorrow . . . "

I interrupted her. "One moment, Magda, please. Thank you, Herr Hinzpeter, I'll call you in again a little later. . . . "

I waited until the door had closed behind the book-keeper. Then I looked seriously at Magda.

"Magda," I said, "we'll let bygones be bygones. We won't talk about this thing any more. We'll forget it for good."

She made a gesture as if she wanted to speak, to contradict this possibly all too-simple solution.

"No, no, Magda," I said hastily, "let me finish—I beg you

to let me go to Hamburg. It is most important to me, and as for my feet, well, I can manage. . . . "

She made an impatient gesture, as if my feet were entirely unimportant at the moment. This lack of interest in my well-being offended me very deeply, but without showing my feelings, I continued: "It will be very good for my state of mind if I got away for a day or two." In a lower voice, I added: "Losing that prison contract has greatly upset me, I feel I've disgraced myself over it."

She looked fixedly at me.

"Erwin," she said, "you said yourself we should let bygones be bygones, and I'll agree to that, although . . . " she broke off. "So don't you start about it yourself. As far as that trip to Hamburg is concerned, I'm firmly convinced that it would not be good for you just now. It's not distraction you need, but rest and concentration. Apart from that, I've made an appointment with Dr Mansfeld for both of us this afternoon."

"That's your wilfulness again, Magda," I cried angrily. "What do I want with Dr Mansfeld? I'm perfectly healthy, apart from my feet, I . . . " "Oh, your feet!" she cried, now angry too, "that bit of sore skin will soon heal. No, you are really ill, Erwin, I've noticed for months past how you've changed. The doctor will have to examine you thoroughly."

"Under your supervision," I said ironically. "Thank you very much indeed."

"Erwin," she said pleadingly. "Just for this once, don't let's quarrel. Do come and see the doctor with me, just as a favour. Then he can decide whether it would be good for you to go to Hamburg."

"Oh," I said bitterly, "if he's going to make decisions on your advice, we needn't go at all. You can tell Hinzpeter straightaway that he's got to go to Hamburg."

We each stood at a window of the office, and stared into the street. For my part, I was not only staring, but drumming

42

on the window-pane as well. Outside the spring sun was shining, and many women were passing by, dressed in flowered frocks. Only a short time before I had felt like a convalescent, and had greeted the familiar things around me with fresh interest, convinced that today a new life was beginning... and now the old creaking mill of our dissension was starting up again, grinding all my good resolutions to dust. And why? Because Magda was obstinate and wanted to decide everything on her own. No, this time I didn't intend to give in. We had agreed that what was past was past, and I didn't have to be submissive just on account of the events of last night.

Magda turned abruptly from the window towards me.

"Erwin," she said softly.

"Yes?" I said sullenly, and went on drumming without looking at her.

"Erwin," she repeated, "I don't want to quarrel with you today. I feel as if we were in some terrible danger and had to keep together at all costs. So I will do as *you* wish; you go to Hamburg, but when you come back, do me the favour of coming with me to Dr Mansfeld."

I turned to her and laughed happily.

"When I come back you'll see for yourself how well I am, and you'll give up this visit to the doctor on your own accord. All the same, I promise. Anyway, thank you very much Magda. I'll bring you home something nice...." and I laughed again. I was so happy at the prospect of the journey.

"I haven't done this to get your thanks," said Magda rather stiffly. "I've done it quite against my own better judgment. I'm convinced that this journey will do you no good."

"But I'll be going with your consent," I interrupted again, "and afterwards we'll see which of us was right. Now tell me, which firms were mentioned in connection with this business? Of course, I'll look around on my own account as well...."

9

FROM the point of view of business, my trip to Hamburg was a great success: I was able to buy three truckloads of cordage at an incredibly low price, and we made quite a tidy sum out of this casual deal. Afterwards, I told Magda a lot of tales about how I had had to hunt for the old rope, but actually it had come my way quite by chance, as sometimes happens; I did not have to work for it at all. Still, I had to say something to justify being away for nearly five days. I did not once get drunk in Hamburg, I want to make that perfectly clear. But I got into the habit there of taking a little drink at any hour of the day, even early in the morning, a habit which is perhaps more fatal than an occasional heavy bout of drunkenness. I went about the beautiful city a great deal—the whole business was settled within half an hour on the second day—I went down to the River Alster and the harbour and among the wharves, tramped through the endless halls of the Altona fish market, attended an auction there, travelled out to Ohlsdorf and wandered through the famous cemetery for hours on end, and in between all this I would scuttle in and out of saloons to drink a glass or two of some clear or brown burning liquid. It put me in a good mood, did my stomach good, cheered my heart, allowed me to see the colourful teeming city through happy eyes, in short, it took me out of myself. I went through the days, not quite drunk, indeed very far from any real drunkenness, and yet never really sober; and whereas at the outset I had waited until ten or even eleven for

44

my first tot of schnaps, by the last two days I was quite cheerfully ringing for the chambermaid and ordering her to bring me my first double brandy in bed by eight o'clock already. Breakfast tasted all the better for it.

During the return journey, for which I had provided myself with a good pocket flask, the best of resolutions matured in me. It was clear that I wouldn't be able to keep on with this habit under Magda's sharp eye, and after I had just taken a good swig in the toilet on the train, I felt it would be quite easy to give it up. After all it was only one or two little glasses every one or two hours, it ought to be easy enough to wean myself of that. Contrary to my expectation, the journey lasted longer than the contents of my flask, though I thought I had provided amply for it. In our station buffet (where I am not known) I had another couple of drinks and then set off home. I did not forget to buy a box of cachous at the chemists, to cover up the smell of alcohol. For I anticipated that, after such a long absence, a welcoming kiss from Magda would be inevitable. She received me amicably but coolly, she looked quizzically at me and found I had grown stouter, or a little puffy about the face, as she put it. This made me furious, but I didn't show it. Instead I talked enthusiastically about how I had bought the cordage, about the beautiful city of Hamburg, the cemetery at Ohlsdorf, and also about an organ concert which I had heard (quite by accident) in St. Nicholas' church. I proved thereby that I hadn't only been sitting around in bars, but had led an interesting and lively existence and I actually succeeded, to some extent, in cheering up my all-too-serious Magda. She in her turn reported on the way business was going; she had started something new. She had been going out into the country nearly every day in our little car, and had bought up honey from all the bee-keepers, not only the honey they had on hand, but also the yield of the coming rape- and lime-blossom season. She had bought jars and wanted to add to our

45

firm a department for the distribution of honey direct to the consumer. She started to talk to me about the wording of the advertisements and the newspapers in which our honey department was to be advertised.

I could hardly listen. I wasn't actually tired, but I was so weary of all these things, of this unflagging busy-ness—all for nothing. Because what was the point of selling honey? None. People ate it, and then it was gone. It was like soap bubbles, a shimmering nothing enclosing a little air in a great deal of light. It burst, nothing remained, all was delusion and black magic! Ah, get away with you! Don't talk so much, don't natter all the time! Leave me in peace! What are you wearing yourself out for? There are hundreds of thousands and millions of firms in the world; do you think yours is important? It's absolutely insignificant, even a fly wouldn't take any notice of it! Yes, if I had some schnaps now, I might be able to listen to you with some attention. I could get some, too. I could get Else to fetch me a whole bottle from the nearest saloon, but it's not possible because you're sitting here nattering all the time. Because you're sitting here in my life and so I can't do what my life demands. No, no, of course I don't mean it's as bad as all that, I quite like her, Magda, but it would be awfully nice if she would just vanish into thin air for a while—the boring, eternally nattering cow!

In the course of this monologue I had talked myself into a towering rage. Now I suddenly stood up and to Magda's astonishment brusquely remarked that I had a bad headache and wanted to take a walk for a quarter of an hour—no thank you, no company. And with that I was outside already, and it was really all the same to me what she thought or whether I had hurt her feelings again. I turned six or seven corners till I came to a district where I thought I was not known, and went into a little saloon and asked the fat bearded landlord for a double cognac. As I was knocking back the third one, for I wanted to make proper provision for the night, the landlord said slowly, "This is a bit unusual for you, Herr Sommer, I suppose you've got a cold, have you?" Angry to find myself so well known, I gave up the idea of a fourth drink and started for home. I sucked my sweet breath cachous and of course I was furious with Magda because she obliged me to drive away the delicious taste of the cognac with such sickly scented sweets.

She was still waiting for me, probably she wanted to inveigle me into further discussion about her boring honey, but I went straight to the bedroom, and only muttered a few sullen words, pretending that I still had a bad headache. Then I quickly fell asleep.

But in the middle of the night, shortly after one o'clock, I stood barefoot in the larder again, in my pyjamas, and emptied in quick succession what was left in the three bottles, and while I had the last bottle at my lips, I realised with a terrible certainty that I was lost, that there was no salvation for me, that I belonged to alcohol, body and soul. Now it was quite immaterial whether I kept up some appearance of seemliness and moral responsibility for a few days or weeks—it was all over, in any case. Let Magda come and catch me drinking. I'd tell her to her face that I'd become a drunkard, and that she had driven me to it, she and her infernal efficiency!

But she didn't come. So I left the three bottles standing there empty, and put the corks beside them. Let them all know, Magda, Else, everybody, it was all the same to me!

But then, towards morning, I felt so heavy-hearted that I got up again, virtually licked the last few drops out of the necks of the bottles, filled them with water, half- or three-quarters full as the case might be, corked them and put them back in their old place. And so I gained two or three days' grace. . . .

10

FOLLOWING this, I went to the office fairly regularly and did a certain amount of work, not for the pleasure of it, but because it was an old habit not easily broken, and because I felt ashamed of myself in front of Magda. Magda had grown very quiet; we only discussed the most essential things now. The only time we showed any animation was when some third person was present—Hinzpeter or Else or a client. Then we could even joke together, and the good-humoured tone of our early married life seemed to have returned, but hardly had the door shut behind this third person, than we fell silent immediately, my face froze and Magda began to rummage among some papers. During this time she constantly kept near me. Not that she would walk with me to the office, but five or ten minutes later she would appear without fail. The running of the house was left entirely in Else's hands. Naturally this supervision had not the slightest effect on me, I did as I liked, that is to say, I drank when I wanted to. From my customary small nips I had passed on to taking long pulls out of the bottle. I always kept a bottle in my desk at the office and another in the corner of the bathroom cupboard at home. I enjoyed smuggling these bottles in under Magda's eyes, as it were, in my brief-case or even in my trousers pocket covered by my jacket. Whenever I replenished my store, I experienced a real feeling of happiness, as if I had grown richer. At the very slightest sign of thirst I could take a drink. At home in the bathroom it was simple enough, but in the office, which Magda shared with me, there were difficulties sometimes. I would sit for several minutes, turning over in my mind some pretext to send her outside. Once, when I couldn't think of anything, right in her presence I went as far as to set the uncorked bottle on the floor—the desk hid me from sight—and then I dropped my india-rubber and started fussily to look for it, ending up on all fours under the arch of my desk, where, delighted at my own cleverness, I sent a considerable amount of cognac gurgling down my throat.

I changed my mind almost hourly about the extent to which Magda could see through me. As a rule, I was firmly convinced that she guessed nothing, but at other times, when I was bad-tempered and irritable, I was almost certain that she was completely aware of what I was up to. Sometimes I would moodily pace up and down the office, constantly passing Magda's place; then I was evil, as I called it, not for any special reason, not even on account of Magda, but I was just evil, as downright bad and wicked as a man can be, that's how evil I was, and I was looking for a pretext to start quarrelling with her. In this quarrel I wanted to find out for certain whether she knew all or nothing, and if she knew all, then I wanted to drop the last pretence of decorum. Right in the presence of my neat, sober, efficient wife, I wanted to get blind raving drunk, to put my feet up on the desk, to sing coarse and dirty songs and use obscene expressions. What utter satisfaction to drag her down into the filth with me, to make her see: this is the one you used to love, and this is what your love has made of him. . . .

I paced up and down even more rapidly, I no longer felt ashamed, I threw her fierce challenging glances, and then, just before I broke out, she always got up and left the office. But I stared after her, I stared furiously at the brown grained door, I clenched my fists, I ground my teeth. "Run away again, you

49

coward. But that's what you've made of me, you and your efficiency!" Finally I sat down at my desk again, had a good drink, and grew tired and gentle.

If I said that I only went on working from force of habit, that is not quite correct—one should not hide one's light under a bushel. Through the alcohol, I lost much of my dignified reserve, I could gossip far more freely with my country clients, we slapped each other on the back, told jokes—always looking round to make sure Magda was nowhere about—and thus I managed to bring off a number of unusually advantageous deals. I now liked to do something that I had never done before, something for which I had considered myself too dignified and my firm too respectable; I would go with my country customers into some little saloon, and there, over a scarred lime-wood table on which our glasses left wet rings, we talked a great deal, drank still more, and often I managed to buy at most advantageous prices from my half-drunken clients. When I got back to the office again and notified Hinzpeter of these transactions so that he could enter them into the books, I noticed the looks which this dry little adding-machine exchanged with my wife, but I only laughed.

However, one morning, after a deal in which I had properly soaked the bailiff of a large farm and had talked him into selling me a whole truckload of peas at half the regular market price, well, that morning I heard the sound of excited conversation in the yard, and when I went to the window I saw the bailiff, sober now, talking wildly to my wife and Hinzpeter. I stared through the glass for quite a while, and thought to myself: "Yes, go on talking, be as sober as you like, but you can't talk away that signature you put on the deal last night!"

Now Magda spoke and he nodded and shook his head and stamped his foot and suddenly he looked across to me and must have seen me behind the glass and, would you believe it, the fellow raised his arm and shook his fist at me, in front of my wife and Hinzpeter, and shouted a term of abuse, that sounded something like "Old swindler!" I waited and waited for Magda to turn the insolent fellow out of the yard, but she only spoke quietly to him and after a while the bailiff let his fist drop and they resumed their discussion. I was disgusted at my wife's spinelessness, and after a while, as they still went on talking, I sat down at my desk, opened a certain compartment and fortified myself. After a further lapse of time, during which I had sat thinking of nothing, the door opened and Magda came in, looking very pale, a brief-case in her hand. She put the brief-case on the desk, and started to rummage about among the papers, otherwise it was perfectly quiet in our office, and the alcohol went gently around inside me and made me feel peaceful and contented. But suddenly Magda dropped the papers, let her head fall on to the desk and burst wildly into tears. I was perfectly helpless, had no idea what to do, and anyway in my present agreeable condition I was much too lethargic to do anything. I just said rather feebly: "What's the matter? Do calm yourself, Magda. I'm sure it's not as bad as all that!"

But she raised her head and started at me with streaming eyes and cried: "It's too bad! It's not enough that you're blind drunk every day, you have to bring the firm into disrepute! Everybody's saying that we're not to be trusted any more, and that we're out to cheat people . . . "

"Halt, stop, Magda," I said slowly, and suddenly I was pleased that things had come to a head at last, and I was determined to spare her nothing.

"Halt, stop, Magda," I said. "Not too much at a time! As far as being blind drunk every day is concerned, I'd like to ask you whether you've ever seen me stagger about or heard me stammer? I quite admit I take a little drink now and then, but I can stand it. It helps me to think clearer. People who can't stand alcohol should avoid it. But that's not me. Look," I said slowly, and opened that certain compartment in my desk, "here we have a bottle of brandy that was still full at nine o'clock this morning, and now about a third is gone, a good third, let's say. But am I staggering about? Can't I manage my limbs? Am I muddled in the head? I'm ten times clearer than you! I wouldn't allow any jumped-up muck-ox to call my wife a swindler. I'd knock his teeth in!" I shouted suddenly, and then continued more calmly. "But you went on talking to him, and calmed him down, and if I know you and that frightened old hen Hinzpeter, you either washed out that deal with the peas or else raised the price."

I looked at her ironically.

"Of course we did," she cried, and now she dried her tears, and looked at me without love or affection. "Of course we did. We've cancelled the deal, but we've lost a good client for ever."

"Is that so?" I answered, still more ironically. "You've cancelled the deal. Of course, I'm just the lowest office boy here, and what I put my name to is just a scrap of paper! I'll tell you one thing, Magda. If Mr Bailiff Schmidt of the Fliederhof doesn't fulfil his agreement to the last hundredweight, I'll summons him, and I'll win my case. Because an agreement's an agreement, any lawyer will tell you that. And if he has accepted my low offer, that's his fault, not mine. I didn't make him drunk, but he tried to make me drunk, and if he fell into his own trap, it's not my fault. And, Magda," I said, and now I got up from my chair, "I'd have you know that I'm the boss here, and if agreements are going to be cancelled, I'm to be asked, and no one else. It doesn't suit me that you play yourself up here, and try to ride roughshod over me, with all this talk about being blind drunk when I'm as sober as an eel in the water and ten times more clever and more efficient than you are. I'm the boss here, and you're not going to push me around. Get back to your pots and pans, I won't interfere with you there. I didn't ask you to come here, but now I'm asking you to go."

I had been speaking very seriously and deliberately, and while I was speaking it had become clearer and clearer to me that I was right in every respect, and she was wrong. Now I sat down again.

Magda had been looking at me very attentively while I was speaking, as if she wanted to lip-read every word I said. Now that I had finished, she said: "I can see it's no use talking to you any more, Erwin. You have lost all sense of right and wrong. The Count had told the bailiff that he would lose his job if this drunken agreement wasn't cancelled at once, and you would be summoned for fraud. . . . "

"Let him try!" I cried ironically. "Of course, you're impressed by a Count, just because he calls himself blue-blooded. But I don't care that much!"

I snapped my fingers.

"Let him summon me! He'll soon find out his mistake!"

"Yes," cried Magda again, "it's all the same to you whether your good name gets dragged through the mud in court. Unfortunately I'm forced to realise that now. But I give up talking to you about it. Schnaps has destroyed all sense of justice in you. But I would like to ask you something else, Erwin."

"Go on, then," I answered sullenly, but I was very much on the alert, for I anticipated that nothing good was coming. She took a deep breath and looked fixedly at me, then she said.

"Are you still a man of your word, Erwin? I mean, will you still stand by what you once promised me?"

"Of course I will," I answered sullenly, "for instance I would keep to an agreement, whether I was drunk or sober at the time it was settled."

She took no notice of my irony.

53

"When you were going to Hamburg," she said, "you promised me faithfully you would come to the doctor's with me. Will you keep your word, will you come with me to see Dr Mansfeld this afternoon?"

"Stop," I said excitedly, "you've got things mixed up again, Magda! I never promised you to go to the doctor's in any event, I only promised to do so if I came back ill. But I have come back perfectly healthy."

"Yes, so healthy," said Magda bitterly, "that the night you came back you emptied every bottle in my larder. And since then you haven't been sober for a minute. But I see you don't want to keep your word."

"I would keep my word, but in this case I haven't given any word, not like that."

"But Erwin," Magda began again, but quietly now, "why do you struggle so against having yourself examined for once by the doctor. If it's as you say and the doctor confirms it, then everything's all right ... but if not ... "

"Well, what then?" I asked ironically.

" ... then something will have to be done about your health. Because you're ill, Erwin, you're so ill, you have absolutely no idea ... "

"Oh, stop it," I said, rather bored. "You won't get round me that way. You talk soft to me, but I can see by your eyes that you don't mean well. I'm not going to allow my wife to order me about, however efficient she may be."

"I don't want to order you about at all ... "

"Oh, please: first you cancel my contracts, then I'm supposed to go to the doctor's because you imagine some nonsense, finally you'd like to take my place as boss here, eh? During my absence you've been making yourself quite comfortable in my chair, haven't you?"

"All right then," she said, and now her eyes had a really wicked gleam, and no trace of mildness was left in her voice, "you don't want to, you don't want to do anything but drink and cause trouble. But I'm not going to allow you to ruin me and the firm. Ruin yourself as much as you like. But then I'll have to take other steps . . ."

"Take them, take them," I said sarcastically, "and see how you get on. . . . By the way, would you be good enough to tell me what steps you happen to be thinking of?"

My irony made her beside herself with rage.

"Certainly I'll tell you," she cried furiously. "First of all I'll get a divorce . . ."

"Well, well," I laughed. "So you're going to get a divorce. I didn't know I'd given you grounds for divorce yet. But that can probably be rectified—and what else have you in mind?"

But she had had enough.

"You'll see," she said, and sat down again at her desk and her papers.

"I can wait," I answered.

I took the brandy bottle and laid it with my uneaten sand-wiches in the brief-case.

"Get this quite clear: by law everything belongs to me. You had nothing when we married. House, furniture, business: all mine!"

I laughed as I saw her furious gesture of protest.

"Yes, you enquire from a lawyer first, then you'll think again about a divorce, and now," I said, and took my hat from the hook, "I'll leave my firm on loan to you. Be very indus-trious, dear Magda, and cancel plenty of nice contracts, and . . . why, what's the matter? Are you trying to give *me* grounds for divorce?"

My sarcasm had made her frantic with rage. She had snatched up the nearest thing to hand, a blotter, and thrown it at me. I only just managed to dodge it. She looked at me, trembling, white as a sheet. I thought it best not to provoke her any more, I put the blotter back in its place, and left the office.

11

I WAS firmly decided not to return too soon. Let her play about there for a bit on her own; I couldn't do a thing right, anyway. The whole business had bored me for some time past: now I had a more interesting task on hand, better suited to my present mood—my fight with Magda! Let her match herself against me, and she would find out how much the cleverer I was, and how much more I knew about the law!

I was on my way again, my brief-case under my arm, through a lovely though rather hot day at the end of spring. The Queen of Alcohol—I had neglected her for far too long— she certainly wasn't dull. Apart from that, it was time I got my shoes back. Nobody was going to say that in my drunkenness I had scattered my clothes over half Europe. Nobody, not even Magda. It was quite clear what this capable lady intended, to whom I had been married up till now. Divorce, all very well, but divorces aren't arranged so quickly as that; certain preparations have to be made, e.g., an examination by the doctor. Magda had been on good terms with Dr Mansfeld for years. He had always treated her whenever she was ill. I knew him less, I never had much the matter with me. She would probably talk him over to her way of thinking and then I should probably be put under restraint in a home for inebriates. That's what my fine Magda would like: her husband shut up in a home, preferably third-class of course, while she gets her hands on his property and runs the firm. But there were other doctors, more clever and capable than good old Dr Mansfeld who was only an ordinary G.P., after all: right away within the next few days I would go to one or more of them and get certificates attesting to my perfect health. With such a target before my eyes it should be easy not to drink for a day or two before my visit to the doctor. She would soon find out whom she had to deal with, would Magda; despite fifteen years of married life, she didn't know her husband at all! Anyway, before I'd give up my property to her, I'd sooner burn the house down over her head, that was certain.

So my thoughts ran, on my way to the village inn, and the filling-in of all the details shortened the journey for me in the most agreeable fashion. For instance, I could dwell on the idea of being shut up in some institution cell, disciplined with cold water and fed on bad food, while Magda ate veal cutlets and asparagus in our pretty dining-room. Tears of self-pity nearly came into my eyes at the thought of my hard lot and Magda's injustice. In between times, I fed my sandwiches to the village ducks and geese, for as usual lately, I wasn't in the least hungry, and every so often I dived behind a hedge and took a drink. I never quite lost the feeling of shame that I, Erwin Sommer, was hiding behind a hedge, pouring schnaps into myself like the lowest tramp. I could never take it for granted, I never became quite so blunted. But it just had to be, it couldn't be otherwise.

I had finished the bottle shortly before reaching my goal. I threw the bottle into the ditch and began my last five minutes' walk. It was striking noon from the village steeple; before me, behind me, and all around, the villagers were coming from the fields, with hoes and spades over their shoulders. Some of them greeted me, some gave me keen sidelong looks, and others nudged each other, pulled faces and laughed as they passed me by. It may only have been the usual critical village attitude to townsfolk, but I had the suspicion that it might be noticeable I had been drinking, perhaps, or that something about my clothing was disarranged. I was already acquainted with the fact that the worst thing about alcohol was the feeling of uncertainty it gave, as if something was not quite right. You can look in the mirror as often as you like, look your clothes over, try every button, but when you have had something to drink, you are never sure that you have not overlooked something, something quite obvious that has been neglected despite the closest attention. One has similar experiences in dreams, one moves quite happily in the most exclusive society, and suddenly discovers that one has forgotten to put one's trousers on. Well then, I found it irksome to be so stared at, and besides, it occurred to me that this busy noonday hour would not be the right time for me to go looking for my pretty one. I turned aside into a field path and threw myself down on the grass under a shady bush. At once I fell asleep, into that pitch-black sleep that alcohol induces, in which one is, so to speak, extinguished, one dies a modified death. There are no more dreams, no notion of light and life—off into nothingness!

When I woke up, the sun was already low. I must have been asleep for four, perhaps five hours. As usual nowadays, my sleep had not refreshed me, I woke up old and tired, a shaky feeling in my limbs. My bones were stiff when I stood up; and I found walking very difficult. But I knew by now that all this would be better as soon as I had had my first few drinks, and I hurried to reach the inn.

I had chosen a good time: the bar-room was empty again, there was nobody behind the bar either. Stiffly, I let myself fall into a wicker chair and called for some service. First a woman's head appeared in the crack of the door; it wasn't my pale pretty one however, but an unkempt red-nosed elderly character, and then a fat woman looked in, calling "Coming, coming!" and opened the door by the stairway which I had climbed that night, led blindly by the hand.

"Elinor, Elinor, come down!" cried the landlady. She once again assured me that I would be served, and disappeared into the kitchen. So her name was Elinor. I hadn't been so far out with Elsabe. But Elinor was very good, rather better really. Elinor suited her, *Elinor la reine d'alcool*. Very nice too!

And then I heard her coming down the stairs, not at all gazelle-footed by the way; the door banged open, and in she came. She must have been asleep, her hair was not so neat and carefully pinned as usual, and her light dress was rather rumpled and untidy. She stood for a moment and looked across to me. She did not recognise me at once, she was looking into the sun. Then she cried quite cheerfully: "Oh, it's only old pop who likes schnaps so much!", and ran upstairs again. I didn't really mind this novel and rather painful greeting. I was only pleased at such an unaffected reception. I had been a bit doubtful how she would receive me after my departure over the shed roof that night. But now everything was all right, and I waited patiently for five minutes until she appeared again, spick-and-span. She came straight over to my table, gave me her hand like an old friend, and said amiably, "I thought you were never coming back! What have you been doing all this time? Are you bankrupt now?"

"Not yet, *ma reine*," I said, smiling too, "but for the time being I've handed the business over to my wife, from whom, by the way, I'm getting a divorce. What do you think of that, my pretty one? Perhaps in eight weeks I'll be on the market. Quite well-preserved, aren't I?"

She looked at me for a moment, and then the smile vanished from her face, and she said rather coolly and in a businesslike tone, "One schaps, was it? Or a whole bottle again?"

"Quite right, my golden one," I cried, "a whole bottle again! And another bottle of champagne for yourself!"

"Not in the daytime," she answered shortly, and went

away. A moment later I had plenty to drink, of this coarse watery-coloured stuff that I already liked better than cognac. But except for that, I didn't get much for my money that afternoon. Elinor was constantly busy, in and out of the barroom, and we could only exchange a few words from time to time.

Upset by this, I drank more than usual, and after about an hour and a half, Elinor had to bring me another bottle, and I realised myself that I was very drunk. Then a few young fellows came in, among them that bricklayer with whom Elinor had been talking so intimately; and just to attract the girl to my table (which only succeeded for a few minutes) I let them all sit with me and ordered for each one whatever he wanted. In a short time my table offered a wild spectacle. Beer and schnaps glasses, wine and champagne bottles stood on it in wild confusion, and around it were grouped a horde of wildly talking, shouting, laughing, gesticulating figures, and I was the wildest and drunkest of the lot. I felt myself absolutely liberated, I really was a stone hurtling into the abyss—I absolutely ceased to think.

In all our uproar we did not hear the car pull up, and when two gentlemen came in we hardly noticed them. I was just shouting some protestation or other to the man opposite me —he wasn't even listening—when suddenly I stopped as if a hand had been clapped over my mouth, for one of these gentlemen, who had sat down at the next table, greeted me with a friendly "Good evening," and this gentleman was Dr Mansfeld. I didn't know the other gentleman. Even my drinking companions fell silent; and though they saw that nothing further was happening, that the gentlemen at the next table were quietly drinking their beer, deep in conversation, even then the old jollity did not return. One after the other, they faded away, and at last I was left alone in this wilderness of glasses and bottles, and I looked in vain for Elinor; she did not come to restore order to the chaos. Probably she was outside the door flirting with the young bricklayer, who was doubtless a lover of hers. After the wild abandon of a few moments ago, a deep depression fell over me, I gnawed my lips and shot suspicious glances at the neighbouring table, where they were taking no notice of me at all. My suspicions were aroused, I wondered whether Dr Mansfeld had turned up here by mere coincidence in the course of going the round of his practice, or whether Magda had asked him to come. I racked my brains to remember whether in my drunkenness I might have given Magda the name of this little resort of mine, or whether I might have let slip some indication so that it was not difficult to trace—but I could not remember. The second gentleman seemed familiar to me but I couldn't quite place him. . . .

I could have done with another drink, and the brandy bottle was close enough at hand, but in front of the two guests at the next table I did not dare to fill my glass. I told myself that in view of the state of this table and my wild behaviour of a short time ago, nothing could make matters worse, and yet I still didn't dare.

At last Elinor came back into the bar-room. I called her to me and quietly asked her for the bill. While she totted up a row of figures on her pad, standing bent over me and hiding me rather from the view of the next table, I swallowed down two or three quick mouthfuls. Then I carefully corked the bottle and thrust it into my brief-case. Elinor gave a sharp glance at what I was doing and, indicating the next table, she whispered with raised eyebrows: "Friends?" I merely shrugged my shoulders. The bill was so steep that it took nearly all my money down to the last mark, and left only a quite inadequate tip for Elinor. She looked at me again with raised eyebrows, and whispered: "Cleaned out?"

I answered just as quietly, "I know where to get more. Till the next time, *ma reine.*"

She nodded lightly.

Now I had to get up and walk, under the watchful eyes of the gentlemen at the next table. I took my brief-case and made sure in advance on which hook my hat was hanging so that I shouldn't have to search round for it as I went out. Then I stood up. I felt I could manage. I would have to move slowly and very carefully, and then it would be all right. After all, I only needed to get out of the village to one first sheltering bush, or better still, a happy thought!—I only needed to lock myself up in the toilet here, and I could sleep as long as I wanted to. I had fresh provisions with me.

Already I had politely said "Good evening" to the next table as I got up, and now I was at the door only a step from salvation, when a voice behind me said: "Oh, just a moment, Herr Sommer!"

It gave me such a start, I nearly fell.

"I beg your pardon?" I cried in an unnecessarily loud voice. The doctor had taken hold of my arm and supported me.

"Did I startle you? I didn't mean to. I'm sorry."

"Oh, it's nothing, nothing," I said, embarrassed. "It must have been this wretched carpet I stumbled over. . . . " And I looked crossly at the carpet which lay quite smooth.

"I only wanted to ask you, Herr Sommer," Dr Mansfeld went on, "if I might perhaps offer you a lift home in my car."

He paused, and then said smilingly, "We've been celebrating a bit, haven't we? Never mind, we all like to do that occasionally. But getting home might be a bit hard going, mightn't it? So you come with us."

He took me amiably but firmly under the arm. The other gentleman had paid and now he came over to us. "May I introduce you?" said the doctor, "Herr Sommer—Dr Stiebing, our district medical officer."

With that he took me out of the inn and over to the car. I followed him like a sheep to the slaughter—the district medical officer!

So it was not chance, after all. It was a cleverly laid trap! That damned Magda! She wanted to get the better of me. She acted fast, I must admit. But I was clever too, I would have to play a part, be cunning, counter guile with guile.

"Well," I suddenly laughed merrily, "two doctors, they should be able to manage a poor drunkard, eh? Have mercy on me gentlemen!" With that, I sat in the back of the car, while the other two gentlemen, also laughing, took their seats in front. We were just about to start when Elinor came running out of the house. She was carrying an ugly parcel wrapped up in newspaper, and she handed it into the open car. She said in a loud voice: "Here's your shoes that you forgot the other night!" She gave a sneering laugh as she looked at me with her big white face and colourless eyes. Her mouth was very red.

After an embarrassed silence, the doctor asked, "Shall we go now?"

I answered, "Yes," and the car moved off.

12

I AM quite unable to describe how I felt during that journey. Abysmal desperation alternated with a paralysing apathy which terrified me even in that state of mind. It was as if I lay imprisoned in some heavy nightmare, close to waking all the time and yet unable to waken, and becoming involved in ever deeper and more fearful horrors. On a seat beside me lay the parcel containing my shoes. The newspaper had burst open and I saw them, smeared and dusty. I looked at one of the soles: dreadful, simply dreadful what pretty Elinor had done, worthy of a queen of schnaps.

"Yes," I thought, "that's how alcohol tortures and makes fools of its disciples. It's the only thing capable of such dumbfounding surprises. One thinks one is safe, one has acted the part well, one has overcome the worst, and suddenly it thrusts its devil's face forward, flays your breast with its claws, leaves you trembling, destroys your dignity. . . . *La reine d'alcool*—if I ever see you again, you won't have a good time with me, Elinor!"

I could stand it no longer. With a glance I made sure that the two gentlemen were deep in conversation. I drew the bottle out of the case, uncorked it, and took a few long pulls. But I had not thought of the driving mirror.

"Not too much now, and not too fast, my dear Herr Sommer," said Dr Mansfeld, and lifted a warning hand from the steering wheel. "We would like to have a sensible talk with you later."

The scoundrel, the glib medical scoundrel! Now that he had me in his car, he let the mask drop, I wasn't being driven to my home, but to some medical discussion at which just by chance the district health officer happened to be present!

From then on I was absolutely calm and collected. The schnaps I had just drunk lent me new strength and concentration. I had a firm aim in view—to get this discussion deferred by hook or by crook; later on, certainly, under circumstances more favourable for me, but today, outwitted like this by order of her ladyship—no thank you, my dear!

The car went on and on. Already we were on the outskirts of town and so far I'd had no opportunity to withdraw my partnership in this journey. But then a big locomotive pulling two trucks came rather suddenly out of the goods-yard. The doctor put his brakes on and pulled over to the left side of the road, and in the meantime I had gently opened the car door; and now that the train had passed and the doctor was accelerating again, I jumped lightly out, staggered for a moment, threatened to fall and then caught myself. I stood, waved my hand after the car to give passers-by the impression that this sudden descent had been with the knowledge of the people in it, and then walked off briskly, taking the right fork in the road, along the goods-yard fence, to a small dilapidated colony which the townsfolk call the "shed district." I shook with inner laughter to think that the two clever doctors would bring no more back from their expedition than the drunkard's shoes.

13

THE most disagreeable thing about my present predicament was that I was standing in the street practically without a penny. I couldn't go home, where I had at least some small change in my bureau, because I was obliged to assume that as soon as they noticed my absence the doctors would go looking for me there, and make their report to Madame Magda. It was too late to go to the bank, it shut two hours ago. Just as I was looking at my watch, it occurred to me that I owned not only it, but also a heavy gold signet ring and quite a solid wedding ring, moreover, which, after my scene with Magda this morning, had lost all real significance. So I was not entirely without means, and I boldly directed my steps towards the narrow dirty lane that led through the "shed district."

This colony had grown around an old army camp in the depression years following the World War. The former army huts had been changed but not beautified by all kinds of ramshackle additions and reconstructions. In between stood little red brick houses which were already collapsing before they had been properly finished. I went hesitantly along this lane, myself unsure what I was doing or looking for here, when, at a window in one of these little brick houses, the familiar red sign caught my eye, advertising accommodation. I stepped closer and read, sure enough, that there was a comfortably furnished room to let to a respectable gentleman. There was no doorbell. I stepped through the open door and immediately found myself in a kitchen filled with steam from boiling washing. I couldn't see anyone, so I loudly called "Hallo!" and out of the steam appeared a tall, bent, but still quite young man, with a yellow pallor, a soft beard, and lightish brown hair which had a golden sheen above the forehead. This man looked at me with some surprise and in a soft voice, he very politely asked what he could do for me.

"I would like to see the room that's to let."

"For yourself?" asked the man, rubbing his hands and coughing slightly. I said, yes.

"It's no room for a gentleman. It's not fine enough for a gentleman. It's a room suitable for a working-man, sir."

"Show it me, anyway," I insisted.

He went silently before me, up a stairway, across an unfinished floor, and opened the door of a little one-windowed room with sloping walls—an attic really. Its interior was almost exactly like Elinor's primitive room, and involuntarily I went across to the window to see whether there was a sloping shed roof here too, to offer the possibility of escape in the event of a surprise visit. No, the shed roof was missing, but instead there was an absolutely astonishing view over my native town. It lay before me, a little below, with its red-brown roofs, its three pointed church spires and the round-headed tower of the Town Hall; the green-bordered river wound through it, disappearing here and shining out again there, and as my eyes followed its course, I saw in the distance, out among the green of the fields and gardens, veiled in a blue mist, a roof, my roof.

"It's a lovely view," I said after a while.

The man behind me coughed.

"A working man," he said, "doesn't ask about the view. He asks if the bed's good, and that's a good bed, sir."

"What does the room cost?" I asked.

"Seven marks a week," said the man, "and we change the sheets once a week."

"I'd like to eat here too," I said. "I want to live here undisturbed for two or three weeks, in absolute quiet. I have some work to do, some writing. I shall hardly leave the house, can that be arranged? I don't make many demands."

"Our food is too simple for you, sir," said the man. "But I can have meals sent over from the pub, if that's all right for you."

"All right," I said, "I'll take the room. My trunk is coming tomorrow. Have some supper sent over," and I sat down at the table.

"I'll have to ask for a little deposit, sir," said my landlord, and he pulled his fingers till the joints cracked. "We're poor people, sir . . ."

"Sit down," I said to my landlord. "Ah, I see there's a glass over there on the wash-stand. I wonder if you'd be good enough to bring it over, please."

My landlord did so, and at my repeated invitation, he sat down at the table.

"What's your name?"

"Lobedanz," he answered, "It's a rather funny name . . ."

"I don't care whether your name is funny or not," I said patronisingly, "let's drink your health."

I poured his glass half full—despite his protests—and kept hold of the bottle.

"I can drink out of the bottle for once," I said laughingly. "We've all done that in our young days."

He smiled feebly and took a little sip, while I drank deeply.

"I must ask you, Herr Lobedanz," I said easily, "to have a bottle of brandy sent over with the supper. But no rubbish please. The best they have in stock."

I saw his lips move and guessed what he was going to say.

"About that deposit—I ought to tell you that I decided on

this work quite suddenly." I caught my landlord's glance, as he looked thoughtfully at my open brief-case, which was quite empty. I laughed.

"Well, I'll tell you the truth, Herr Lobedanz. All that stuff about the work I want to do here in absolute peace and quiet is rubbish of course. The fact of the matter is I had a serious row with my wife this afternoon. And in order to scare her a bit I want to disappear for a week or two. You understand, I want to bring her to her senses."

Herr Lobedanz nodded.

"I want to let her see what it's like without a husband."

Herr Lobedanz nodded again.

"She's got to learn how useful, how indispensable I am!"

Again Herr Lobedanz nodded and then he said in his soft, almost whispering voice: "Even so, sir, I can't take you without a deposit. We're very poor people here in the 'shed district', sir, and supper from a good pub and a bottle of best brandy costs a lot of money."

"You'll have all the money you want tomorrow Herr Lobedanz," I said persuasively. "I'll go and draw some money from my bank at nine tomorrow morning."

"No," said my landlord, "I'm sorry, sir, I'd like to have you as a lodger, an educated man who wants to frighten his wife a bit in a gentlemanly way. We beat our wives, it's simpler and cheaper."

"Well, yes, yes," I laughed, a little embarrassed, "but I don't know whether I would come off best in a fight with my wife. I'm afraid she's the stronger."

I laughed again and drank.

"But since you're so keen on a deposit, I'll give you a ring as security."

I took the signet ring and the wedding ring off the third finger of my right hand. I hesitated for a moment, then handed the wedding ring to Lobedanz.

"I'd like you to keep this as security till tomorrow morning, and not get rid of it."

Herr Lobedanz took the ring from my hand.

"We're very poor people, sir," he said again in his whispering voice. "We've hardly got three marks in the house. But I could pawn the ring with a safe man I know, and we could redeem it again tomorrow afternoon."

"All right, all right," I said, suddenly bored and irritated by all these formalities. "But see to it that the food and the brandy gets sent over quickly, especially the brandy. You can see the bottle's nearly empty, and a man needs to drown his sorrows, you know."

"It will be very quick, sir," whispered my landlord, and he shut the door. I threw myself on the bed and drank. That is how I made the acquaintance of Lobedanz, the lowest scoundrel and hypocrite I ever met in my life.

14

I HAD firmly resolved that night to go home, pack a case with clothes, linen, shaving things, and to take what money was in my bureau. For I really intended to live in hiding for a few weeks at Lobedanz's. I had the idea of curing myself of the drinking habit in peace and quiet; the first day I would drink the usual amount, the following day one-third less, and so on, until in a week or two I could appear before Magda and the doctors and say "What do you want with me?"

I thought it quite possible that Magda would surprise me at my nocturnal packing, but I didn't shrink from meeting her, no, I even wanted to. In the silence of the night, undisturbed, I would be able to tell her a few home-truths about her despicable behaviour in setting the doctors so slyly on to a man to whom, after all, she has been bound in marriage for fifteen years. She had broken off the comradeship between us, and I became more and more certain that she was only trying to have me put away, so as to get hold of my property. I was going to tell her all this to her face.

Unfortunately nothing came of my fine plan. Again, alcohol played me a dirty trick. Not that it plunged me into a stupefying dreamless sleep, as had occasionally happened before, so that I missed the proper time; no, on this occasion, I had a much worse experience: my body refused to serve me, my stomach went on strike. Though with some aversion, I had dutifully eaten part of the supper which had been brought in —it was quite nice—and afterwards I had drunk heavily. I had lain down on the bed and, in a half-sleep I was awaiting the time for my departure. Then my stomach began to heave. I was obliged to get up and vomit endlessly, in agonising pain. My whole body was covered in sweat, my hands and knees were trembling, my heart beat loudly and uncertainly as if at any moment it would stop. There were tears in my eyes, lights flickered in front of them, veils seem to float through my brain, often I was almost unconscious. At last I lay on my bed again, nearly dead with exhaustion, seized with an insane fear; was the end near? So soon, already? I hadn't been drinking for very long, and not at all excessively. Did one become a drunkard so quickly? No, I didn't want to die yet! I had regarded this period of drunkenness merely as a passing phase; I had been convinced that I could give it up at any time without harming myself—and now was everything to come to an end already? No, it was impossible! I would get well again, soon, perhaps by tomorrow; there must have been another reason for that gall-bitter vomiting! Surely it was something I ate for supper!

It is strange that at the worst stage of the poisoning, I had not the slightest notion of giving up alcohol. On the contrary, I anxiously avoided any thought of it. It couldn't be the cause, I couldn't give it up! It was my only true friend in all this abandonment and degradation. And hardly had I recovered a little, hardly had my heart and my breathing become calmer, than I reached out for the bottle again, and drank anew, to summon the dreams, to summon forgetfulness, to enter again into that sweet oblivion in which one knows neither sorrow nor joy, in which one has neither past nor future.

For a while the schnaps did its duty: I lay there relaxed and faintly happy. Then the vomiting caught me again, an even more agonising retching sickness, since there was nothing left in my stomach but a few mouthfuls of schnaps.

So I passed the night between drinking and vomiting. In the end I was concentrating all my will and all my strength just on keeping back the vomit for as long as possible, so that the alcohol would have a few minutes to work its way through the mucous membranes of my stomach into my body, before a new bout of retching drove it out. It was such a pity about that lovely schnaps!

At last, towards morning, I fell into a restless exhausted sleep through which flitted the images of wild agonising dreams.

Lobedanz woke me up. He stood in the doorway and remarked with a cough that it was nine o'clock, should he bring the coffee? I told him indignantly that I didn't want coffee, he was to bring me another bottle at once.

Without taking any notice of my words, he began tidying up the wild disorder of my room. He opened the windows, and the fresh air and sunshine streamed in. Exhausted, weak, defenceless, I blinked into the light.

"Hurry up, Lobedanz," I angrily implored. "I've emptied this bottle. See that I get a new one straight away!"

"You wanted to go to your bank at nine, sir," Lobedanz reminded me in his soft, whispering way. "It's nine now."

"I can't go now," I said angrily. "You can see that I'm ill, Lobedanz. I'll go tomorrow, or this afternoon. Now fetch me some schnaps."

"Then I'll have to sell the ring, sir," said Lobedanz. "The pawnbroker would only lend me fifteen marks on it. If I sell it, I'll get twenty-five marks."

"Twenty-five marks!" I cried indignantly. "That ring cost ninety marks new!"

"It's an old ring now, and the pawnbroker's got to live, sir," whispered Lobedanz impassively. "If I can sell the ring for twenty-five marks, the brandy will soon be here."

73

"And how can fifteen marks be gone already?" I cried in exasperation. "One supper and a bottle of schnaps, that doesn't come to fifteen marks!"

"And the room-rent, sir?" asked Lobedanz. "Isn't a poor man like me to have anything? By the way, I'll have to charge you twelve marks for the room, sir. . . . I know, I know," he said, and again he cracked his joints in a particularly loud and disgusting way, "I said seven marks and I'm a man of my word. But you make a lot of work, sir, and you're ruining the room, and you go to bed in your clothes and shoes and that spoils the sheets. It all costs money, and we're very poor people . . ."

"You're a lot of thieves!" I shouted furiously. "You can go to the devil! I'm moving!"

"Very good sir," said Lobedanz, and went away.

But of course he was the winner. After a while I got up, tormented by thirst, and went groaning down the stairs, calling him. (He let me call for a long time). And I cajoled him, and gave him permission to sell my wedding ring for twenty-five marks—and then, at last, after a long, long agonising wait, I got a new bottle of brandy, and again I could drink and vomit, drink and vomit. So out of one day grew a second and a third and a whole row of days and I never once left the room at Lobedanz's.

15

DURING this first week which I spent with Lobedanz, both of my rings, my gold watch and my brief-case passed into his possession. I am quite convinced that the pawnbroker was merely an imaginary person, and that the one who actually acquired my valuables was that "very poor man" Lobedanz himself. What I got in return was absurdly little. Perhaps twelve to fourteen bottles of schnaps, at four marks a bottle (incidentally, the quality he brought was always poor), and now and then a little food. For I ate hardly anything. Whenever I happened to glance in the mirror now, I would observe my face with a sort of cruel voluptuousness. Covered with days-old bristles, it looked bloated yet emaciated, positively burnt-out. "That's the way to destroy oneself," I said triumphantly. And immediately I thought of Magda again, and how shocked she would be if she could see me in this condition, and how I would fling it in her face that she, and she alone, was the shameful cause of this transformation!

My health changed much during this time. Of course, I did not give another thought to the cure I had planned. I drank as much as I could get into my stomach. Usually, it was on strike, and I had a great deal of trouble to get the required amount down; at other times, for some unknown reason, it was quite willing to swallow and keep down whatever it got. Those were the good times. Then I sat at the window, with the bottle always close by me; I sang old folk-songs and *wanderlieder* softly to myself, and I looked out over the town below me, over to the house which lay far away in the blueish mist, and which was mine. Then I would wonder what Magda was doing just now; and at these times I was firmly convinced that I loved her as much as ever, and that it was she who had betrayed our love. Then I imagined how, one day, I would return home, healthy and bright; somehow, by some secret but quite lawful means, I had come into possession of a lot of money, and made everybody glad, and everyone admired me, and they all lived happily ever after.

From such childish dreams, Lobedanz would wake me roughly enough. He made it clear that I should get neither drink nor lodging from him unless I produced some more money at once . . . . We became involved in an endless quarrel, on his side, always polite, quiet, insinuating, on mine, rude, with passionate outbursts that ended almost in floods of tears. But it did not help in the least to keep reproaching him for the usurious prices at which he availed himself of my belongings, giving me little, almost nothing, in return. He sheltered behind the pawnbroker who just would not give more, he swore up hill and down dale that he had not made a penny out of me up to now, and still maintained that I must get money or move out. Yes, and now he even made dark insinuations that the police might be very interested in people of my sort, and that it was not permitted to take up residence without reporting to them, and that this was making it dangerous for him. At that time, I paid no attention to such threatening talk. But I knew that I would have to get some money, for the gentle Lobedanz was as hard as flint.

The only thing I got out of him was another bottle of brandy on tick, to make me fresh for my night expedition. I had just had one of my good days, that is, a day when my body was on good terms with alcohol; that was a bit of luck. On another day, it would have been impossible for me to undertake such a trip. I knew that I could not go to the bank

76

any more: I was sure that they had been notified of my disappearance, and advised that, if I did turn up, no payments were to be made to me without previous consultation. So I would have to break into my own house. The thought of meeting Magda was not so pleasant—now that such a meeting was almost certain—as it had been a week ago, when I had only dreamed of her. But it had to be. I thrust the brandy bottle into my trouser pocket—the gentle Lobedanz had refused me the return of my brief-case—and started on my way. It was shortly after midnight. Lobedanz let me out of the house and whispered that it was very dark. I should be particularly careful when crossing the bridge over the river.

"I'll wait up for you, sir," he whispered, "however late it may be. I'll have a bottle ready for you. And then, sir," he whispered still softer, "then, sir, if you've still got any jewellery or silver—I've got a dealer on hand who pays very decent prices, not like that twister—just bring whatever you can and I'll look after you all right."

"That's the way to catch simpletons," I thought, and was simpleton enough not to withhold my appreciation from Lobedanz for being so clever as to keep a bottle of brandy ready as a reward for my return. Of course, I had quite different plans, of which he had no inkling.

Walking was much easier for me than I had expected. I felt hardly any need for drink. I was rather excited. I well remember how, all the long way, I tried anxiously not to think of what lay ahead of me. I recited to myself, over and over again, all the poems I knew by heart from my schooldays; and in spite of that, I found myself between one verse and the next, talking to Magda or wondering which suitcase would be the best one to take.

At last, after nearly three-quarters of an hour's walking, I arrived at the garden gate of my villa. Shortly before, one o'clock had struck from the town's three steeples. I closed the gate softly behind me, and avoiding the gravel-path, made my way across the grass round my house. Everything lay quiet and dark. For a long time, I stood under Magda's bedroom window, and thought I heard her quiet breathing; but it was only my own heart beating loud and restless within my breast. When I came to think that here I stood by my own house, within five yards of my own wife, like a penniless stranger in the night, unwashed and unshaven for a week, such a wave of self-pity swept over me that I burst into bitter tears. I wept long and painfully. I would have liked to get into Magda's room and let her console me, but in the end, the schnaps again proved the best comforter. I drank long and deeply. My grief calmed down. I fought back an inclination to sleep for a while, and returned to the front of the house.

16

I AM standing in my stockinged feet in the hall of my house. I have left my shoes by the door. It is dark, but now my hand gropes for the switch, a faint click, and it is light. Yes, here I am at home again, I belong here, in all this order and cleanliness! With an almost reverent shyness, I gaze around at this cosy little hall, with its light-green carpet, from which the ugly traces of that dismal night have long since been removed; I look at the hall-stand, on which Magda's green costume jacket and a blueish summer coat are neatly hanging side by side. And now I tiptoe over to the mirror, in which one can see oneself from head to foot, and I look myself up and down. And I am gripped by a terrible fear when I see myself standing there in my soiled and shapeless clothes, with a greyish-black collar, a pallid bristly face, and red-rimmed eyes.

"So that's what's become of me!" cries a voice within me, and my first impulse is to rush in to Magda, to fall on my knees before her, and to implore her: "Save me! Save me from myself! Hold me to your heart!" But this impulse vanishes: I smile craftily at my image in the mirror.

"That's just what she would like," I think. "And then—off with the old man into a drunkard's home, while she gets hold of the business and the money!"

Be cunning. Always be cunning. And I quickly move a chair over to the big cupboard in the hall, I reach up, and take down a suitcase, the best suitcase we possess, a real cowhide one; it belongs to Magda really, I gave it to her once for a

79

birthday present. But that is of no importance now, besides—do not married people own everything in common? In the next quarter of an hour, I become feverishly active, I pack my overcoat, two suits, underwear. I fetch my toilet things from the bathroom. Magda will be surprised in the morning! From the shoe-cupboard I fetch two pairs of shoes—I arrange everything as if for a long journey. And now I really do feel as if I were about to start on a long journey, perhaps, perhaps this time Elinor will be more amenable. Now I have finished with all these things, and before I begin the most difficult part, I sit down for a moment on the hall floor, take a drink, and rest. It is very noticeable how feeble I have become during the last few weeks. This bit of packing has exhausted me out of all proportion, my heart is palpitating, I am covered with sweat.

Then I set to work again. Till now, everything has gone splendidly. I have made no noise that would wake a normal sleeper, nothing has fallen from my hands. But, as I have said, the most difficult part is still ahead of me. I open the drawer under the mirror, and look, the torch is lying there sure enough! I switch on, and look, it really works! There's nothing like a well-ordered household—hurrah for Magda! I switch off all the lights and steal into our living-room with the torch. It is next to the bedroom, and is separated from it only by a double-door decorated with coloured glass panels, through which every light and every sound penetrates. In the darkness, I grope over to the writing-desk, in whose centre compartment our ready money lies in a small cash-box. Usually, only the money necessary for household expenses is kept in it—very little; but if we had taken some money at the office of an evening, too late to pay it into the bank, we would bring it home with us here. So I was very anxious to see how much I would find. I managed to open the compartment without any noise and to get the cash-box out. In the dark I also came across the cheque-book which was lying beside the cash-box. I thrust it into my pocket, and carried the cash-box carefully, step by step, into the hall, put it down first, closed the door, and switched on the light. It may sound odd, but I uttered something like a prayer before unlocking the cash-box. I prayed to God, whom I had so long forgotten, to let there be a lot of money in the box. A lot of money, to continue this life between drunkenness and sickness for a long time yet, still more money to induce Elinor, *la reine d'alcool*, to go travelling with me. I didn't give a single thought to the position into which I was putting my own business by taking the money. Indeed, I believe that if I had thought of it, the greater the harm done to my business, the more I would have exulted. So I uttered my prayer, and opened the cash-box. I lifted out the upper compartment, in which there were only coins, and looked eagerly for the paper-money.

My disappointment was boundless. There were only a very few notes there; as I counted them over, they came to not much more than fifty marks. I still see myself standing there, those few notes in my hand, an icy feeling in my heart.

"This is the end," I thought. "This is neither enough for Elinor nor for Lobedanz. In two or three days, this money will be gone, and then there's only surrender, sackcloth and ashes, the cold-water asylum, the final abandonment of hope."

So there I stood, with death in my heart, for a long, long time. . . .

Then life came back to me again. Again I saw Lobedanz's yellowish face before me, with its dark beard; I heard his soft voice whispering something about jewellery and silver. . . . Jewellery was out of the question. The little jewellery that Magda possessed was worth hardly anything; besides, she kept it in the bedroom dressing-table.

But silver—yes, we had silver. Beautiful heavy old table silver, a bargain picked up at an auction. There was still room in the suitcase. . . . I drank quickly and deep. I emptied the whole bottle at a go. There had been a good third of it left. For a moment, the sudden strong intake of alcohol flooded my body like a red wave. I shut my eyes. I trembled. Would I have to vomit? But the attack passed, I had myself under control again. Quickly I went into the dining-room and switched on the chandelier. Now I did not need the caution that I had so carefully observed hitherto. I unlocked the sideboard and took out the silver, which was wrapped by the dozen in flannel covers (we only use it on festive occasions). First I laid it all in a heap before me, then I packed it away, big spoons, knives and forks, the small set, the fish knives and forks. . . . I stuffed them all into the suitcase as they came. Now only the silver serving-spoons, the salad- and carving-set were missing, which were lying loose in a separate drawer. I quickly took them out; suddenly something was driving me on, I had to get out of this house. A spoon fell with a clatter to the floor. I swore aloud, made a grab for it, and let a second spoon drop.

Impatiently I tugged at the drawer to pull it right out, and to carry the single silver pieces in it to the suitcase. The drawer gave unexpectedly, and fell with a crash on to the silverware, which rang brightly. I gathered everything together however I could get hold of it, without a care now for the noise I made, and hurried with it to the suitcase. As I went, two or three spoons fell. I threw what I had brought into the suitcase, on top of everything, and ran back to get those I had dropped. Then I stood rooted, staring at Magda, who was there in the middle of the dining-room, in front of her burgled sideboard!

17

SHE turned her head and looked at me for a long time. I noticed how she started, how rapidly she breathed, how she tried to collect herself.

"Erwin," she said, in a faltering voice. "Erwin! What a sight you are! Where have you been to get into such a state? Where have you been for so long? Oh Erwin, Erwin, I've been so worried about you! And to think that we should meet like this! Think Erwin, we loved each other once. Don't destroy it all! Come back to me, I'll help you the best I can. I'll be so patient with you. I'll never quarrel with you again. . . . "

She had been speaking faster and faster. Breathlessly she stopped and looked imploringly at me.

But I was stirred by quite other feelings. I glared with fury and hatred at this well-kept woman, flushed with sleep, in her blue dressing-gown—I who looked as if I'd been rolling in the gutter, I who stank like a polecat. I think it must have been the reference to our former love that put me into such a mad rage. Instead of moving me, her words only reminded me how far off was the submerged past.

Angrily I stumbled towards Magda, nearly fell over a silver-serving spoon, looked furiously at it, took a step back and trampled it underfoot. Magda cried out. I rushed over to her, raised my fist and cried: "Yes, you'd like that, wouldn't you? I come back to you. And then what happens? Then what happens?"

I shook my fist in her face.

"You put me to bed and make sure I go to sleep and as soon as I'm asleep you fetch the doctors and let them take me off to some drunkards' home for life, then you laugh up your sleeve and do as you please with my property. Yes, that's what you'd like!"

I glared at her. Now I was breathless too. And Magda glared back at me. She had turned very pale, but I could clearly see she wasn't afraid of me, despite my threatening behaviour.

Suddenly my mood changed; my excitement died down, and coolly and calmly I said, "I'll tell you what you are. You're just a common vulture. I say it to your face!"

She didn't flinch. She only looked at me.

"You're a traitor! You betrayed our whole marriage when you set those doctors on to me. I'd like to spit in your face, you——!"

She was still staring at me. Then she said swiftly, "Yes, I did send the doctors after you, but not to betray you, only to save you if that's still possible. If you had a spark of common-sense left, you would realise that, Erwin. You must see that you can't live another month like this. Perhaps not another week . . ."

I interrupted her. I gave a sneering laugh.

"Not another week? I can live for years like this, I can stand anything, and I'll go on living just to spite you, just to spite you."

I leaned close to her.

"Shall I tell you what I'm going to do next time I get drunk? I'm going to stand outside your window and shout out to everyone that you are a traitor, a greedy vulture, greedy for my money, and greedy for me to die . . ."

"Yes," she said spitefully. "I believe you're capable of that. But if you did, you wouldn't land up in a home, you'd land in prison instead. And I'm not sure that it wouldn't do you good."

"What?" I shouted at her, and now my rage had reached its climax. "Now you want to have me put in prison? Just you wait! You won't say that again! I'll show you. . . . " I reached for her. I saw red. I tried to seize her by the throat, but she fought back. She really was almost as strong as I, indeed in my present condition she was probably much stronger. We wrestled together. It was a sweet sensation, to feel this once loved, now hostile body pressing so close against me, now her breast, now her straining thigh. The thought shot through my head, "Suppose you were to kiss her suddenly, whisper loving words in her ear? Could you get her round?" I whispered in her ear: "Tomorrow night I'll come and kill you. I'll come very quickly. . . . "

Magda called loudly, "No, no, it's all right, Else! I can manage him alone. Ring Dr Mansfeld and the police. I'll keep him here!"

I turned in astonishment. Sure enough, there stood Else, pretty as a picture, attracted by the noise of our struggle. And then she disappeared in the hall, towards the telephone. I tore myself free with a jerk.

"You're not going to get me, Magda!" I gave her a push and she fell back.

As I ran, I snatched up the scattered silverware, including the broken serving-spoon, and rushed into the hall. I threw everything into the suitcase, and tried hard to shut the lid. Magda was there already.

"You're not taking those things! My silver is staying here! You're not going to drink that up as well!"

A yard away, Else was busy telephoning. I heard her say: "He wants to kill his wife!"

"My God, what a child you are," I thought.

We both tugged at the suitcase. Then suddenly I let go and

85

Magda went sprawling on the floor again. I tore the case out of her hand, lashed out at her once or twice, rushed to the porch, snatched up my shoes and ran into the street in my socks. Suddenly I stopped short.

"Give me the suitcase, sir," said Lobedanz's soft insinuating voice. "I'll go on ahead, look out, here come the women!" Quite mechanically, I handed the case to Lobedanz. He made off. I ran after him, off into the night, in my socks.

18

LOBEDANZ ran with the suitcase. He took the shortest route, plunged into the oldest part of the town, rushed along lanes and alleys, and suddenly turned a corner. I ran after him. It was very dark. It was only because he was wearing shoes and so made a noise as he ran, that I was able to follow him at all. I am quite sure that Lobedanz had intended to disappear completely with the suitcase, and leave me helpless in the street. He really thought he had shaken me off: he hadn't heard my soft stockinged footsteps. But when he eventually stopped to draw breath, I was beside him, and asked him why he had been running so senselessly. Nobody was after us!

The scoundrel was not put out for a moment. He managed to conceal his disappointment at my appearance, and said: "You had some trouble with the women, didn't you? The women were shouting, weren't they? What did you do to them?"

"Nothing you hadn't advised me to, Lobedanz," I laughed. "I tried to frighten them by knocking them about but it didn't come to much. It's quite understandable that a woman should resist when her silver's being taken. I've got the silver, Lobedanz."

"Ah, have you?" the scoundrel answered. "Now we have to see if we get anything for it. Most silver is light and hollow, or the shape is unfashionable, silver that's only good for melting down is hardly worth anything."

"You needn't worry about that, Lobedanz," I said malicious-ly, "I'll sell my silver without you—if I sell it at all, which I haven't decided yet. Now let me carry my suitcase myself."

During our conversation I had been putting my shoes on, and now I took the suitcase despite Lobedanz's protestations. At last I had hit on the right tone for dealing with him. Alcohol, which is constantly stirring up new and different moods, had suggested it to me. Now Lobedanz became a worm again, he protested that he was only a poor worker incapable of dealing with an educated man. Of course my silver was bound to be good, bound to be. I must put it down to his stupidity—that he had thought a man like myself might have inferior silver. I pretended to be sunk in gloomy silence, which made him uneasier than ever, but to myself I was shaking with inner laughter. When we got back home, without having to be asked, Lobedanz brought out the bottle of brandy which, sure enough, he had kept ready. I reached in my pocket and asked: "How much?"

"Two marks fifty," he whispered, very humbly.

"Here's your money, and don't you dare to bring me such rotten liquor again. Have I got to pay anything else?"

He assured me that everything was settled.

"Good, then get out. I want to sleep now." He wriggled out through the door, I had managed to make him embarrassed and humble.

But I neither felt like sleeping nor drinking. My craving for intoxication had slackened for a while, for some unknown reason I was given a short respite, during which something of my former active self came up to the surface. Perhaps this was a result of the scene I had just had with Magda, which had deeply upset me—of course I tried to think of it as little as possible. For a while I sat brooding on the sofa. It was terribly apparent that, after what had happened, I could never return home again. My old plan of weaning myself from alcohol and facing Magda and the doctors as a healthy man, had finally collapsed—in my sober moments I had never quite believed in it myself. It was also impossible to stay any longer here with Lobedanz; the idea filled me with disgust. It could only end in madness. I had to find some other way, and I believed I had a notion of what this way might be. Within the next twenty-four hours I should have to risk a great deal. I couldn't set about my task as a drunken man.

It must have been between two and three in the morning when I got up from the sofa and began unpacking the suitcase. I washed myself from head to foot, got half-dressed, and shaved with the utmost care. Everything went infinitely slowly. My hand was shaking so much that from time to time I despaired of ever being able to shave, but at last I managed it. From some unknown source within me, new energy arose, that gave me endurance, that allowed me just to take a few little mouthfuls of drink at long intervals.

When at last, washed and tidied, I looked at myself in the mirror, I was astonished how well I still looked. True, my eyes were bloodshot, with pinpoint pupils, and my cheeks were rather flabby, but nobody could take me for a drunkard. I could risk it tomorrow morning, and I would risk it. I didn't bother to go to bed. I wrapped a blanket round me and sat down on the sofa, to wait for morning. I listened. Everything was quiet in the house, but I was firmly convinced that Lobedanz was on the watch. Well, I would wait, and I trusted myself to outwit him.

I had filled a tumbler with brandy, and put the bottle with the rest of it in the furthest corner of my room. I would have to manage till morning with this tumbler of brandy: I had made up my mind. But I only sipped it. I was dead-tired from the unwonted activity of the night. I leaned back, and was soon asleep.

A slight clatter awoke me. I half-opened my eyes and blinked into the room, in which the morning sun had already got the upper hand of the light from the electric bulb. Lobedanz stood bent over my suitcase. He had taken a table-knife out of its baize, examined it critically and weighed it in his hand. For a while through half-closed eyelids I watched this scoundrel rummaging among the silver; then I stretched and yawned loudly like someone who is just waking, and looked round my room. It was empty. I just caught sight of the door-handle lifting into position. A glance into the suitcase convinced me that Lobedanz had contented himself for the time being with merely examining the silver. The actual pilfering was probably being reserved for my more drunken moments. I opened the window and looked out over the town. The sun had not risen far above the horizon, it must have been between six and seven o'clock. I called through the door for Lobedanz. The artful dog let some time pass before he answered. I called down to him that I would like to have my breakfast. He brought it very quickly: his cringing, almost sheeplike expression betrayed a lively alarm at the change in my bearing. I acted as if I had noticed nothing and for the first time I ate with some relish. The coffee was surprisingly good, the rolls crusty, the butter fresh and cool—that scoundrel Lobedanz certainly knew how to live.

While I was eating, Lobedanz tidied up my bed and the wash-stand, and as he did so, he couldn't resist throwing furtive side glances at me. His cough seemed to get worse. The brandy-bottle which he found in the corner of the room, gave him at last the excuse he had been seeking to start a conversation:

"You've hardly drunk anything, sir," he said, and held the bottle up to the light.

"No, my dear Herr Lobedanz," I said ironically but genially, as I spread some butter thickly on a roll. "And if you go on bringing me such hooch, I'll soon give up drinking altogether."

"It was a mistake, sir," he growled. "A mistake on the grocer's part. As true as I stand here, I paid four marks fifty for this bottle, and the grocer gave me the wrong one. But of course I've only charged you the proper price, I paid the two marks myself, though I'm a poor man. I'm honest, sir . . . "

"Don't talk rubbish, Lobedanz," I answered roughly. "You're no more honest than you are poor. You're an old swindler, or rather a young one, but sly enough for an old one. Perhaps that's why I like you. Now you can take that bottle," I suddenly cried in pretended rage, "and drink it yourself. And see there's a decent one here in five minutes."

And I threw a note down on the table. He snatched it.

"As soon as the shops open," he assured me.

"Not when the shops open!" I shouted still louder. "Now, this very minute! You idiot, do you think I'm going to sit awake all day after a night like this? I want to get to sleep some time."

With a pretence of excitement, I had jumped up, already taken off my jacket and unbuttoned my waistcoat. I had to convince him now, or the whole thing would go wrong. So I snatched up the tumbler of brandy that stood on the table, gulped it down, and cried, "There, fill it up again with that damned hooch of yours. And see there's some other drink here in five minutes; the grocer is bound to let you in by the back door, a good customer like you!" I had torn off my waistcoat and was already unbuttoning my braces.

"In five minutes!" Lobedanz assured me, and hurried out of the room. It was easy to detect the relief and satisfaction in his words. He had been afraid of losing his milch cow, but now I was boozing again, hallelujah!

Hardly had I heard the front door shut than I was in my clothes again. I shut the suitcase, took it, and ran downstairs.

There might be a Frau Lobedanz, and Lobedanz children, of the same gentle, insinuating, whispering, damned-roguish kind as their father, I'd never set eyes on them, and I didn't see them this morning either. Unimpeded, I came out into the lane. Here, almost free of my tormentor, the alcohol nearly played a trick on me again. Suddenly I remembered that for the first time for weeks I was out without "provisions", and on such a dangerous and decisive journey, while up in my room stood a newly-filled tumbler of brandy. I nearly went back, and if I had I would almost certainly have fallen again into the long-fingered blackmailing clutches of Lobedanz. But the energy which had newly awakened in the night was victorious; I shook my head and went on my way.

19

Of course I had no idea in which direction Lobedanz had gone, and at first I looked about me rather anxiously. But once I was out of the "shed quarter" and walking through the clean streets of my home town, I felt safer. Without hesitation, I went straight to the station and sat down in the second-class waiting-room. I knew I was risking a great deal; if anything of my story had leaked out, I was lost. But I would have to run many more risks this morning: this sitting in the waiting-room was only a rehearsal for other important undertakings to come. Of course I could have hidden in the park for a few hours with less risk, but in my changed mood, I liked to defy danger now, though I must also confess that I was to some extent incited to it by alcohol. I did not want to be quite without it, so I ordered from the waiter, besides a big breakfast of fried eggs, sausage and cheese, a carafe of cognac as well, with which to lace my coffee while I breakfasted for the second time, in comfort, and not without appetite. During this long spun-out meal I buried myself in the local newspaper, which I had not seen for a long time. I read all the local news, including the personal columns, and became certain that no hint about me had got into the paper. It was quite feasible that Magda in her 'concern for my well-being' would have inserted in the paper an announcement to the effect that: E.S., a wholesale merchant, had been missing for such and such a time and was probably wandering about the neighbourhood in a state of mental confusion. Anyone having news of him etc., etc. But nothing of the kind.

During my breakfast I was interrupted for some ten minutes by Stretz the baker, about whom I had just been reading in the newspaper. It appeared that he had been celebrating the twenty-fifth anniversary of his business. We get our bread from him, and now and then he buys his white flour from me. We have known each other for years. He sat down at my table and expressed surprise that we had not seen each other for so long and that I was here at the station eating his competitor's rolls, instead of breakfasting peacefully at home off his. But all this was innocent, as I quickly noticed. I explained everything by hinting at a journey. I was sure now that no rumour of my changed way of life had penetrated beyond the very narrow circle of those concerned. Later, some distant acquaintances came into the waiting-room and, feeling quite safe, I greeted them with a friendly nod and wave of the hand.

However, as the hands of the clock got closer to nine, the waiter had to bring me a second, and finally a third carafe of cognac—let him think what he liked about me, I was not likely to be his guest again soon.

By five to nine I had paid. I got up, took my suitcase, and went into the street. I went along the station road, then fearlessly down our main promenade, the Ulmenallee, and so to the market square where the bank is. Here I was well inside enemy territory. Directly opposite the bank is the Town Hall, on the ground floor of which is situated the very police station that was probably called last night on my account. And one minute from the market square is my own business-place to which, perhaps, this farm-cart is rolling with its load of wheat-sacks. I really was rather excited and before I entered the bank I dried my sweating hands with my handkerchief. Then I went in.

In the bank, I saw at a glance that, at this time of day,

94

shortly after opening, there were only a few office-boys and typists fidgeting with papers. I put the suitcase down, hung up my hat, and went over to the counter behind which sat the clerk who looked after my account. Smiling, I bade him "Good morning" and told him that I had just returned from a lengthy journey (I pointed to my suitcase by the door) and that I would like to ascertain the state of my current account. And while I said all this lightly and without hesitation, I examined his face, inwardly trembling, for any sign of mistrust, suspicion, doubt. But nothing of this showed in the young man's face. He willingly opened the book, totted up some figures with his pencil for a minute, and then said quite indifferently that at the moment my account stood at seven thousand eight hundred odd marks and some pfennigs.

I could hardly conceal a start of joyous surprise, I had never expected so much in my wildest dreams. It was something of a puzzle to me how Magda had managed it. Probably the prison administration had settled up for the delivery of the cordage, but even that could not nearly have accounted for so much. Well anyway, I told myself, suppressing my happy excitement, there was money enough there, enough for the business and above all enough for me and my plans. For the moment I struggled with the temptation to draw out the whole amount, but I conquered myself. I did not want to behave meanly to Magda and the business, however meanly she had behaved to me. Apart from that, such a withdrawal, which would have looked like the closing of my account, would have attracted too much attention.

All this went through my head like lightning, and now I said casually that I had a large payment to make today, and asked for pen and ink. Still standing by the counter, I made out a cheque for five thousand marks, and handed it to the book-keeper. With a last remnant of fear I examined his face again, but without a moment's hesitation he made the necessary entries, stamped the cheque, and himself took it over to the cashier's compartment. I went over too. I was animated by a feeling of proud triumph and boundless joy. Now I had done Magda beautifully: that she had been stupid enough not to give the bank the slightest hint, that showed my enormous superiority in its true light. I could have danced and shouted for joy. It was only with an effort that I suppressed a laughing fit that overtook me.

"How would you like the money, Herr Sommer?" asked the cashier.

"In big notes," I said hastily, "that is, in fifties and hundreds, and about two hundred marks in small change."

In two minutes I had my money, put it away carefully in my breast pocket, and stepped like a proud conjuror into the market square. Just as I was going through the revolving doors, the idea occurred to me that this triumph ought really to be celebrated. Despite the early hour, I wanted to go to a little wine-bar in the market square and, with a bottle or two of burgundy, to eat a lobster or some oysters, or whatever Rohloff had, according to the season of the year.

I step out of the door, and before me stands the inevitable, the repulsive Lobedanz, looking at me with his slimy smile.

20

IF THIS had not been the open market square I would have strangled the scoundrel! As it was I only looked at him darkly, menacingly for a moment, held on tighter to my case, and without taking further notice of him, made my way toward the station. But I knew full well that he was following on my heels and soon I heard his hateful soft insinuating voice:

"Do let me carry your case, sir! Please let me carry your case, sir!"

I pretended I had not heard, and walked on faster. But suddenly I felt a hand near mine on the handle of the case, and, in broad daylight on the open street, Lobedanz had taken the suitcase out of my hand.

Furiously I turned and shouted: "Give me back that case at once, Lobedanz!"

He smiled humbly.

"Not so loud, sir," he begged in a whisper. "People are looking. That's embarrassing for you, sir. Not for a poor working man like me, but for you, sir. . . . "

"Give me back that case at once, Lobedanz," I repeated, but quieter, for people really were looking at us.

"Later, later," he said soothingly. "I like to carry it, sir. To the station, eh?" And without waiting for an answer, he passed by me and went on ahead to the station. I followed him with a helpless feeling of impotence. I looked with hatred at this slightly bowed figure in the dark-blue jacket. Ever since those minutes during which I walked behind Lobedanz to the station,

I have known how a murderer feels immediately before his crime. And I could do nothing to him, nothing at all. He was stronger than I, physically as well as morally. He only needed to call the nearest policeman, and I was lost. He knew that perfectly well, the scoundrel. If I had been a bit more calm and collected at that moment, I could have left Lobedanz peacefully in possession of my suitcase, and dodged off quickly into some side street. With such a large sum of money in my pocket, the loss of the suitcase could easily be put up with—just the ransom to buy myself free from the miserable rogue. But these thoughts did not occur to me, my blood was boiling, I could not think.

Having reached the square in front of the station, instead of going in, Lobedanz turned into the public convenience that lay to the left, hidden by bushes. He did not look round at me, being certain that I would follow him like a little dog. Once in there, he put the suitcase down, pulled on his fingers till the joints cracked, and said: "Now, sir, we can talk peacefully here."

I looked round. The water was rushing in the half-dozen urinal basins, but customers were lacking at this early hour. Lobedanz was right: we could talk in peace here.

"And so we will!" I cried furiously. "What do you think you're doing, Lobedanz, running after me and spying on me all the time, last night already, and now again . . ."

"Spying on you?" he echoed, reproachfully. "But sir, I've brought you your brandy," and he actually took it out of his trousers pocket. "You forgot it this morning. But I'm an honest man. I said to my wife: 'The gentleman paid for the brandy, so he ought to get it.' So here I am."

He held the bottle out to me.

"Drink up, sir, I've uncorked it already. The cork's quite loose."

I made a furious gesture. He wasn't discouraged. He offered me the bottle again.

"Do drink," he insisted. "You're such a nice gentleman when you've had a drop to drink. It doesn't suit you at all when you're sober. You're always so irritable then. . . . "

He took the cork out of the bottle and rubbed its wet butt to and fro on the neck of the bottle.

"Listen, sir," he said laughing, "the schnaps is calling you."

And really, to this day I can't make it out, but by his idiotic behaviour the rogue got me round again. Now laughing myself, I seized the bottle, cried "You miserable scoundrel, you!" and drank and drank. Then I took the bottle away from my mouth, corked it, thrust it into my own trousers pocket, and asked: "But what do you want from me, Lobedanz? Haven't you had everything you were supposed to get?"

"Don't let's talk about that, sir," said Lobedanz eagerly. "Don't let's talk about trifles like that. I know you're an honourable man, you're really a fine man. You wouldn't have the heart to let a poor man die in misery. . . . "

"What do you mean, Lobedanz?" I asked warily. "I think you've already had enough, and more than enough, out of me. When I think of that jewellery of mine. . . . "

He paid no attention.

"Look, sir," he began in his most insinuating tone, and he made his joints crack sickeningly, "a man like myself is like a brute beast, born in filth and never getting out of the filth. A fine gentleman like yourself can't imagine it properly . . . "

"I can imagine a whole lot of things about you, Lobedanz," I said grimly, "and they certainly have to do with filth."

Again he took no notice of me. Impressively and with conviction, he said: "And when such a brute beast, sir, sees a bit of business that might lift him out of the filth for his whole life, well, sir, there can't be any hesitation, the business has to be gone through with, sir!"

He looked at me and repeated, this time with nothing soft

and insinuating in his voice: "The business has to be gone through with, sir. It's a matter of life and death."

Inwardly, I trembled at the wild threat in his voice, but outwardly I was quite calm as I asked: "And what sort of business are you talking about, Lobedanz?"

He passed his hand over his eyes as if wiping away some evil picture, and began to smile, insinuatingly, softly. He had himself under control again.

"What sort of business, sir?"

He smiled more broadly, his finger joints cracked.

"The gentleman knows best how much money he drew out of the bank, and how much he wants to give me."

I was dumbfounded by his impudence. I had expected that he would claim the silver, and was already half prepared to let him have it, but that he should ask for a share of my precious money, that was something I hadn't anticipated.

"You're a fool, Lobedanz," I laughed. "Moreover, you didn't pay proper attention. I didn't get a pfennig from the bank. My wife had blocked my account. I'm not allowed to draw any more money out, do you understand?"

He listened to me in gloomy silence. I reached into the side-pocket of my jacket and took out what was left of the money I had taken from Magda's cashbox.

"Here, see for yourself. That's all the money I possess."

I held the money out to him. His dark suspicious glance wandered from my face to the money in my hand.

"How much is there?" he asked in a faltering voice. "Show me."

He stood quite near to me, his eyes close to the money. Then surprising me with a sudden lunge he reached into my breast pocket and tore out the bundles of money. One or two fell on to the dirty wet asphalt floor of the lavatory—we both bent down after them simultaneously. His hands were quicker, but realising the futility of trying to pick up the money, I seized him by the throat, I hung tightly on to him, determined never to let him go until he had given in, until I had my money back. . . . He tried to defend himself, but his defence was hindered by his greed. With both hands he was holding on to the money that he could not bear to relinquish.

He jerked his knee up against my stomach. A moment later, we were both rolling on the floor, I still hanging on to his throat, his limbs wildly threshing, like a fish the angler pulls in to land . . . then his limbs went slack, from his throat came a horrible rattle . . . I let go of him and tried to open his hand . . . I would like to know what our honest postmaster Winder can have thought when he found two men struggling wildly on the lavatory floor, when all he wanted was to settle peacefully his morning business! "Gentlemen! Please!" he cried in a high startled voice. "Here, in the toilet! Gentlemen!"

Lobedanz, who had got his breath back, saw his chance—with one bound he was up, grabbed the suitcase, pushed the postmaster aside, and was out of the lavatory, before you could count three. I stood giddy and benumbed, unable to make any quick decision. I went towards one of the basins, turning my back on the bewildered and indignant postmaster. He said "Herr Sommer, if I'm not mistaken. I'm surprised, Herr Sommer. I'm really surprised at you!" For a moment I felt his stabbing glance at my back, then a closet-door closed, a lock clicked, clothes rustled—I was alone and able to make my exit. And just at that moment when I was about to leave the convenience, absolutely desperate, without money, my glance fell on a blue package, and, look, there crumpled and soiled, lay a bundle of hundred-mark notes—a round thousand in ten hundred-mark notes!

21

Nobody who has just lost a beautiful cowhide suitcase with his best things and all his silver, nobody who has just lost four out of five thousand marks, can have the slightest idea how happy I was, as I left my native town a quarter of an hour later in a second-class compartment. Heaven knows how it was, but I really felt I had got rid of Lobedanz remarkably cheaply and I thanked God that I had at any rate salvaged a thousand marks from the disaster.

Of course I must confess, this feeling of happiness was considerably helped by the fact that despite the struggle, I had found the brandy-bottle intact and unspilt in my trousers pocket. I had already taken a long drink from it, and this drink no doubt contributed substantially to my optimistic assessment of the situation. Comfortably I gazed at the green fields gliding by, with grazing cows and peaceful woods, and I had not the slightest care for the future. For the time being, I had enough to live on (and to drink), and what came after would somehow settle itself. I would manage somehow; I felt I had emerged from the day's adventures with complete success, for I marked up the visit to the waiting-room and the bank as victories to my own credit, and I took the defeat at Lobedanz's hands with a calm shrug of my shoulders, as an inevitable accident of nature.

About midday, I reached my destination (which I had only chosen to mislead anyone who might be following me). It was a small health-resort, little known but well kept. I ate in an hotel by the water (green eels with dill sauce and cucumber salad) and let the sun shine on my head as I drank a fine fully-matured burgundy, and reflected what a comfortable life I could lead now, as a retired businessman and semi-bachelor. After the meal I sauntered through the town, bought a brief-case, two pairs of silk pyjamas (I had never before possessed any so gaudy) some fine toilet things, scented soap, and some rather sharp French perfume with which I had already been sprayed on approval—and I joked in such a superior, charming, *mondaine* way with the young salesgirls that I, at least, came to have a lively respect for my own hitherto-unused talents as a gallant and a ladykiller.

As a logical consequence I immediately bought some scented cachous at a chemist. Then I went to the best hotel in the square, to which was attached a wine-shop, to buy some schnaps. I had the good fortune to meet the owner himself, a stout white-haired man whose blossoming red face told of many bottles of burgundy emptied in peace and comfort. He smiled a little at my primitive request for corn-liquor, recommended and sold me an amber-yellow Saxon schnaps, and then drew my attention to a highly alcoholic plum-brandy from the Black Forest, a real wood-cutters' tipple for icy winter days, he called it. He poured me out a little glass to try, and I must confess I was so enthusiastic about it, that I quickly followed the first glass with a whole sequence of others. This was just the thing for me, an exaltation far above my hitherto primitive experience—burning and pungent and retaining in itself something of the sweetness of ripe fruit. I bought five bottles straight away, a handy-sized parcel was made of my purchases; in another shop I obtained a strong corkscrew, and so I wandered back to the station, well-provided and in a most cheerful mood.

Now I was travelling again, and on the same route by which I had come this morning. I was travelling back towards my home town. But one station before it, I got out and walked. Night was falling. I was nearly half an hour from that country inn where Elinor, the queen of alcohol, lived. Forgotten was that abortive night in her room, forgotten that humiliating bout when, under the eyes of the doctors, my boozing companions had all left me, forgotten were the shoes that had been so maliciously handed into the car! Alcohol has no memory. If it makes a man angry, a word or a glass can soon extinguish that anger again. I only knew that after my experiences with Magda and Lobedanz, Elinor was my refuge. With her I would stay or with her I would go—that was the only glimmer of life I had, and it seemed enough.

22

I HAD come too late. At the inn-windows the shutters were already closed, and no gleam of light came through. I tried the latch but the door was locked. For a moment I stood reflecting. Then I went softly round the house into the orchard and looked up to Elinor's window. There, too, all was in darkness, but that did not matter. I had all the time in the world, and in any case we would get on quite well in the dark. Better, even, better!

First of all I sat in the grass and started to open my parcel. A cleverly-tied parcel is an excellent thing, but it has the disadvantage that one cannot get at its contents so easily. I had been thirsty for too long, I had accomplished great things, and now for that good old woodcutters' schnaps! After I had considerably, very considerably, fortified myself, I began to set my belongings up on the shed roof, which I could just reach with my hands. First the brief-case, and then one bottle after the other: one bottle of Saxon schnaps, then four unopened and one opened bottle of Black Forest plum-brandy. All nice and tidy, side by side on the edge of the roof. Now I was ready for the climb. I hung on to the overhanging edge of the roof and tried to pull myself up. But I had overestimated my gymnastic abilities and underestimated the effect of the schnaps. For a while I dangled helplessly in the air, then I lost my hold and fell heavily in the grass. I lay there groaning; the fall had done me no good. But with that obstinacy that drunkards develop towards impossible tasks, I kept renewing my attempt —after I had well and truly fortified myself each time. The remainder of the first bottle went in that way. Each time I fell to the ground. The last time I tried, it was clear to me that I would never achieve my aim like this. Also I realised that I was very drunk. "I'm absolutely tight, I'm completely sozzled," I kept murmuring stupidly, and I leaned panting against a tree.

Then I dimly recalled that I had seen iron tables and chairs standing outside the inn. Laboriously I dragged one of the chairs over, clambered on to it carefully (by now I was afraid of another fall) and tried to get up on the roof. And again I fell. There was a longer pause, partly because I had bruised myself badly and partly because I had to hunt around for the corkscrew to open a fresh bottle. I was sure I had put it on the edge of the roof, but quite inconceivably it had fallen off. Grumbling to myself I looked for it on all fours in the grass. It was not to be found. Eventually it occurred to me that there was a corkscrew on my pocket knife which had served me quite well up to now. I felt in my pocket for the knife, did not find it, but found instead the corkscrew I had put on the roof. After I had had another drink, the thing became clear to me: I would never reach her bedroom window by way of the roof. So I went round to the front again and once more tried the front-door. It was still locked. I took the bunch of keys out of my pocket and tried my keys one after the other. They were all much too small for this stout country keyhole, but I kept on trying them with stupid obstinacy, in the firm hope that eventually a miracle would happen and the door would open of itself. During all these drunken preparations I had not shown the slightest consideration for the inhabitants' sleep, so it was no wonder that eventually a window opened above me and an angry woman's voice asked sharply: "Who's there?"

I stood quite still, like a trapped thief.

"Will you go away!" cried the furious voice from above. "You won't get anything here. We're closed!"

With that, the window slammed to, and I stood alone in the dark, still locked out. For a while I remained without moving, then I tiptoed to the back-garden and began softly to take my belongings off the shed roof and round to the entrance, where I pedantically arranged them on an iron table. (Needless to say I did not forget to drink during this operation.) Hardly had I finished this task, which took a long time on account of my stupor and my uncertain gait, than I began that idiotic game with the bunch of keys and the keyhole again. I had not been at it for long, when the window flew open again with a crash, and the woman's voice cried out furiously: "This is going too far! Will you get away from here, or do I have to fetch the police!"

The word "police" loosened my heavy tongue. "Oh please, let me in!" I called up in confusion. "I'm the Professor. . . ."

How I came to give myself the title of "Professor" I have no idea, it was a heaven-sent inspiration.

"The Professor?" said the voice from above in a tone of utter astonishment. "What Professor . . . ? The one who was painting pictures here last summer?"

"Yes, of course," I said in the most matter-of-fact tone in the world, as if it were quite normal for a picture-painting professor to try to unlock strange doors with his own keys in the middle of the night.

"Let me in! I've been standing here for two hours!"

"If you'd only written a postcard, Herr Professor," said the voice from above, still not exactly friendly but milder. "Wait a moment. I'll open up at once."

Relieved, I sat down on an iron chair, took a quick drink and shut my eyes. I was very tired, almost stunned. I did not realise then that something dangerous lay hidden within my calmness, a wild unbridled rage that might break out at any moment. It only lacked a cause, and anything might start it off This plum-brandy was far more dangerous than the comparatively harmless schnaps. It went deeper into the blood, and led to unexpected abysses.

At last the key turned in the door. A ray of light shone on me.

"Well, come in then," said the woman's voice, "but it's not very nice of you to disturb our night's rest like this, Herr Professor."

I got up and followed my guide into the bar-room, which, by the light of a single bulb, looked most inhospitable, with its chairs set up on the tables. My companion now turned to me. It was the white-haired innkeeper of whom I had caught a glimpse once before. She gazed at me in astonishment.

"But you're not the Professor at all!" she cried angrily. "You're that gentleman who got drunk here the other day, and the medical officer had to take you away. You've got a cheek, coming here with your lies. . . !"

I silenced her with a threatening glance. I felt an enormous rage rising in me. I knew I would break any resistance that might be opposed to me; I was capable, I knew, of striking this woman, of throwing her to the ground, of killing her even, if the devil so prompted me. I looked at the woman and ordered: "Call Elinor!" And as she gave a sign of dissent: "Call Elinor at once, or" my voice became soft and threatening, "or something will happen!" The woman made a helpless gesture and then said pleadingly:

"Please don't cause any trouble, sir. It's night time now, and the girl's asleep. I'll gladly make up a bed for you on the sofa. You see, you're a little bit drunk."

She tried to smile but there was fear in her smile. I recognised it very well.

"You sleep it off, and tomorrow Elinor'll be with you as much as you like. After all, you're an educated man, sir."

"Call the girl," I said obstinately, and as she started to pro-test again: "All right, then I'll go up to her myself."

I pushed the landlady aside. "I'll call Elinor," she said quickly. "Please sit down on the sofa for a moment. Elinor'll come immediately."

"Stop!" I cried as the landlady made to go upstairs. "You call her from down here. You're not leaving this bar-room. Any one leaving this room will be shot."

I reached into my pocket as if I had a gun there. The landlady screamed softly.

"Now you know," I said darkly. "Go on, call her."

The landlady called. She had to call several times before an answer came from above. Elinor slept heavily.

"You've got to come down, Elinor!" called the landlady. "Be quick, will you?"

"That's better," I said, with the face of an examining magis-trate. "And now, one question: have you any Black Forest plum-brandy?"

"No," said the landlady, and as she saw my furious expres-sion, she added, "but we've got some kirsch, that's much better."

"Nothing's better than plum-brandy, but bring me your kirsch, anyway."

She brought it, bottle and glass shaking in her hand.

"That's it," I said, and drank. My mood brightened; it really was almost better. "And now sit down and tell me who else is in the house besides yourself."

"Only Elinor, really, besides myself there's only Elinor."

"You're lying!" I cried furiously. "Don't you try to lie to me again, or something will happen!" And I reached in my pocket again. And again she screamed softly.

I continued inexorably, "I saw a woman the last time I was here, with shaggy hair and a red nose . . . "

"Oh, you mean Marie," cried the landlady, relieved, "but

sir, what do you want to upset yourself for and frighten me like this. I'm not trying to tell you lies; Marie only helps here. She lives in the village with her parents."

"Well," I said, pacified, "if that's the case, I'll forgive you this time."

I drank.

"This kirsch isn't bad. It's quite good, even."

"Isn't it, isn't it?" said the landlady eagerly. "I'm doing all I can to satisfy you. I'm getting the girl out of her bed in the middle of the night. But now you've got to be nice too, and not threaten me with that gun any more. Best thing would be to put it away. A thing like that goes off easily, and you wouldn't want that; you're a good respectable gentleman . . ."

Before I could protest against this new insult, for I was determined not to be good, but awe-inspiring and wicked, and to show my power over people, before I could get angry again, Elinor's firm tread was heard on the stairs; and she stepped into the light. She was fully dressed, only her dark hair was not done up but combed to the back. She looked more beautiful than ever.

"Elinor!" I cried, "my queen!"

Just for a moment she started, seeing me there with the landlady in that untidy room; and then this astonishing girl did exactly the right thing, as if she knew everything that had happened: she ran up to me, embraced me, gave me a kiss on the right cheek and a kiss on the left, and cried happily: "Why, it's pop! Good old boozy pop! Now we can have fun, eh, Mother Schulze? Now we'll have some champagne!"

"Champagne," I cried. "Of course we'll have champagne. As much as you like. I've got lots of money. Elinor, you're my best girl, you know I love you. You're my queen, and now we'll go off on our travels. Elinor, give me another kiss, but right in the middle of the mouth!"

She did so. I felt her breast against mine, I was happy. At last alcohol had brought me complete happiness. I saw only Elinor, I felt only Elinor, I thought and spoke only Elinor. I did not notice that, despite my stern threat of death, the land-lady had long since left the bar-room.

23

I DO not know how long I had been like that in Elinor's arms.
I had her huge white face with its high-arched eyebrows quite
close to mine, it leaned over me—and the whole world sank
away. Her eyes, no longer colourless but glittering green,
looked at me, and I felt a trembling within me, to the innermost part of my bones. My heart fluttered like a poplar-leaf
in the breeze.

"Oh Elinor, forgive me! I've never loved like this before.
I never knew that such a thing existed. You make me weak and
strong; when your breath touches me I feel as if a storm was
blowing through me, blowing away all the dry old leaves of
the past. Through you, I have become new again—come, let's
get away from here, let's get away from the past! We'll go to
the South, where the sun always shines, and the sky's always
blue. White castles on the vine-slopes! That's where we'll go!
Come with me! I've got a little brief-case outside, but there's
enough in it. Come with me as you are, we'll get away, this
very minute. I'm afraid something dreadful will happen if we
stay here any longer. They wouldn't allow you to be with me.
Come, let's go, my relentless paleface, *ma reine d'alcool*. To
you, and long may you live, from the bottom of my heart,
I drink to you."

I looked at her, beaming. Then, deeply disturbed: "Why
don't we go now?" She passed her hand caressingly, soothingly,
through my hair. She was sitting on my lap, she had one arm
round my neck, her tenderness hid the world from me.

She said softly: "We'll go soon, pop, soon. There's a train goes from the station at six o'clock. Till then, you must be patient, pop. We're all right sitting here, aren't we?"

I nestled closer to her. I laid my head against her breast, I felt sheltered there, like a child with its mother.

"Of course we're all right here. But we'll go at six o'clock, we'll travel far, far from here. We'll never want to see any of this again. In the South, we shall love ... we shall always love each other. ... "

She looked into my eyes, so near, it seemed to be one single eye, that became blurred as if I had looked into the sun.

She whispered close to my ear: "Yes, I will travel with you, pop. But you won't drink all the time then, will you? I hate men who are always drunk. They disgust me."

"I'll never drink any more, once I've got you; not a drop more. You're better than wine or schnaps. You're like fire in me. You make the whole world dance. Your health, my queen!"

"Your health, my old pop! We'll go travelling. But shall we have enough money for such a long journey? We shan't want to have to work."

"Money?" I asked contemptuously. "Money? Money enough for both of us. Money for all the journeys and the longest life!"

And I tore the notes out of my pocket. It really was quite a bundle. Elinor took them from my hand, smoothed out the notes and arranged them for counting.

"Eight hundred and sixty-three marks," she said at last, and looked at me thoughtfully, with knitted brows. "That's not very much money, pop. Not enough for us to go on a long journey, and live together without working. Is that all the money you've got?"

For a moment I was somewhat sobered. I passed my hand

over my forehead, and looked with aversion at the bundle of dirty scraps that Elinor held in her hand.

"Somebody's stolen my money, Elinor," I said sullenly. "Some scoundrel has stolen from me five times, ten times more money than you've got in your hand. And all my things in a cowhide suitcase, and our silver, it's all gone. Whatever will Magda say?"

Under her gaze I slowly collected my senses.

"But it doesn't matter, Elinor. Put the money away. I don't want to see it any more. I can get some more from the bank, I can get as much as you want. Tens of thousands! I come in with a cheque, they say to me: 'Herr Sommer...'"

"So your name's Sommer?"

"Yes, Sommer's my name. Erwin Sommer. Like Sommertime. If you go travelling with me you'll have Sommer all the time."

I laughed. But she remained serious. She said, "There you are, pop, somebody's already stolen your money and things. You can't manage, in your condition. I'll look after it for you. It's quite safe if I keep it for you. Here, I'll put some money in your pocket. You don't want to be entirely without money, do you, pop? It's twenty-three marks. If that gets lost, it doesn't matter so much...."

She became more and more insistent. It was ridiculous how seriously she took this silly money.

"And you'll promise, won't you, pop, not to tell anybody that I'm keeping your money for you? Nobody? Whatever happens?"

"I'll never tell anybody, Elinor," I answered, "I swear. But all this is unnecessary. We're going away at six o'clock...."

"Well, you've sworn it, pop. You won't forget. Not a word to anybody, ever. Whatever happens!"

"Not a word, Elinor!"

"My good old pop," she cried and clasped me in her arms.

"And now as a reward you shall be allowed to drink out of my mouth!"

She took a mouthful of kirsch, then she put her lips to mine, I shut my eyes, and from her mouth the kirsch flowed sharp and warm and living into my mouth. It was the sweetest thing I ever experienced. I ceased to exist.

24

I WAKE up, I look around. No, I am not awake, I am still dreaming. What I just saw was a whitewashed room with an iron grill on one of its sides—that is something out of my dream. I lie there with my eyes shut, I try to remember . . . something happened in the night. Then my left hand remembers. Quite involuntarily it gropes about the floor and now it encounters the cool smoothness of glass. It raises the bottle to my mouth, and I drink again, with eyes shut I drink Black Forest plum-brandy again. I am with Elinor again! I am with Elinor! Life is beginning again, I swing myself higher . . . I have only been asleep for a short time and now I'm with Elinor again.

Two, three mouthfuls, and now the bottle is empty. I suck at it, not another drop comes. With a deep sigh I put it down and once again I open my eyes. I see a whitewashed cell, rather dirty, with many inscriptions and obscene drawings scratched on the walls. Very high up on one wall, where it begins to slope, a small barred window. This window is open. Through the opening, I see a pale blue feebly sunlit sky. On its fourth side, this cell has a strong iron-barred grill, exactly like the bars of cages in the Zoo. Outside this grill is a stove, then a door, which is shut. I am imprisoned! I look at my bed. I am lying in my clothes on a miserable iron bedstead, on a straw-bag with a torn blanket. My cell also contains a table, a stool and a terrible stinking bucket. Yes, and the bottle which I have

just emptied . . . I spring up from my bed, I hold the bottle
up to the light: there really isn't a drop in it! Finally I put it
away behind the bucket, and while I am doing so, something
of the night's experiences returns . . .

I see the untidy dimly-lit bar-room, I see myself, Erwin
Sommer, proprietor of a market produce business, a respectable
citizen of 41 years old, I see myself grappling with the police,
resisting arrest tooth and nail—we are rolling on the floor, and
the stout landlady with the white hair, who had been so
frightened of my gun and who now knows I was only pretending to have a gun, is all the time giving me sly kicks and
punches, and suddenly pushing her hand in my face, while I
am fighting with the police for my liberty, and at the same
time, during the fight, I see Elinor watching us struggling, with
an unfathomable smile on her face, but she doesn't lift a finger
to help. Neither does she say a word.

And yet I might perhaps have broken free, for a terror was
raging within me that I, a civilised citizen, might be marched
off to prison like some nobody, I, a respectable man to whom
people raised their hats—in gaol! My desperation gave me
such strength, that I might well have wrenched myself free
from the sergeant—had it not been for Elinor. At one point of
our struggle, perhaps at the very moment when victory was
inclining towards me, she was suddenly standing by us with
one of my bottles of Black Forest plum-brandy; smiling gently
and looking radiantly at me with her pale eyes, she said: "Don't
be upset, pop. The sergeant'll let you take a bottle of schnaps
with you. It's only for one night, pop, until you've got over
your jag."

That dispelled my fighting spirit, and they easily got the
mastery of me. Once again, alcohol and Elinor seduced me
(they were probably the same poison: alcohol and Elinor);
they had deceived me so often, and led me to my most ignominious defeats, and yet I never seemed to learn. I sold my

chances of freedom for a bottle of schnaps, and now, there it
stands, behind the stinking bucket, empty. And here I stand,
between white-washed walls; here is an iron grill, and up
there, near the ceiling, a little window. No Freedom, no
Elinor. No schnaps. And suddenly I recall the final scene, the
very last of the previous night, such a shameful scene that I
clench my fists and grind my teeth. . . . We had come to terms,
the policeman and I. He had had a lot to say about the regulations and so on, but I suppose I had given him trouble enough
already, and he was probably frightened I might make more
difficulties on the way. He had finally agreed that I should
take the bottle of schnaps with me; I carried it in my trousers
pocket, the cork loose and ready to be pulled out. In return,
I had given my word that I wouldn't resist him any more, and
wouldn't attempt to escape. Despite that, he had put a little
steel chain round my right wrist; perhaps he rather mistrusted
a drunken man's word, and now we are standing in the door-
way. I turn and say to Elinor: "Good night, Elinor. Thank
you for everything, Elinor."

And she answers in an indifferent voice, "Good night, pop.
Sleep well"—just as if I were some regular customer going
home to bed after his evening pint. Well, with that we're
ready to go, the sergeant and I, when suddenly the landlady
calls in a shrill voice: "What about my wine? And my schnaps?
And the broken glasses? The drunken old scoundrel hasn't paid
yet, sergeant! He's not going to get away with that! Let him
pay up first!"

The sergeant looks doubtfully at me, sighs, then asks in a
low voice: "Have you got any money?"

I nod.

"Pay up then, so I can get home."

And aloud: "How much is it?"

The landlady tots it up, and says, "Sixty-seven marks, including service. Oh yes, and there's the phone call to the

police station, sergeant, that makes altogether sixty-seven marks twenty."

I reach in my pocket, I bring out a little money. I reach into the breast-pocket of my jacket, it is empty. Suddenly I remember . . . I look at Elinor first with a silent question, then pleading, challenging, insisting . . . Elinor does not look at me. With a faint unfathomable smile she glances at the little pile of change. I have put down on the table. Then her glance slides away and across to the landlady. Elinor's lips open a little, the smile broadens on her mouth. The landlady has darted over and counts the money in no time.

"Twenty-three marks!" she shrieks. "You scoundrel! You damned twister, you! First you rob me of my night's rest and threaten me with a revolver, and then——"

She goes on abusing me. The sergeant listens, bored and yawning. Finally, as the landlady tries to get at my face again with her claws, he wards her off and says: "That's enough, now, Frau Schulze." And to me: "Haven't you really any money?"

"No," I say, and look firmly at Elinor. This time she looks back at me, just as firmly, without a trace of a smile. And now, quick as lightning, the girl does an astonishing thing: she reaches into the neck of her blouse and momentatily draws out the bundle of notes she has taken from me. I see the blue shimmer of the hundred-mark notes. The tip of her tongue appears in the corner of her mouth. She smiles ironically. The bundle of notes disappears again in her bosom. She puts her hand under her breast, lifts it a little so that I see its beautiful full curve, turns away from me, and goes behind the bar.

Oh, how sly and refined she is: just at the right moment she reminds me of my word, but not quite trusting my word, she reminds me also of the bond of our flesh. Bitter-sweet, with a cold fire, a mistress who has never quite given herself, who would never quite belong to me—the true queen of alcohol!

"No," I say with a dry voice, "I've no more money on me. But send the bill to my office. My wife will pay it."

The landlady turns on me: "Your wife'll have something better to do than pay a drunkard's bills! Turn his pockets out, sergeant. Perhaps he's still got something on him. . . . "

"I haven't," I say, "but I've got a brief-case outside, sergeant. Can I go and fetch it?"

We fetch the brief-case, containing the purchases I had made at the little health resort. I spread out my purchases: my two suits of parrot-coloured pyjamas, the elegant toilet-set, the French perfume . . . how long ago is it, since I, with my man-of-the-world jokes, had bought them all from those young girls? Now I'll never use them! How long ago is it since, on that terrace by the lake, I dined off green eels and burgundy and reflected on what a comfortable life I would lead as a retired businessman? How long? Just a bare twelve hours. And now I'll never lead that comfortable life! Now I have a chain about my wrist and I am being taken into custody by the police as a common criminal. Oh, farewell, good life!

"What am I supposed to do with these fine knick-nacks?" the landlady bellows. "Seven pairs of cuticle and nail scissors alone! I can't use them! I want my money! And these common-looking pyjamas!"

But one can tell from her voice that this is only a rearguard action; her greed has been awakened.

"I paid about a hundred marks for it," I say. "And there's two bottles of plum-brandy and a bottle of schnaps outside. You can have them as well. Now are you satisfied?"

She goes on grumbling for a while, but then she calms down.

"But I'd like to give this bottle of scent to your girl for a tip," I say, taking it.

"She can have it, for aught I care," says the landlady. "I don't want to stink myself up with that whore's stuff."

But she holds up the gaudy pyjamas to see if they are long enough for her.

"Elinor!" I call through the bar-room again. I cannot get away from the sergeant because of the chain. "I've got a bottle of real French perfume for you here. Come along!"

"Oh, leave me alone," she calls back sullenly. "I've had enough of you. Why don't you take him away, sergeant? I want to get to bed."

Her brutal lack of consideration for me, now that she has got what she wants, almost takes my breath away. I call sharply across the bar-room, "Aren't you relying a bit too much on my decency, Elinor?"

"Take that drunken fool away, sergeant," she shouts. "I don't want any more of his gab. He always did make me sick. I hope you keep him in jug for ever!"

I understood, in a moment I understood. Now my money was safe for her. I had denied possession of it myself. And she no doubt did not have it about her any more, she had hidden it somewhere behind the bar. Now she let the mask fall. I was a disgusting idiot. True enough, I really was. A good thing I still had a bottle of schnaps in my pocket, as a consolation! Supposing the schnaps were to desert me now, as well?

"Well, come on," said the sergeant, and pulled at the little chain.

I followed him without a word. The policeman mounted his bicycle and rode off, slowly for a cyclist, rather quickly for a pedestrian. I trotted beside him. He handed me over at the lock-up in a large village nearby, the same place where I had arrived by train that evening.

25

I HAVE moved my bed under the little window and pulled myself up by the iron bars. I see a peaceful sunny country, with meadows, ploughed fields, grazing cattle, and strips of woodland on the horizon. Directly below me is a vegetable garden with a paling fence. An old man is walking along a path, picking green stuff for goats and rabbits and putting it into a sack. He can go where he likes. And I, I am a prisoner! Yesterday all this belonged to me, I could do as I wished with my life. Today, others hold my life in their hands, and I must wait to see what they decide to do with it.

I let myself fall on the bed. I feel very sick. My head aches. The effect of the few mouthfuls of drink I had just now has gone already. I am thirsty—but whenever shall I be able to quench my thirst again? Today, I tell myself soothingly, today for sure. Today they will let you go again. They only wanted to frighten you. That's what they do. They put drunkards into a cell for the night, so they can sleep it off and sober up, and then they set them free again. That's what they're doing with you too. I don't bear them any grudge. After all, they're acting properly enough. I really went too far in that country inn; this warning example, this shot in the air, is quite good for me. Soon the key will turn in the lock and that nice sergeant of last night will come in and say: "Well, Herr Sommer, had a good sleep? Then get out of here—and don't get into mischief again!"

And I go out into freedom again, into that fresh green

sunny morning where an old man with a sack can gather green stuff along the roadside wherever he will. I am free again. If it had been a really serious matter, would the sergeant have put a bottle of schnaps into the cell with me?

So I pacify myself, and when any recollection of that scene in the night with Magda tries to sneak up on me, I firmly ward it off. Magda is my wife. In spite of all our differences lately, we've been together for so long, she will forgive me, she has already forgiven me. She understands that I was ill. But this warning example has sobered me. I'll never drink again. Not a drop.

I jump up and pace about my cell. No, I want to be honest now, I don't want to lie to myself any more: when I'm released from here, I shan't be able to give up the drink immediately. I am terribly tortured by thirst already. It is like a voracious longing in my body, a greed that seems to want to kill me if it is not satisfied. My limbs tremble, one fit of sweating follows another, my stomach is in revolt.

Suddenly I remember that before I left the inn, I had paid for a whole bottle of kirsch, which had remained only half-emptied, on the table. I should have asked the sergeant to let me finish it. He would have allowed me, and then I would have had more alcohol in me, and I wouldn't have had all this terrible trouble now!

Well then, I want to be honest with myself: I cannot entirely give up alcohol at once, but from now on I shall drink only very moderately, perhaps a mere half bottle a day, or only a third, I could even manage with a third already. Just now, one single little schnaps would make me happy, a tiny glass, barely a mouthful of schnaps, in the state I'm in at present.

When I am let out of here shortly, I'll treat myself to a little glass in the village, just the one, only, and then I'll go home on foot, and never drink again. I haven't any more money on me, but I've got my blueish spring coat. I'll leave it with the landlord as security. He'll give me a bottle of schnaps on it, perhaps two, and then I'll be provided for, for three or four days. Certainly for three days, anyway! And in three days I'll have Magda around, I shall be very friendly and loving with her, I'll get money from her again. . . . For a moment I shut my eyes: I have just thought of that five thousand marks I drew from the bank about this time yesterday. It must have been a heavy blow for the business. It might not be such a simple matter to pacify Magda . . . but I quickly assure myself, I can mortgage our house, it's free of debt so far; I'm sure to raise five thousand marks on the house. Then Magda would be placated. And of course I'm not going to let Lobedanz get away with his robbery unpunished. I'll go and see him today and he'll have to give back my things and the silver and jewellery, at least. I'll let him keep two thousand marks of the money. And if he won't come to terms, I'll prosecute him, and then good gentle hypocritical Lobedanz goes to prison instead of me.

So my thoughts run on. Despite occasional uneasy moments, they are on the whole optimistic. I'll get by, all right. After all, I'm a respected citizen. They'll take care not to treat me too harshly!

In between times I stare almost unconsciously at the inscriptions on the cell walls. Some are written in pencil, some are scratched in the whitewash with a nail. Mostly, a name is written above, and below are two dates—the date of entry and of release. I find it very reassuring that all these dates are so close together. According to the inscriptions the man who occupied this cell for the longest time was here for ten days. Another proof that they have no bad intentions towards me. Ten days—well, ten days are quite out of the question for me. With my hunger for alcohol, I'd never be able to bear it. But I, of course, shall be released in a few minutes. And besides, what about breakfast? Prisoners have to have breakfast don't they? Probably dry bread and water, but still breakfast. It is at least half-past nine now, to go by the sun, and nobody has brought me any breakfast. Of course, that's another sign they don't mean badly by me. They intend to let me out so quickly that they don't want to waste a breakfast on me. The sergeant saves that much. I can buy myself breakfast outside! That's as clear as day.

Completely reassured for the moment, I throw myself on to my straw mattress again, and try to go to sleep. I think of Elinor. I try to recall the sweetness of the moment when she gave me schnaps to drink out of her mouth, but strangely enough, this doesn't seem so sweet to me any more. No, I don't want to think of that country inn again. It was too horrible. And how that little whore fleeced me, like any silly schoolboy. But I'm not going for her like I will for Lobedanz, let her sink or swim with her loot, I'll never see anything of her again. From now on, I live only for Magda. It's a good thing I'm absolutely finished with those people at the inn. I've paid for everything, they can't want anything else from me, I shall never see them again. I only wish I was so sure of Magda's attitude to me. . . .

So my thoughts run. In between times I sleep a little, half drowsing or else suddenly gone right off as in a deep faint. And then I am awake again, conscious once more of the torment in my body, I groan: "My God, my God, I can't bear this . . . am I never to get out of here?"

I run to and fro, shake the iron bars, lean against the door in the mad hope that perhaps it has been left open, and think of Magda. . . . To tell the truth, I am afraid of Magda . . . she can be so damned energetic. . . . But I am her husband, we loved each other, she will forgive me, she must . . . so turns the mill-wheel of my thoughts.

125

26

I HAVE been sleeping again. The clatter of keys has awakened me. I spring up from my bed and look expectantly at the four gentlemen who come into my cell. Two of them I accord only a short glance: they wear police uniform. One is the sergeant who brought me here last night; the other is a policeman whom I know from my home town. Many a time I have played cards with him over a glass of beer, a good respectable man, not of my social class of course, but I never was proud. One of the two men in civilian clothes I do not know, a young man with sharp features and rather staring severe eyes. His lower lip protrudes heavily. But I know the other civilian all too well, it is our family doctor, good old Dr Mansfeld. The moment I recognise him, it passes through my mind like a lightning-flash that I'm not going to be released. He will take me to a home for alcoholics. But that is not so bad, on the contrary, perhaps it's much better. In such a home, my present torments would be eased, they are bound to have some remedy there, and then I shall be spared that impending discussion with Magda. Magda will think much more leniently about a sick man in a home of that kind. All this runs through my mind in a few seconds and I hurry across to the doctor. I shake his hand. I say excitedly: "Thank you for coming, Dr Mansfeld. You see," I laugh, a little embarrassed, "how they've housed me here!"

I glance around the dirty cell. Dr Mansfeld presses my hand firmly. I notice that he is upset too, his face is trembling.

"Yes, my dear Herr Sommer," he says and there is a tremor in his voice, "I hadn't intended things to end like this."

"To end?" I say and try to give an easy tone to my voice. "To end, Dr Mansfeld? I think this is a new beginning. You'll send me to a nursing-home and make me well again."

"I wanted to do that a fortnight ago, my dear Herr Sommer," says Dr Mansfeld, shaking his head, "but unfortunately you've made it impossible. Now it's for the Public Prosecutor to say."

And with that, he looks across at the younger man with the staring eyes, who pushes out his protruding underlip still further, looks at me severely, and says, at first hesitantly: "Yes, yes, of course."

Then quickly, "Herr Sommer, I have to arrest you for the attempted murder of your wife. You are under arrest."

I stand thunderstruck. For a moment I cannot utter a word.

"They can't be serious," I think feverishly. "They're only trying to frighten you. Attempted murder? Of Magda?"

At last I can speak. I say in a trembling voice, "Attempted murder of my wife? That's ridiculous. I never tried to murder Magda!"

The Public Prosecutor gives me a crushing look, and barks: "We'll soon show you how ridiculous it is, Sommer!" and, "Come, doctor!"

And again, to the policeman from my own town. "You know what to do, sergeant. Take the man away."

"Dr Mansfeld!" I call after them in boundless despair, as they leave, "Dr Mansfeld, you know how much I loved Magda. . . ."

The door slams behind the two civilians. I am alone with the two men in uniform. Distracted, I slump down on my straw bed and hide my face in my hands.

27

AFTER I had sat motionless like that for a while with the words "attempted murder of your wife" running round and round in my head, the sergeant from my own town, Herr Schulze, put his hand on my shoulder and said, as a gentle reminder: "We have to go now, Sommer."

"Sommer." How it touched me, this simple "Sommer" without "Herr"! To be spoken to like that by quite a humble man with a yearly income of hardly more than two thousand four hundred marks, brought home to me in the clearest possible way the changed circumstances of my life. Ever since I finished my apprenticeship, no one had addressed me without calling me "Herr", and now—I took my hands from my face and with tears in my eyes I asked, "Where are you taking me, Herr Schulze?"

I stressed the "Herr" but he took no notice. Such a simple man probably has no feeling for these fine shades of intonation.

"Only to the police-court, Sommer," he said. "Only to the police-court." And he continued, "Look, Sommer, you're an educated man. You won't cause any trouble, will you? I ought to put you in handcuffs, but if you promise not to cause trouble. . . . "

"I promise you, Herr Schulze", I said eagerly, and almost cheerfully now, "I promise on my honour."

"Fine," he replied, "I'll trust you. Put your coat on. There's your hat. Have you got anything else? Then come along!"

He went with me out of the cell, we descended a stairway and stood in the village street. I had only been in the semi-darkness of the lock-up for a few hours, but the spacious brightness of the countryside overwhelmed me. My heart beat faster at this greeting from the outside world. "Supposing," I quickly thought, "supposing I were to jump over the fence and run through that bushy garden, across the meadows and into the forest, would Schulze trouble to catch me again? Would he even shoot after me as if I were a real criminal? Oh no," I thought, with a weak smile, "he'd never do that. We've often played cards together, and he knows who I am and what I represent. But I don't want to run away from him at all," I quickly thought, "I promised I wouldn't cause any trouble, and I'm a man of my word. But there's something else I want from him. . . . "

When Schulze had mentioned that he had to take me to the police-court, a hopeful possibility had occurred to me.

"Herr Schulze," I said very politely, "I would like you to do me a favour. . . . "

"Well, what is it, Sommer?" he asked. "Am I walking too fast? We can easily go slower. The train doesn't leave for another twenty minutes."

"Look, Herr Schulze," I began, "I've got a frightful tooth-ache. And I see there's an inn just over the road. Couldn't I quickly nip in and have a rum or a brandy? That always relieves my toothache immediately. You can stand at the bar with me," I quickly continued, "if you're afraid I'll run away from you. Of course, I won't run away. It's just on account of this terrible toothache."

"You put that right out of your head," said the sergeant firmly. "I'd lose my uniform if it got around that I'd been drinking schnaps with a prisoner in some pub. Nothing doing, Sommer."

"But nobody knows me here, Herr Schulze," I cried pleadingly. "It'll never come out."

"There!" cried the sergeant, and he raised his hand to his

helmet in salute. The doctor's car, with the Public Prosecutor sitting next to Dr Mansfeld, had passed us.

"If those two had seen us going into a pub, I'd have been for it! So let's get on. Sommer!"

"Herr Schulze," I pleaded, and I did not stir a step from the square in front of the inn, my last chance. "There's really not a soul here who knows me. Please do me this one favour! Just one single schnaps! I'll tell my wife to let you have a hundred marks . . ."

"That's going too far!" shouted the sergeant, red with rage. "Have you gone raving mad, Sommer? That's bribery, what you're trying to do. I ought to charge you on the spot. Come on immediately, or I'll put you in handcuffs."

Utterly crushed and intimidated, robbed of my last hope, I followed Herr Schulze. For a while we walked silently side by side, he muttering angrily to himself, I with bowed head and dragging feet.

Then the sergeant said more calmly, "I can't understand you, Sommer. You used to be a solid and respectable man, and now you get up to tricks like this. Haven't you had enough of that old drink? Hasn't it got you into enough trouble? Anyway, I don't want to put you into a worse plight than you are already. I didn't hear a thing. But be a good fellow now, Sommer, and pull yourself together. In a few days that boozing fit will be over and you'll have a clear head again. And you're going to need a mighty clear head, as you ought to know by what the Public Prosecutor said."

I heard all this in silence, without answering. I found it most humiliating and offensive that such a simple fellow as Sergeant Schulze should dare to presume to speak to me in such a way. Of course I did not know then that I stood at the beginning of a long road of suffering, and that quite other people, of much lower standing, were to be far more out-spoken with me.

We had arrived at the station, and Sergeant Schulze bought two third-class tickets for us.

"Well," he said, and marched me on to the platform among the waiting people. "Keep your head up, Sommer, and go on talking to me, then nobody will notice anything. They'll all think we're old acquaintances who've just met by chance. At home, after a game of cards, we used to walk along the Breitestrasse together for a bit, and it never occurred to you or anyone else that we were anything other than acquaintances. . . . "

He was right there. And since by now I had somewhat recovered from my shock over the schnaps, we really managed to hold quite a sensible conversation, first about the hay harvest which was just starting, then about the harvest prospects in general. Schulze and I were both of the opinion that on the whole the outlook was not bad, but it ought to rain now, the spring had been too dry, and the forage especially, but the mangolds as well could do with a bit of moisture.

The short train journey passed quite quickly, and probably none of the passengers had an inkling that here was a man under arrest for attempted murder. (Sometimes I liked to imagine myself as some real and gloriously villainous criminal.) But when we reached our own station and forced our way through the waiting crowds, into the booking-hall then out into the square in front of the station, I felt quite apprehensive again. For at any moment I might meet a close acquaintance, or one of my own employees even, yes, even my own wife. I tugged at the sergeant's sleeve, and begged, "Herr Schulze, couldn't we go round by the back streets a bit, and through the park? I know so many people here, and it would really be most embarrassing. . . . "

Herr Schulze nodded his head.

"That's all right as far as I'm concerned. It doesn't matter whether you get to the police-court a quarter of an hour earlier or later. But I'd like to relieve myself. . . . " And with that, Herr Schulze accompanied me diagonally across the square to that very edifice I had visited with Lobedanz, coming from another direction some twenty-four hours before. It was a strange feeling, to be standing again in this room with its six basins, to hear the water rushing and to look at the dirty wet asphalt floor. This was where I had wrestled with Lobedanz— it was such a short time ago and yet already it seemed quite incredible. Like a wild dream that is completely convincing while one dreams it, and yet seems absurdly grotesque as soon as one awakes. But I *had* fought Lobedanz here, it hadn't been a dream, and no word of honour nor feeling of consideration bound me to that arch-rogue. So when we came out of the public convenience again and were making our way along the edge of town, avoiding all the busier streets, I took heart and told Sergeant Schulze one after the other, all my experiences with Lobedanz, from the time I first appeared in his steam-filled kitchen after my flight from the doctor's car, to my fight for my suitcase and money in the toilet. In the course of his duty, Sergeant Schulze must have experienced too much of human passions and weaknesses to be very surprised about an affair like this, but during my story he stopped several times, quite moved, and exclaimed, "Good heavens, it's unbelievable!" "You don't say! Is that really true, Sommer?" He whistled through his teeth as well. Finally, when I had finished and was waiting for an outburst of indignation against that scoundrel Lobedanz, Sergeant Schulze remained silent for a while and then, looking me full in the face, he said deliberately: "I only know you from playing cards with you. That's to say, I don't really know you at all, but I always took you for a sensible clear-headed businessman. That you're such a—excuse the expression but it's the truth—such a stupid ox, is something I would never have dreamed of. You can twist and turn it about as you please, but it wasn't just the booze. You can't blame such thick-headedness as that on the booze. You must have seen what a scoundrel the fellow was, the very first day. Well, you did see it, and yet you didn't get out, though you would have been able to soak as you wanted in any little pub around the corner. No, it absolutely served you right that that fellow took you down. It served you right, and I only wish he'd taken that last thousand marks from you as well, then you wouldn't have been able to get up to mischief in that inn. . . ."

The sergeant drew breath and looked at me severely. I was most indignant at this quite unexpected effect of my account, and I said crossly, "I didn't tell you this story so that you could give me a moral lecture, Schulze. . . ."

"Sergeant Schulze, if you don't mind, Sommer!" Schulze corrected me severely.

"But I thought," I continued furiously, "that you might take the trouble to set about catching this scoundrel immediately."

"That's good," laughed the sergeant ironically. "First of all, in your drunken stupor you have to hand over all your goods and chattels to some criminal, and then you yell for the police and expect us to say, 'Dear, oh dear!' and break our necks running after a handful of spoons for you. I tell you again, you don't deserve anything better, and if it wasn't that your poor wife has to bear all the burden of your stupidity, I wouldn't lift a finger over this affair. But for your wife's sake, Sommer—mark that, for your wife's sake—I will, as soon as I've seen you safe in clink and made my report to the inspector. It's still possible this bird hasn't flown yet—perhaps he doesn't expect us so soon. But now get on a bit faster, I'd like to hand you over before you get into any more mischief. One never knows what to expect from you. My God! I'm never going to be taken in again by such a fellow as you, in all my life. I used to marvel at what a clever man you were, but probably your wife did it all. How's she ever going to forgive you for all the muck-up you've made of things?"

With that, we went on, and did not exchange another word until we got to the police-court. Probably Schulze was inwardly busy with his report for the inspector, but I was truly deeply offended at all the unjust things which this low-grade policeman had said so rudely to my face. If the fellow couldn't see that I had merely been ill, a helpless invalid at the mercy of a rogue, there was no help for him, he was a stupid fool. Anyhow, I certainly wasn't. I had simply been ill, and still was. . . .

28

In the course of my business career, I had several times had dealings with the police-court, and I knew the lay-out of the place fairly well. But I had never before been in the part to which Sergeant Schulze was taking me now. We went through the whole building (it adjoins the district court) to a rather narrow inner yard which was shut off on one side by a high wall, and on the other three by tall buildings pitted from top to bottom with small, almost square windows, all protected with strong bars.

"I'm going to live up there for weeks and weeks, perhaps," I thought, and I was overcome by fear. I would have liked to ask my companion a number of things about the customs and regulations of such a prison, but it was too late for that now. Schulze pressed a bell-push, a huge iron door opened, and a blue-uniformed man greeted Schulze with a handshake and me with a cool searching look.

"A new arrival, Karl," said Schulze. "The papers will be coming this afternoon from the Public Prosecutor's office."

"Stand over there!" said the man in uniform, and I obediently placed myself where he ordered me.

The two policemen whispered, and looked across at me several times. Once I heard the words "attempted murder"—it did not seem to make any special impression.

Then Schulze called to me from some distance, "Well, keep your chin up, Sommer," and the door closed behind him; he had gone back into freedom, and I felt as if I had lost a friend.

"Come with me," said the man in uniform carelessly, and led me into an office which was quite unoccupied.

"Turn out your pockets and put everything on the table."

I did so. It was little enough: a bunch of keys, a pocket knife, a rather dirty handkerchief.

"That all you've got? No money? Well, hold up your arms."

I did so; and now he felt me up and down, presumably for any hidden belongings.

"All right," said the blue-uniformed man. "I'll put you in Eleven for the time being. The governor's not here just now. It's the lunch-break."

I asked politely whether I might have some lunch too. I hadn't had anything yet.

"Lunch is over," he answered coolly. "There's none left."

"But I haven't had any breakfast either!" I cried excitedly. Up till the present my appetite had not been very large, but now it seemed ravenous. I felt my rights were being violated; even a prisoner must eat!

"You'll enjoy your supper all the more," he answered, unmoved. "Come on now!"

He led me along a corridor, through an iron grill, up a stairway, through an iron door. I saw a long gloomy corridor and many iron-studded doors with locks and bolts, then again up a stairway, up another stairway, again an iron door—the man had to keep unlocking and locking all the time, and he did it all so casually . . . but my heart sank: all these doors that now lay between me and the outside world made me realise so clearly how trapped I was, how difficult it was going to be to get free again. From the very first moment I felt the truth of that saying which I was to hear often in prison: "Easier to get in than out."

My guide had stopped before an iron door with a white "11" on it. Behind this, then, I was to live. He unlocked the door, and beyond it appeared another door. This, too, he un-locked.

"Get in," said my companion impatiently, and I entered. From a narrow bed, a strange figure arose, a tall man of re-markable girth, with a bald head and spectacles.

"A bit of company?" he asked. "Well, that's nice. Where are you from?"

I was so astonished to find that I had a room-mate in my cell that I only noticed much later that the turnkey had gone and I was finally and irrevocably shut in.

"Sit down on that stool," said the fat man. "I'm staying in bed for a bit. You're not supposed to, but Fermi doesn't say anything. Fermi's the one who just brought you up."

I sat on the stool and stared at the man lying on the bed. Like me, he wore civilian clothes, a once-elegant suit from a good tailor, which was now crumpled and stained.

"Are you a prisoner too?" I finally asked.

"I should say so!" laughed the fat man. "Do you think I'd be sitting in this hole for fun?" He stretched, and gave a groan as he did so. "I've been stuck in this place eleven weeks already. But d'you think they've charged me yet? Not a hope. These fellows take their time, as far as they're concerned you could rot before they'd stir themselves. What are you up for?"

"The Public Prosecutor had me arrested for the attempted murder of my wife," I answered with modest pride, and I quickly added, "But it isn't true. Not a word of it is true."

The fat man laughed again.

"Of course it's not true," he laughed. "There's only inno-cent men in here—when you ask them."

"But in my case it really isn't true," I insisted. "I never tried to murder my wife. We just had a bit of a quarrel."

"Ah well," said the fat man, "in time you'll get it all off your chest. Everyone who isn't used to clink starts to talk after a time. Only you want to be careful who you're talking

137

to. Most of 'em want to be the governor's pet and they go crawling to him with everything—and then you're for it."

He looked candidly at me with his little eyes through rolls of fat, and said: "You can talk quite openly with me. I'm the soul of honour. I'm 'stickum'."

"What are you?"

"Stickum, that's what we say here for close-mouthed. I don't squeal, understand?"

"But I've really nothing to confess," I assured him again.

"Well, we'll see about that," said the fat man comfortably. "Perhaps you'll be lucky, and the examining magistrate'll be of the same opinion as you and won't commit you for trial."

"But I was arrested by the Public Prosecutor himself."

"That doesn't mean anything," the fat man informed me. "First of all, tomorrow or the day after, they bring you up before the examining magistrate. He questions you, and if he decides in your favour, you'll be free again."

"Is that really true?" I ask excitedly. "I can still get free?"

"Of course you can. But it doesn't often happen that way. Still, we'll see."

And again he stretched comfortably.

I was intoxicated by the prospect of possible freedom so near at hand. I stood up and thoughtfully paced to and fro in the cell. If Magda gave favourable evidence on my behalf I would get free. And she had to give favourable evidence on my behalf, I felt. And even if she was still furious with me, she could never say I had tried to murder her. That was something I had never wanted to do. Dimly I remembered having said something like "Tomorrow night I'll come and kill you," but that was only drunken babble. It didn't mean anything.

"Listen," said the fat man. "Don't run up and down the cell like that. You give me the fidgets. Sit down quietly on that stool, but take the cushion off first, it's my private cushion.

You can't lie down on your kip yet. The old man won't bring you your straw-bag till tonight. God, how this stable gets on my nerves!" Then the fat man yawned heartily, let a terrible one go—I started with fright—groaned, "Ah, that's better!" and fell asleep at once.

I do not want to go on recounting in such detail the first days of my remand period. They were so agonising that one night I got up softly, went over to the fat man's locker and took the blade out of his safety razor. I wanted to cut my throat. But I could not pluck up the courage. I tentatively made a small cut in my wrist, which only bled a little, but it calmed me. The will to live conquered, and that same night I put the blade back in the razor.

On the whole, it was easier for me to get over my craving for alcohol than I had expected. I had not become a proper drunkard yet, I had given myself up to schnaps for a short time only, and had never seen white mice. I was greatly helped, during this weaning period, by the fact that on the third or fourth day I volunteered for work. I could not bear to sit brooding and inactive in my cell, nor could I stand the fat man's company—his name, by the way, was Duftermann. I think I would have murdered him if I had been forced to spend twenty-four hours of every day in his company. He was nothing but an animal; a more flagrantly egotistic man I have never met. He had obtained for himself every privilege the law allows for prisoners awaiting trial—he had blankets and cushions on his hard straw-bag, a regular supply of tobacco, and food parcels, but he never gave a crumb away. In the first few days, when I did not have my own washing things in the cell, he forbade me even to use his comb. I was not once allowed to touch his mirror, and it was only unwillingly that he permitted me to use a sheet of his newspaper as toilet paper.

"No, no, Sommer," he would say. "Here it's 'God helps those who help themselves.' Why should I start looking after you? What do you do for me? You only give me the fidgets."

That was another point on which I was driven nearly frantic. Everything I did upset Duftermann. I was not allowed to walk up and down in the cell: if, in the night, I turned on my straw mattress, he complained about his sleep being disturbed: if I wanted to open the little window for a moment, he shouted that it was cold on his bald head, and so we had to go on squatting there in the heat and the stink. But he allowed himself everything. He greedily wolfed the food parcels which his wife brought for him twice a week, sat on the bucket six times a day, behaved like a pig, and snored so loudly at night that it kept me awake for hours on end, at the mercy of my gloomy thoughts. If ever I hated a man from the bottom of my heart it was Duftermann. In the long time of trouble ahead of me, I was to lie down with much rougher folk, with labourers, with tramps even—but none of them ever let themselves go, so flagrantly gave rein to all their instincts, as this Duftermann did. By profession he was merely a property-owner, the son of a rich long-dead father who had left him several large houses and other real estate. Up till now, Duftermann had spent his life administering this property, and in the course of administering it, he had met with the misfortune that brought him to prison and caused him to become my cell-mate. As he denied nothing to himself and everything to others, and as he claimed the right to do whatever he pleased, he had set fire to one of his houses, whose dilapidated condition had nettled him for some time past, so as to cover the cost of rebuilding by the insurance money. In this fire, a woman and her child had lost their lives.

Duftermann merely complained: "The damed fool! Couldn't she run out in time like all the rest? No, the stupid idiot has to stuff some rubbish or other into a trunk first, and then the smoke makes it impossible for her to escape. How can I help it, if some old girl's so stupid? The Public Prosecutor would like to make a rope out of it for me. But he doesn't know Duftermann. I've engaged the best lawyers, and if everything goes wrong, I'll have them give me Paragraph 51, be certified and live off my means in some nice little loony-bin."

Duftermann quite openly admitted his guilt.

"Why should I tell lies? They caught me with the petrol can in my hand. There's no point in denying it. Yes, if I were in your shoes I'd deny everything to my dying day. But like this—why I'm just certifiable!"

He roared with laughter.

"After all," he continued in a tone of self-pity, "it was only my good nature made me do it. I'm just a good-natured fool. I couldn't bear to see people going on living in such a tumble-down bug-ridden barrack of a place. I wanted to provide them with decent housing—and this is what my good nature gets me."

In this way, Duftermann drove me to volunteer for work; and I could be sure of his biting scorn, when of an evening I returned to the cell from work, with weary bones but quite peaceful at heart. He would greet me something like this: "Ah, here comes the model boy. Well, did you work hard? Did you suck up to that swine of a governor? The Public Prosecutor will give you just as long in clink as if you'd stayed here quietly in your cell. It's creepers like you who spoil the whole prison. Your sort make it bad for the rest of us, they'll make all work compulsory. But you wait, I'll get you yet."

I hardly listened to his talk, and never addressed a word to the common fellow. Of course, this did not upset him in the least. He had the hide of a rhinoceros, and calmly went on talking whether I answered or not.

29

WELL, I had volunteered for work. Splittstösser, the head-warder, issued me with a new blue jacket as my prison uniform, and with ten or twelve others I was taken into a yard, surrounded by high walls, where great piles of wood lay. Formerly we, too, had taken the firewood for our central heating—bought by the cord from the forestry people—to the prison, to have it chopped up. I had never given it a thought, who sawed and chopped my wood there. Now I myself stood for eight hours a day at the saw-bench, and opposite me stood an habitual burglar named Mordhorst, a man with many previous convictions. Together, for eight hours at a time, we pulled the two-handled saw through pinewood, beechwood and oak. A guard paced to and fro in the yard, watching to see that we did not do too much talking and too little work. Now I was sawing wood for the citizens of my native town, and this time it was Hölscher—the general merchant for whom we were working at the moment—who gave no thought to the fact that his old client Sommer was cutting his firewood for him. At first it disturbed me greatly that the fourth side of the yard was bounded by the district court building, and many windows looked down on me and my sawing arms in the blue prison clothes; but within a few days I had become accustomed to it and hardly turned my head when Mordhorst whispered: "The Public Prosecutor's up at the window again, looking to see if we're earning our keep. Saw slower, mate. When he's looking, I'm not working."

Mordhorst was a small wiry man with a wrinkled embittered face and pepper-green hair. He had spent considerably more than half his life in prison. He took it so much as a matter of course, that he never mentioned it. He regretted nothing, he had no desire for a different life. He never spoke of his crimes, as a craftsman never speaks of his craft. Burglary was to him like sewing trousers to a tailor. I only found out from other prisoners that in the criminal world, Mordhorst was a man of high standing, who could crack the most modern safes, and who was well known for working without a mate, a lone wolf, a typical enemy of society. It only irked him that he had got stuck in such a mudhole, as he called my home-town, more or less by chance. He was on his way to Hamburg, where he had a big job to do, and had got stranded here for a few hours, and in the night, being a little drunk and having nothing to smoke, he had broken into the tobacco kiosk in our market place, and they had caught him at it.

"Just think of it, man," Mordhorst would rage. "I'd got plenty of cash on me, I could have bought what smokes I wanted where I was staying. Just because I was tight! And for a little thing like that they'll put me away for a five year stretch. It sends me up in the air, just to think of it!"

To me it seemed all the same whether Mordhorst got five years' penal servitude for a big safe robbery or a bit of tobacco pilfering, it was five years in any case. But I took good care not to say so aloud, for Mordhorst was a quick-tempered man, and he had startled me early on with his fits of rage when I, an inexperienced newcomer, had pulled the saw so clumsily that it jammed. Once, in a burst of temper, he had tried to hit me on the head with a piece of wood, and only the warder's intervention had saved me.

Then five minutes later Mordhorst had become normal and sensible again. I suppose it was the long years of imprisonment that had made him so wild and unrestrained. I am sure he had a worm gnawing in his brain, anyone who paces a cell year after year, just waiting for the day of release, of freedom, and knowing all the while in his innermost self that the longest stay in freedom is only a flying visit of a few months at most, to be followed again by years and years of bitter waiting—such a man cannot remain normal.

I learned a great deal from Mordhorst. He knew everything about police-courts, reformatories and prisons. It was quite astonishing how well this silent little man, who seemed to have dealings with nobody, was informed about everything. He knew what kind of meat we were going to get on Sunday, and what the new occupant of cell 21 was supposed to have done. He knew the family circumstances, the salary, and the troubles of each prison officer. He could make a light for a cigarette with a trouser button, a piece of thread and a stone. He always had something to smoke, and something extra to eat, though nobody left any food parcels for him. He always had money in his pocket, which was strictly forbidden, he possessed a knife (also forbidden), and had some means of smuggling letters out of prison without being censored by the governor. He knew all the underground ways which open up in time in any human community, however strictly supervised it may be. I was always a novice to him, a mere babe. He passed on some of his life's experiences, but never let himself be carried away into confessing anything to me. I was well aware that he treated the other prisoners differently.

Old gaol-birds understand each other by a glance and a wink. They walk behind each other, they hardly move their lips, and something has already been slipped from one hand to the other. The prison officers gave Mordhorst far more freedom than me, for example. They shut one eye to him, he could do almost anything. Perhaps they were afraid of him because he knew so much, but I rather think they shied away from a clash with such a dangerous man. When he had been standing idle at the saw-bench for five minutes on end, and I had whispered: "Hey, get on with the sawing. The warder keeps looking over here," Mordhorst did nothing of the kind. And when the prison officer finally came over to us and said: "Well, Mordhorst, that's enough loafing, get on with it!", he said heatedly: "Don't I do enough for my thirty pfennigs a day?" (We got thirty pfennigs 'wages' a day, which was entered to our credit for the day of our release.) "Am I to work my fingers to the bone for that fat swine?" And he looked wickedly at the windows of the district court. The warder merely laughed and said: "You've got your rag out again, have you, Mordhorst? The Prosecutor won't get any fatter or thinner from your saw...."

But Mordhorst muttered: "I know what I know," seized the saw-handle which I held out to him and we went on sawing, thrust after thrust, log after log, hour after hour.

They were good times, really, that we spent in the wood-yard. Today I think back on them quite gladly, however endless and heavy they appeared to me then. After the inevitable aches and pains which my unwonted labours caused me at first, my body soon became used to sawing, and the work helped me to bear much easier the symptoms of my de-alcoholisation.

Spring was slowly changing to summer now, in the yard stood high fruit trees, apples and pears, into whose shadow we moved the saw-bench when the sun poured down too hot upon us; the saws groaned and shrieked occasionally when a chip resisted the blade, the clop-clop of the wood-cutter's axes came to us monotonously; on the other side of the wall, unseen, children shouted at their games in the street. We took off first our jackets, then our waistcoats. Some worked quite naked to the waist, but I could never decide to do so. The hours flowed by, life glided along, I was imbued with a—deceptive—feeling of security and regularity. The time of dangers and disorders seemed over, and it appeared so easy to me to continue this life outside, a quiet peaceful life almost without future. Mordhorst and I softly talked of what we were going to get to eat this evening, and what the food had been like at lunch-time today—food played a most important part in our conversation, since like Mordhorst I got no food parcels, and had to rely on the prison diet even more than he. Moreover he was a better comrade than the pampered Duftermann. Every day he brought me something, some trifle that, outside, would have been of no value, an onion perhaps, which I cut up with a spoon and put on bread, or a cigarette and a match; then at evening, after lock-up time, when the building had fallen quiet, I would smoke my fag in comfort. Yes, I learned to smoke in prison, very much to the fury of Duftermann, who always filled the air with his cigar-fumes, and despised the smoking of cigarettes as womanly. But I let him go on talking, by that time I was completely indifferent to him.

Yes, Mordhorst, misanthrope as he was, helped me a great deal; he was an excellent adviser in my 'case' too, a better one than the lawyer who came to see me. Unfortunately, at the first hearing, I appeared before the examining magistrate without Mordhorst's advice, and thus I made a serious mistake which I only realised later.

30

I HAD been in custody for three days, and I was not yet working in the wood-yard, when the head-warder Spittstösser appeared at my cell at four in the afternoon and said: "Come with me, Sommer. Put your jacket on and come with me."

I walked behind the "chief", and was at that time so inexperienced in prison matters that I politely asked: "Where are you taking me, officer?" I did not know then that a prisoner should never ask questions, that he never gets an answer, that he can only wait and see what fate—which may be a warder, or may be the Public Prosecutor—has in store for him. So I got the rather rude answer: "What's it to do with you? You'll find out."

Over in the district court, the atmosphere of a real summer afternoon reigned; many of the room-doors were open and I caught a glimpse of tidied and deserted desks. It turned out that the sergeant of the court had gone to the post office, and so was not able to take me over from the charge of the prison officer. My custodian was in a hurry to return to his own building, and a slight argument ensued between a fat elderly woman clerk and my warder.

"I'm not here to look after your prisoners," said the clerk angrily. "You always try that sort of thing. If one of them gets away, I'd be blamed for it."

"Yes, but your sergeant doesn't have to run off all the time, he knows full well the prisoner's only been called over for interrogation."

So the argument went back and forth for a while, neither of them would have me, till suddenly the elderly woman said, quite surprisingly: "All right, just for once I'll do it. Herr Sommer won't run away from me."

With that, she looked at me with a friendly smile. So she knew me. I was set on a chair, and for the first time for days I looked again through an unbarred window, out on to one of my home town streets, and saw the children playing. One of the drays of the Trappe Beer Company rolled by. Trappe himself, who was well known to me and almost a friend, sat on the driver's seat. Now a young girl, also a clerk probably, went through the room in which I had been put, saw me, gave me a friendly smile and said: "Good afternoon, Herr Sommer."

So she knew me too, she was kind to me, although I was in custody on a charge of attempting to murder my wife. That elderly clerk had been kind also, she had said: "Herr Sommer won't run away,"—they were all kind to me, the best proof that my prospects were good. Probably the examining magistrate would not commit me for trial, perhaps I would be free in half an hour. My heart beat strongly, joyfully.

Now an elderly man came into the room, a long, thin, grey-haired gentleman, who looked somewhat uneasy and distraught.

"This is Herr Sommer, Herr Direktor," said the elderly clerk, and she nodded her head towards me.

"Is it?" said the elderly gentleman, with a slight cough (he was the head of the district court, I later found out). He looked at me for a moment with his tired, rather troubled eyes, and then gave me his hand.

"Come with me, then, Herr Sommer."

Again nothing but friendliness, handshakes, being addressed as "Herr"; all this to-do utterly deceived me inexperienced as I was, I completely forgot that these were all my enemies only out to trick me, to sentence me, to keep me in prison.

I forgot the saying I had only just learned: "Easier to get in than out." I thought that getting out was being made easier for me than getting in. I opened my whole heart to the magistrate, told him everything as it really happened, and later I was to find out what consequences my trustfulness had.

The head of the district court went before me into a comfortably-furnished office with many many books along the walls. I was placed on a chair in front of the desk, the magistrate sat behind it, a middle-aged lady appeared and put a large sheet of paper in the typewriter, the magistrate ran his hand through his hair, adjusted his spectacles, and said: "We're very worried about you, Herr Sommer." He coughed and said to the woman: "Take down Herr Sommer's personal details."

The questionnaire was easily enough answered; perhaps I gave Magda's birth-date incorrectly (I was ashamed to admit that I didn't know it for sure), and when I was asked whether my financial affairs were in order, I straightway said "Yes," though I subsequently had serious doubts about this, because it seemed questionable whether Magda would be able to manage the business after my withdrawal of that five thousand marks. But I did not have the chance to rectify matters, for now the magistrate began to question me, or rather he took up a large closely-typed sheet, ran his hand through his hair again, adjusted his spectacles, coughed, and said: "So you are held on suspicion of the attempted murder of your wife, Herr Sommer. What have you to say to that?"

At this stage, I had such trust in all the people around me that I quite naively cried: "For God's sake, do they still maintain that I tried to murder my wife? I've never thought of such a thing in my life! I love my wife, and if I . . . "

"No, no, Herr Sommer," said the head of the district court soothingly. "Of course, attempted murder is out of the question. It was attempted homicide, wasn't it? You acted under stress, you were drunk, weren't you?"

"But, Herr Direktor, I didn't attempt to kill my wife at all. That was just drunken talk because I so much wanted the suitcase, because my wife is stronger than I am."

"Well, well," said the magistrate, and smiled thinly. "It probably was something more than a harmless scuffle. You've been drinking rather a lot recently, haven't you, Herr Sommer? Tell me all you had to drink before you paid this nocturnal visit to your wife."

So the interrogation slowly unfolded. I told everything just as it happened, I racked my brains in order not to forget a single bottle of brandy, I told the barest truth, and like a fool I thought I would manage affairs by truthfulness. But I insisted that I never had the intention of doing my wife any harm, I only wanted the things, I said. The magistrate coughed louder, he referred to the typewritten sheet, and said "I want to put your wife's statement to you: Here: 'He seized me by the throat, and tried to kick me in the abdomen,' and here: 'He whispered in my ear: I'm coming back tomorrow night to do you in!' All this sounds like a great deal more than mere threats, doesn't it, Herr Sommer?"

I was dumbfounded at Magda's baseness, in putting things in this way. She might at least have added that she only took it for drunken talk: I tried to explain this to the magistrate, I pointed out to him that Magda had been very upset too, and in her excitement she had perhaps taken things far more seriously than they were meant. The magistrate nodded and sighed, he wiped his glasses, whether I convinced him I do not know.

Eventually he said, "Very well then, I won't question you any further today, that will be enough for the first time."

"So you won't commit me for trial?" I asked with boundless joy. The magistrate coughed again.

"No, not exactly commit you for trial, as it were. Not exactly. You see, Herr Sommer, by your own evidence you were excessively drunk."

"Not excessively drunk, Herr Direktor. I can stand a great deal."

"You had," continued the magistrate, correcting himself, "you had an excessive amount to drink, and there is a suspicion that at the time of committing the deed you were not in full possession of your mental faculties. What would you do if you were at home now? You would only start quarrelling with your wife again, you would only start drinking again. No, Herr Sommer, first you must get quite well again. First of all, I'll send you to an institution where you'll be under medical supervision and can get really well. . . ."

"Thank you, thank you, Herr Direktor," I could have fallen on the old gentleman's neck for his great kindness. Yes, for his great kindness.

31

Then I heard from Mordhorst two or three days later (they took their time over my transfer to the institution; in the court they all have plenty of time, except the prisoners for whom time passes so slowly)—well, I heard from Mordhorst that I had behaved like a complete idiot.

"Look," he said, "how could you act so barmy? The old buzzard was laughing up his sleeve at you when you unpacked one bottle of brandy after another. He was just having you on, kidding to be so friendly. You should have said, you should have sworn blind: I wasn't drunk, I wasn't drunk at all! I did what I did deliberately, I worked it all out! And why ought you to have said so? Because you run the least risk that way. Look, for homicidal intent you get six months, a year at most. You can do that on your head, and then you're out, a free man again, and nobody can lay a finger on you. And what'll happen to you now? First you go for six weeks' observation in the asylum, to find out the state of your mind. Do you think the asylum is better than gaol? It's much worse! All the trimmings are the same as here—grub, work, warders. But you're not with people in their senses, you're with a pack of loonies! And then the doctor makes his report and you get Paragraph 51 and proceedings against you are stopped. But they'll declare you insane and dangerous and they'll order you to be detained in the asylum, and there you'll stay five years, ten years, twenty years, not a soul will give a damn, and among all those loonies you'll slowly turn into a loony yourself. That's probably what they want. From what you tell me, your old woman's pretty keen on the business; that way she gets the business and everything else belonging to you. And there you are, shut away, just a poor loony, and if they give you a bit of cake and a plug of tobacco at Christmas you can consider yourself lucky. . . . ”

So said Mordhorst, the man of experience, and at his every word a voice within me answered: “yes.” I had acted like an idiot, I had let them entice me on to thin ice and now I was in it up to the neck. From the very first I had guessed what Magda was planning, but I had forgotten it; I had not wanted to think about it any more. I had to some extent deceived myself that she was my wife, she used to love me, she would not betray me. . . . But she had betrayed me! She had been working to this end for a long time. First she had set the doctors on to me, then she had given this devastating evidence against me, in which she had treated all my drunken talk as something said in dead earnest.

And how had she behaved since I was put in gaol? Had she acted as a real wife should when her husband has met with misfortune? Had she made a single effort to get permission to speak to me, to visit me and so provide an opportunity for discussion and reconciliation? Not at all. I had written to Magda. I had written her a serious friendly letter; I was obliged to write to her, I needed a blanket for my straw mattress, a sheet and a pillow. I also needed a newspaper and something to eat. Oh yes, she sent the things I needed, but there was no food or newspaper in the suitcase. And she did not write a single line!

Now I was in gaol, now she let the mask fall, now she felt herself already the owner of my property, now she thought she’d have me put away for ever in a lunatic asylum!

But she was mistaken about me, I wasn’t giving up the fight yet! No, I was only just starting! I knew what I was doing, I wasn’t a child to be led up the garden by Magda’s “efficiency”, I had Mordhorst to advise me now, and I had the best lawyer in town, Herr Doktor Husten!

32

HERR Doktor Husten, whom I had previously known only by sight, was a man in his late thirties, an already stoutish figure, with the livid wrinkled face of a successful actor. He had not long been in practice in my native town, and had the reputation of being cunning, somewhat rash, and very expensive. In my business dealings, of course, I would never have engaged a lawyer of his kind, but for a criminal case like this he seemed the right man. I was called in from my wood-cutting to find Dr Husten waiting for me in the governor's office. He had answered the summons of my letter almost at once. Dr Husten shook my hand somewhat emphatically, assured me in a deep voice, with much rolling of the R's, that he was particularly delighted to make my acquaintance, and then turned to the governor with the playfully-phrased request that we might be shown to some comfortable place where we could have a confidential chat. The governor grinned, and ordered the warder to take us to my cell. The indignant Duftermann was chased out into the yard for a while to take a walk.

"Don't you dare touch any of my things!" With these words, he went out.

Instead of concerning himself with my case, Dr Husten asked in a whisper who that rude, impressive gentleman was, and he nodded as I briefly informed him. "Ah, that's who it is! I've heard of him. Who's defending him?—the fellow's rolling in money. One could make something out of his case."

I was more interested to know what could be made out

of my case, and rather irritated, I reminded Dr Husten of this.

"Ah, your case!" He cried sonorously and in some surprise. "Your case is in splendid shape. I have already examined the documents. You'll get Paragraph 51 and get off scot-free, just leave that to me, my dear Herr Sommer."

I asked still more irritably: "And what happens after I get Paragraph 51?"

Surprised again, the lawyer cried: "What happens to you? As far as the criminal court is concerned, your case is absolutely closed. And personally? I suppose you will go to an institution for a little while, but that's quite desirable for reasons of your health!"

"And how long will that little while in the institution be, Herr Dokter Husten?" I asked maliciously. "Five years? Ten years? For life?"

The lawyer laughed.

"Ah, some fellow-prisoner has been putting ideas into your head! For life! I never heard such nonsense! In your case there's no question of that. You are a sane man in full possession of your mental faculties . . ."

"That's exactly my opinion," I answered, "and that's why Paragraph 51 is out of the question for me. No, Herr Dokter Husten, I take full responsibility for everything I have done, and I am ready to bear the consequences."

"But my dear Herr Sommer," he cried pleadingly. "You would have to go to prison for twelve months, for at least twelve months. You would come out a dishonoured man. Everybody would point you out!"

"Even so," I insisted as Mordhorst's faithful disciple. "Even so, I would far sooner have one year in prison than an un-limited number in an asylum . . ."

"Unlimited! You'll have to stay half a year, perhaps a year there, Herr Sommer . . ."

"Would you give me that in writing, Herr Doktor Husten? Backed by your word as a lawyer . . . ?"

"Of course I can't do that, my dear friend," said the lawyer.

He also seemed rather cross now, and his fingers drummed nervously on the table.

"I'm not a doctor, only a doctor can judge how far your alcoholism has gone, and how much time is necessary for a complete cure without fear of relapse—But my dear Herr Sommer," he cried, pulling himself together and letting his studied triumphant optimism gain the upper hand once more, "give up this dark mistrust of yours. Put yourself utterly into the doctor's healing hands. Remember too, that psychologically as well as physically, you are scarcely equipped to meet the demands of a long imprisonment. And I hardly think, moreover, that this solution would be according to the wishes of your dear wife . . . "

This was the wrong word at the wrong moment!

"Herr Doktor Husten," I cried, jumping up indignantly. "Whose interests do you represent: mine or my wife's? How do you know what my wife's wishes are? Have you been to see her before consulting me?"

I was trembling all over with excitement.

"But my dear Herr Sommer," he said soothingly, and put his hand on my shoulder, "what are you getting so excited about? Naturally, I've been to see your wife. As your lawyer, that was a matter of course. And I can tell you that your wife bears you no grudge, although she is upset. I am convinced that she very much regrets what has happened to you . . . "

"Yes, she shows her regret very clearly in that statement of hers which is among the papers," I cried, more and more indignantly. "Haven't you read her statement, Herr Doktor Husten?—No, I find it simply unforgiveable that you, as my lawyer, should have been talking to the chief witness for the prosecution, without consulting me."

"But I had to do so, my dear friend," replied the lawyer, smiling gently at my lack of worldly knowledge, "I had to inform myself about who was to pay my fees. At the moment you are, so to say, without means . . ."

"You are mistaken, Herr Doktor Husten," I said quite coldly. "Everything there, the business, the bank account, the outstanding bills, the house, all belong to me, and to me alone. Not to my wife. I'm not in any asylum yet, I'm not put away yet . . ."

"Of course, of course," said the lawyer soothingly, "that is absolutely correct. Unfortunately I expressed myself wrongly. I shouldn't have said 'without means'. Let us put it this way: that you are at present somewhat impeded in the disposal of your assets, while your wife, as your faithful trustee . . ."

"I'm going to see to it, Herr Doktor Husten," I said finally, "that my wife does not continue for much longer in the position of trustee. Then perhaps her interest in getting me shut up for life in a lunatic asylum may diminish a little more rapidly. I shall tell my wife that your visit has absolutely convinced me of the necessity for an immediate divorce."

"My dear friend," said the lawyer sonorously, shaking his great actor's head. "How young you are for your forty years! (You are forty, aren't you?) Always beating your head against the wall! Always throwing out the baby with the bath-water! Well, well, you'll be calmer once you come under the appropriate medical care!"

Now there was something unspeakably sarcastic about his sickening friendly grin.

"Apart from all that, I am probably not incorrect in assuming that I am not to regard myself as your confidential lawyer?"

"Quite right, Herr Doktor Husten."

"I am truly sorry. I am not sorry for my sake (yours is only a small case for me, Herr Sommer, a very small case), I am sorry for you and your wife. You are running blindly into trouble, Herr Sommer, and by the time your eyes are opened, it will be too late. A pity."

He quickly took my hand and shook it.

"But let us not part as enemies, Herr Sommer. We have met, we have talked, now we part. 'Ships that pass in the night.' You know that excellent book of the Baroness? I wish you all good luck, Herr Sommer!"

With that, Herr Doktor Husten left my cell with his head in the air; I only followed some distance behind, and returned to my sawing in the wood-yard. There I reported our discussion to Mordhorst down to the smallest detail, was praised by him for the first time, and was strengthened in my determination to hurry on my divorce from Magda as much as possible, and to deprive her of the management of my property.

33

BUT I was unable to get on with any of this for the time being. Other things intervened, which seemed to me more important. On the morning after Dr Husten's visit, when the warder unlocked our cell and I hurried towards the latrine with my full bucket, I suddenly stopped short in amazement. I could not trust my own ears, and yet there was no deception: from a cell which had just been opened, came a soft, insinuating, whispering voice, a voice that was inextricably bound up with my drunkenness, a voice that I destested from the bottom of my heart—Lobedanz's voice!

I hazarded a quick glance. Yes, there he stood with his gentle, sallow face, with the dark beard and dark slashed-back hair with its red-gold sheen, there he stood, talking softly to his cell-mate, and pulling at his fingers till they cracked. He was trying to get something out of the other fellow, for sure, the poor honest working-man!

I hurried past the cell as quickly as I could, emptied and cleaned out my bucket, and crept back into my own cell, taking care not to be seen. That morning Duftermann had to do the "outside work" of cell-cleaning; however much he grumbled, he had to fetch the broom and cloth and the clean water; I had no desire to be seen by Lobedanz.

But inwardly I was filled with triumph and malicious joy. They had caught the sly hypocritical Lobedanz, they had put him in gaol, and only one thought still bothered me; whether they had managed to recover the loot, or a substantial part of it, from Lobedanz. But I was not to remain long in uncertainty about that. As usual we went out into the wood-yard, but without Lobedanz, either because he had not volunteered for work, or because the governor knew that we were mixed up in the same affair. In such cases, care is taken not to allow the accomplices to come into contact with each other.

Mordhorst and I placed ourselves at our saw-bench and began our day's work, this time of a most agreeable kind—soft smooth pine-logs, child's play for such practised men as we were. The first log was sawn up, and while I was putting the second one into position on one bench, I asked my workmate the question that was repeated every morning: "What's new about the place?"

"Mhm!" murmured Mordhorst, and set the saw on. Then: "A new arrival. A con man, it seems."

We began to saw. Then I stopped again. "What has he done?"

"Who? Done what?" asked Mordhorst, whose thoughts were miles away, probably still revolving around that bitter fate by which he had been caught in such a mud-hole, and over such an undignified little job.

"Who? Done what?"

"The new man!" I reminded him.

"Oh, him. What do those fellows have the nerve to do?"

And he tried to start sawing again, but I held tight to the saw-handle. "No, tell me, Mordhorst, it really interests me. I think I saw the fellow this morning."

"That may be. He's in your block. What has he done? Robbed a stiff of course, what else would a geezer like that have the pluck for? Just lifted some stuff from some drunken old soak, you know."

"I know," answered the drunken old soak, "and had he managed to put his loot away safely?"

"No idea. I suppose so—even he is not so daft!"

"Find out, Mordhorst. I'm very interested to know."

"Why are you so interested? It seems funny."

"Not to me. Because I was the drunken old soak the fellow robbed. You remember, Mordhorst, he's that landlord who did me down when I was drunk. I told you about him."

"Ah, that's him," said Mordhorst, grinning with delight. "There'll be a fine old rumpus when he finds you're here, seeing it's you who got him in chokey."

"Well, find out, Mordhorst, whether he managed to put the stuff away. He's got two gold rings and a gold watch of mine, table-silver for twelve people, a cowhide suitcase with some things in it, a leather brief-case, and four thousand marks."

"Not bad," grinned Mordhorst. "Far too much for such a lousy rogue. Well, I'll let you know." And we went on sawing, silently now—the warder was looking at us.

It was some days before I got to see Lobedanz or heard his voice again. In the mornings, when I went bucketing, his cell-door was always shut, and was only opened after we had finished, a sign that they knew we were concerned with the same case. I heard nothing more from Mordhorst either. Whenever I insisted, he only answered, "Wait a bit, mate, I've got to spy around a bit first. Mordhorst never cracks a safe until he has spied around a bit."

However, at last he was ready.

"He had over six thousand marks on him when the coppers nabbed him," said Mordhorst. "And that's straight up. Not only because he says so himself, but I got it from the orderly who cleans the office. They've got the money in there."

"Then he must have sold all my things and I'll never see them again," I said, and suddenly I was very sad about the loss of all my gold and silver things. "He only took four thousand in cash from me, no more."

"He might have had some money of his own," replied Mordhorst. "It's not sure that he flogged your stuff. He may have parked it somewhere."

"That's possible," I admitted, "but I can't quite believe it."

For a long time we sawed in silence, one beech log after another.

Then Mordhorst suddenly said: "What would you give, mate, if I found out where that fellow has hidden the boodle?"

"Boodle—what's that?"

"Your stuff, of course. What would you give?"

"What *can* I give, in clink? I haven't got anything myself."

"You have outside."

"But I can't touch that, my wife won't let me near it."

And we went on sawing. Next day, Mordhorst said to me. "You'll be coming up before the beak soon, and you'll be questioned about this fellow. You'll have to say that you claim the stolen money that's here, as your own."

"You can rely on me saying that, Mordhorst," I said grimly.

"And the Public Prosecutor will have to release the money to you, that's certain," said Mordhorst.

For a while he was silent again. Then he said: "Would you make out a draft, for five hundred marks payable to bearer, if I find out where he has hidden your stuff?"

I thought it over.

"The whole affair is worth five hundred to me," I said at last. "But I should have to get everything back, the gold things as well, and I can't believe that."

"If you get back less, you'll only have to pay less. I'm a square-dealer," replied the incorrigible safebreaker.

"But Mordhorst," I said, and I pitied his ignorance. "Do you really think they'll pay out money to you or anyone from the gaol, just because I write out a draft?"

"Let me worry about that," he replied, quite unmoved. "You've got a corn-chandler's business haven't you?"

"Yes, I have," I replied. "How did you come to know that, Mordhorst?"

"I know everything," he answered, with all the bumptious-
ness of the little man. "And if someone comes from outside
with a bill for grain that he delivered to you three months ago,
and asks for his money, and you acknowledge the bill, I'll bet
the fellows in the bank will pay up."

"Possibly," I replied. "But who's going to come from outside with such a bill?"

"Let me take care of that," answered Mordhorst with
equanimity. "The main thing is, I've got your word, you'll
acknowledge the bill."

"That you have," I said, "and I keep my word."

"You'd better," replied Mordhorst, and he began sawing
again. "You can be sure I'll get you if you do the dirty on me,
I'll get you tomorrow or in five years' time, inside or out,
myself or someone I tip off for it."

That is how the game began, a game such as is only played
in prison, underground, with many intermediaries, with the
whispering of orderlies at locked doors, with infinite subtlety
exercised by many brains during many hours: and the cunning
hypocritical Lobedanz was the target.

I was never quite able to see how it was done, I have never
understood how Mordhorst, who was particularly closely
guarded, was able to maintain constant contact with all the
prisoners, even with the outside world. But he could. Sometimes half a word would be dropped, out of which I could
construct a whole paragraph. For example, there were four
carefully selected prisoners who dragged the wood we cut.
through the town and round to the houses, in an outsized
handcart, under the supervision of a warder of course. And
there was the trusty prison-cook, an old prisoner who was
sometimes taken by the governor to dig and hoe and water
his garden on the outskirts of town. Perhaps these prisoners
were not quite so trustworthy as the prison administration

allowed themselves to imagine. And then there were the hatches, the openings in our cell-doors through which our food-bowls were handed in to us. When meals were being taken round there was always a lot of secret whispering and furtive passing of things to and fro at these hatches. As I have said, I know next to nothing about the game they were playing, otherwise I would have more to say about it here. I was a novice, and in particular, in the eyes of the others, I was not a "real criminal" because I had committed no offence against other people's property.

Mordhorst was careful not to tell me too much about it. I only got to know that pressure was being put on Lobedanz. They managed to cut down his food under the eyes of the warder. They let him starve a bit. And his cell-mate had as much as he could eat and never gave away a mouthful. That was one thing. And the other thing was that Lobedanz really had a wife and children at home, and he had been arrested so unexpectedly that they were left without food or money. It was put to him that a prisoner was going to be released in a few days' time, who could take the hidden things and dispose of them and give the proceeds to his wife—after the deduction of an appropriate commission, of course. I can well imagine that the cunning and suspicious Lobedanz had a hard struggle with himself, but they softened him up. They put the screws on him, they would slip him alarming messages, and then leave him entirely without any news, and when he asked them, they would say "It's all off. You wouldn't do it." And probably even Lobedanz loved his wife and children and did not want to see them starve and beg. The day came when Mordhorst said to me: "So I've got your word?"

"You have. Do you know anything yet?"

"I know everything. Your stuff..." Mordhorst looked at me sharply, "... is in the barn in the first field on the road to Kehne. There's a few planks broken at the back, and it's there in the straw. So now you know. Your gold wedding ring is missing, he's got rid of it, but otherwise everything's there, just as you said. That's worth five hundred marks, mate?"

"That's worth five hundred marks," I answered. Curious, how illogical the heart is. I was almost delighted that Magda would get her silver back, and yet I hated her with all my heart.

"Yes," I said, "but what can I do with my knowledge? I can't very well tell anybody I got it from you."

"When you get your bread today," said Mordhorst, "you'll find a slip of paper inside with what I've told you written on it. You show that to the warder and let things take their own course."

"And who's suppose to have written this note?"

"You don't know that. Just somebody you don't know, who hates Lobedanz and wants to do the dirty on him. Don't worry your head about that."

34

It was all thought out with real ingenuity and carried through with endless patience. The only pity was that this affair, like the majority of such affairs conceived in prison—great robberies and hold-ups, blackmail and swindles—turned out otherwise than we had expected, and Magda never got her silver back again.

Everything happened just as Mordhorst had foretold. I found the slip, gave it to the warder when he unlocked the cell, I was taken down to the prison governor and questioned. Then they took me back to my cell and I heard them unlocking another cell-door further up the corridor: they were fetching Lobedanz. I heard no more about the affair that night, nor during the next two days, and this time Mordhorst heard nothing either. Then I was summoned by the governor and informed that the police had searched the barn; the planks at the back were loose but there was nothing under the straw, and in fact nothing was hidden in the barn at all. I went back to my cell deeply disappointed. So Lobedanz had been cleverer than the lot of them, and either he no longer had the things or else he had hidden them in some quite different place. But Mordhorst shook his head at this.

"Just wait," he said, "there's more in this than meets the eye, and I've already got an idea what it is. Just wait, I'll get to the bottom of it, and if it's as I think it is, somebody's going to have nothing to laugh about."

He really did find out, at least I believe that what he told me was the truth.

"The fellow who was released had picked it up and sold it. He took it just before the coppers got there—the fools, why couldn't they move a bit faster! But I tell you, I'll get the rotten dog, he'll turn up in clink again, and then he'll have something to holler about!"

And a name was spread throughout the whole prison, sixty prisoners took note of the name of the man who had turned traitor, and these prisoners would take care that in the course of time the traitor's name was spread through many other prisons. Everywhere he would be looked on as a common traitor, for even among criminals there is a code of honour of sorts, and he had offended against this code.

But for me, who had played the least part of this game, the immediate consequences were most serious. For one morning when a warder had perhaps been a little sleepy and had not been paying proper attention to his task, I was unsuspectingly taking my bucket along the corridor, and did not notice that, contrary to custom, the door of Lobedanz's cell was already open, and the gentle fellow leaped out at me like a tiger, knocked me and my bucket to the ground and struck me in the face with both fists so that I lost consciousness almost at once. By now they had told Lobedanz that I was in gaol too, and, prisoner-fashion, had teased and tormented him mercilessly over the loss of his loot. They had probably told him also, that the money that had been taken from him was being kept here at my disposal, and perhaps they had pretended that my stuff had come back into my possession again. Anyhow, Lobedanz was wild with rage, and all these days he had been brooding in his cell, thinking how utterly fruitlessly he had worked on me for weeks, how I had got everything back, and how he was faced with a long prison sentence on my account—and all for nothing! He had seen red, he had been brooding all the time on how he could mark me for life, and his rage and hatred had swept away all his native cowardice and caution. When he saw

167

the cell-door open, he had lain in wait for me, he had got me down, and struck me in the face so that the blood immediately gushed from my nose and mouth. As usual the prisoners watched, unmoved and unconcerned, perhaps a little maliciously; it is not the custom, in prison, to interfere in any scuffle between two inmates. I am convinced that Mordhorst would have stood by me, but Mordhorst was not at hand, he was on the corridor below. And before the warder was able to rush up and pull Lobedanz off, Lobedanz had bent over my face and bitten my nose, so as to mark me for life—oh, he nearly bit half my nose off!

Terrible things happen in gaol, and frequently, and nobody makes any fuss about it. Lobedanz was put in a punishment cell, and later a charge of grievous bodily harm was added to all the rest. They laid me down on the straw-bag in my cell, washed off some of the blood, and waited till the prison doctor, summoned by telephone, arrived. The first thing I heard on regaining consciousness, was Duftermann's nagging voice, complaining about all this "filth in his cell", and demanding that I should be put somewhere else; and his voice did not cease to complain about me, as long as he was not asleep, every day that I had to share the cell with him.

In the doctor's opinion, it was not serious enough for me to be transferred to hospital. He sewed up my nose after a fashion, and declared that everything would be all right in three or four days' time. But it never did get quite right again; apart from the fact that to this day I cannot bear to look at myself in the mirror, because I am so disfigured and disgusting. No, I cannot smell any more, and I cannot breathe properly through my nose, either. I breathe with my mouth half-open like an idiot, and my sleeping-companions abuse me and jostle me of a night-time because I disturb their sleep with my snoring and groaning. That dog Lobedanz really has marked me for life, and I can never forget him. In fact, Lobedanz made a deeper impression on me than any other human being, even than Magda. Sometimes as I sit here, suddenly the image rises before me of how I stood at the attic-window and saw the town with its red-brown roofs spread at my feet in the evening light, saw the river shining among the green, and beyond, half-hidden in a blueish haze, the roof of my own house, while at my back, Lobedanz was assuring me in a soft whisper that he was a very poor but honest man, and making his joints crack. From the very first moment, I had realised that he was a rogue and a liar, and if I had had a little commonsense and decency I would have left that room there and then, and gone back home to the house in the blue haze. But in my frailty I stayed there and I have paid for it since a thousand times over.

35

I LAY for three or four days, amid Duftermann's abuse; I was in bad pain and I cursed my unhappy lot. All thought of revenging myself on Magda or of instituting divorce proceedings had quite faded away; I would have been glad if they had let me go home to her. I would have fallen on my knees and begged her forgiveness. But this was only a passing mood, it did not last. My feelings towards Magda were to change very often. I never saw the wood-yard again, nor my mate Mordhorst. Strangely enough, in my memory today they seem beautiful peaceful hours that I spent at the saw-bench, in my blue prison jacket, with the tops of the apple and pear trees above me, and the sunny sky.

Then late one afternoon, when I was absolutely in despair at the interminable nagging of that murderous incendiary Duftermann, the lock of the cell-door rattled at a quite unusual time, and the warder came in and cried: "Sommer, get up at once and pack your things! You're released!"

I started up from my bed and stared at the warder.

"Released," I whispered, and my heart beat furiously. At last! At last!

"Yes, released," he said maliciously. "You're going to the institution. Come on, come on, man, pack your things up! D'you think we've got all day?"

"Ah," I said slowly, and started to pack. "Ah—to the institution!"

Duftermann watched me closely to see that I did not pack any of his precious belongings, and all the time he was telling the warder how glad he was that I was leaving, I was the worst cell-mate in the world, I never spoke a sensible word, and the row I kicked up of a night-time was unbearable. I left without a word to him, I did not even look round.

Below, in the governor's office, stood a strange warder, who scrutinised me carefully, and I notice that he pulled a face at the sight of me. I was still wearing the bandage on my nose.

"Yes," said the governor, "this is the man another prisoner tried to bite the nose off. I suppose you heard about it officer?"

He had heard about it.

The governor added: "But up to now he's been quite a quiet orderly man. I don't think you'll need to handcuff him."

"No, no!" said the warder sharply. "I'm responsible for him. If he runs away. . . . "

"Do as you think fit, officer," said the governor, "I was merely giving my opinion. Listen, Sommer," he now turned to me, "sign this receipt, that you've had all your things back from us. We'll send your money on to you by post . . . "

"Please send it to my wife," I said, on a sudden impulse. "I shan't need money any more."

"Very well," said the governor impassively, and with that, I was released.

The warder put the handcuffs on my wrist and so I was led through my home town to the station, but that did not worry me. I still had the bandage on my nose; even Magda would not have recognised me.

Like my own ghost I walked through the town in which I was born, along the streets I had played in as a child; on that bench over there I once sat with Magda, she had plaits then, and we both carried school satchels under our arms. . . . Now we passed my own business, "Erwin Sommer, Market Produce, Wholesale and Retail" it still said on the ground-glass panes—for how much longer? And led along by a little chain, a suitcase in his free hand, this same Erwin Sommer went by, living yet dead for all that; traces of his life still remained—for how much longer?

"I'm only forty-one," I said to the officer.

"What do you mean by that?" asked the young man. "What are you getting at?"

"Oh, nothing, officer," I answered. "But when a man's already dead to the outside world at forty-one. . . . "

"Ah, come on, don't fret so," said the warder placidly, "you'll be much better off in the place I'm taking you to than you would be in clink, and if you make a sensible impression, maybe you'll get out again some time. D'you know what?" he continued, more and more humanly, "later on, when we get on the train, I'll take the handcuffs off, and I won't put 'em on again outside either. It's just here in town, one never knows what you fellows suddenly get into your heads."

I was silent. He meant well, but he did not know how unimportant the little handcuffs were to me. But with his clumsy efforts to console me, he had uttered a phrase that struck me like a thunderbolt, in my depressed mood. "Maybe you'll get out again some time," he had said! Maybe . . . some time. . . . And I had been counting on a six weeks' observation period, that's what Mordhorst had told me.

Maybe . . . some time. . . .

Was it just a random remark of the sergeant's, or did he really know something? He had my papers! Of course, he knew something: I was going to be locked up for life! Really dead to the outside world, as I had imagined just now. A mist rose before my eyes, and the sun that shone for everybody, shone no more for me. Never again would it shine for me.

36

WE ARE walking together along a beautiful country road, the warder and I. I am free of the handcuffs, which has the advantage that I can carry the suitcase, which is none too light, now in my right hand, now in my left. The warder has lit a short pipe, and has graciously given me permission to smoke. This permission does not help me in the least. In any case it would probably go ill with my bitten nose.

Along the road stand tall old chestnut trees, which have finished blossoming. The sun is sinking. Now and then, a belated cartload of hay creaks passed us. The people hardly turn their heads after us, they are long accustomed to such a sight around here, in the near vicinity of the asylum. The most that happened was that once a woman threw an inquisitive look at my bandaged face. The warder had tried to question me about my "crime" and my former life, but I had only answered him in monosyllables. But since he has decided to shorten the journey with a little conversation, he now tells me about himself, or rather about a garden which he works with his young wife. He would so much like to rent the neighbouring plot of land, and, weighing the matter up at his ease, he sets out before me all the reasons for and against it—his low salary and the high rent, the soil full of weeds, the doubtful yield—oh, there were only reasons against. The warder breathes out a cloud of blueish-white smoke and says finally: "Well, I'll rent that plot at all costs. A plot of land—that's better than a thousand marks in the savings bank!"

I only half-listen to his chatter, and now when he comes to his surprising conclusion I smile bitterly. "It's with such empty-heads as this that I'm to keep company from now on, and they simply call me 'Sommer' without 'Herr' and gracious-ly admit that 'so far I make quite a sensible impression'!"

But aloud I ask: "Is that the institution?"

"That's it," replied the warder. "And now we'd better put a bit of a spurt on; it's nearly office closing-time, and the governor will complain if I bring you in late."

Seen from the road, the asylum does not make a bad im-pression. My heart starts to beat easier. Situated on a slight rise, surrounded by tall thick-leaved old trees, it lies as stately as a great manor-house or some old castle. Great windows blink in the light of the evening sun. But as we come nearer, I see the high red walls all round, with iron spikes and barbed-wire along the top, I see the bars in front of the flashing win-dows, and my companion has no need whatever to explain: "This used to be a convict prison."

No, I can see for myself this does not look like a hospital but a convict prison. A real moat, quite wide, encircles the whole group of buildings, ducks and geese swim peacefully on it, but on the bridge we are crossing stands an armed guard in a green uniform, and the office to which I am taken is no whit different from the prison office I left an hour and a half ago. Even the officials in it seem to be of the same kind, the same bored, uninterested yet searching glance is thrown at the new inmate, the same slow formality is gone through by which my escort is relieved of me and my personal details are entered.

This evening affords me only one ray of light; I was arrested on a charge of attempted murder, the magistrate had ordered my transfer to an institution on the grounds of homicidal intent, now I am being handed over here with the entry "uttering menaces". Without my doing anything about it, the seriousness of the charge against me has been considerably reduced; for a moment I tell myself that it is impossible for them to keep me here for any length of time, and to destroy my whole life for such a slight offence.

But then, as I followed my green-uniformed guide with his fattish melancholy face, through all the wretched stone courtyards on which only barred windows looked down, as I was admitted into a gigantic stone building through double iron doors, and mounted the gloomy staircase, as I realised that the so-called hospital differed in no respect from a prison, that here, too, were bars and warders and iron discipline and blind obedience, I thought no more about the great step I had taken from attempted murder to uttering menaces, I believed no more in the slightness of my offence—I felt that anything was possible, I realised how helplessly I stood at the mercy of gigantic and pitiless powers, powers without heart, without compassion, without human qualities. I was caught in a great machine and nothing that I did or felt was of any more consequence, the machine would run its unalterable course, I might laugh or cry, the machine would take no notice.

37

ONE iron grill and then another iron grill, and now we enter a long gloomy corridor full of pale figures. It stinks here, it stinks piercingly of latrines, cabbage and bad tobacco. Outside the corridor window is the last glow of sunset, above the high iron-spiked wall I see the peaceful evening countryside with its meadows and slowly-ripening cornfields, right across to the low strips of woodland on the horizon. Around me, pale figures are standing, leaning against the walls. Sometimes I see something of their faces, when the glow of their pipes momentarily becomes brighter. A man, a short sturdy man in a white jacket, takes me behind a partition at the end of the corridor. It is his sanctum, the "glass box" as it is called. From this "glass box" the stocky man, who turns out to be the head-nurse, watches everything that happens along the corridor, and he watches very keenly, as I was to discover. He even sees things that he cannot see at all, he knows what happens in the cells, he knows everything that happens at work—he is the stern conscience of Block 3, and the doctor's information service.

"Leave your suitcase down here, Sommer," says the head-nurse. "I'll give you your institution clothes tomorrow, civilian clothes are forbidden here. And now I'll show you your bed, it's bed-time already. We go to bed at half-past seven here, and get up at a quarter to six in the morning . . . "

"Might I perhaps have some supper?" I ask. "I didn't have any there. . . . "

I expect to get a "No" as I did on my first arrival in prison. I did not really intend to ask, having already learned that a prisoner should say nothing, ask nothing, question nothing. But—wonder of wonders—the head-nurse nods his head and says: "All right, Sommer, go and sit in the day-room for a while."

I am put into the day-room. It is a long, three-windowed room, containing nothing but scrubbed-down wooden tables once painted white, primitive wooden benches without backs, and a sort of kitchen clock on the wall. I sit down on a bench. By the clock it is shortly after half-past seven.

Outside, the cry echoes: "Bed-time! Clothes out!" A violent shuffling begins (what an incredible number of people there must be in this block). Doors slam; in a neighbouring room, which is probably the lavatory, an uninterrupted rush of water begins. In bed at half-past seven, like children! How am I to get through the night? And the thirty-six nights of the observation period? And perhaps many many more nights to come? The weight of an infinite length of time in which nothing happens, descends on me like lead. This bare room, containing only the essentials, seems an image of my future life. Nothing to look forward to, nothing to wish for, nothing to hope for . . . a life in which every minute is empty and the future will be empty, too . . .

An aluminium bowl is set before me, a spoon is put by it . . . This is done by a little man in a dirty linen jacket. His face is ugly, and is made even uglier by the fact that all his upper teeth are missing, except two fang-like yellowish-black eye-teeth.

The man looks like some malevolent animal.

"Who are you?" he asks in a high-pitched insolent voice. "Where are you from? What have you done? What's up with your nose?"

I do not answer him at all, silently I begin to dip into my aluminium bowl. It is nothing but cabbage and water. Warm salt water with very little cabbage.

"Is this your supper?" I ask. "No bread at all?"

Around me, though it is bed-time already, several figures are creeping, in worn-out brownish clothes which in many cases are in rags. . . . The little man with the fangs laughs shrilly.

"Is that our supper, he wants to know! He thinks it ought to be cooked specially for him. He thinks he's in a restaurant. He's so posh, he won't talk to the likes of us. No bread, he says!"

He laughs again, and suddenly all is quiet. There are six or seven figures slinking around me or leaning silently against the walls. I put my spoon down in the bowl—what is the good of filling ones belly with warm water? I stand up, take a step toward the door. At the same instant uproar breaks out behind my back. They have thrown themselves on my barely half-emptied bowl, they struggle together like animals. Suppressed cries are heard . . . the clapping sound of blows . . . Oh God, they fight like beasts over a pint of hot cabbage-water! A high yelling neigh of triumph rings out—it is the little man with the fangs, he is the victor! "Will you get out and let me through! I'll report you to the head-nurse! I brought the new fellow the bowl, it belongs to me! You give me the grub, didn't you, new fellow?"

I hurry to get out of the door. I stand again in the corridor, by the glass box. The head-nurse comes out.

"Well, come along, Sommer. Is your bandage still all right? I'll have a look at it tomorrow morning."

In the long corridor, before each cell door, lies a bundle of clothes.

"You put your clothes outside the door too. You're only allowed to keep your shirt on inside."

178

"Mayn't I fetch some pyjamas out of my suitcase?"

"Pyjamas, nightshirts—things like that don't exist here. You'll get a decent institution shirt that'll last you a week."

We enter a long narrow cell, the air is fetid, stifling already. Eight beds stand in the narrow room, four below, four above.

"Yours is the lower bunk on the right by the window. Make it up quickly and put your things outside the door. It's lock-up time immediately."

The door slams behind me, I go over to my bed. I feel many searching eyes turned towards me, but nobody says a word. The bed is better than in prison. There are no straw-bags here but proper mattresses, hard as stone; one can lie on them better. There is a sheet too, and a fine white blanket which, rather clumsily, I button into a cover. There is also a bolster. The bed-linen is blue-chequered. All the time I feel the searching eyes on me, but not a word is said. Hurriedly I slip off my clothes, bundle them clumsily together, and run back to bed in my shirt. I creep into it. The plank bottom of the upper bunk is close above me, I cannot sit upright. The bed above seems empty. I wrap myself tight in my blankets and stretch out full-length. The warm cabbage-water rumbles disagreeably in my stomach.

A voice says loudly: "Don't even say good evening or introduce himself, the miserable bastard!"

Murmurs of approval can be heard. I start up in my bed—I must not fall out with these people on the very first evening. I have had enough with my strained relations with Duftermann. I knock my head badly on the planks of the upper bed. Seeing this, the two men in the beds opposite laugh.

One cries: "He's bumped his nut!"

And the other: "He crumpled his fine cloth pants up in his jacket, he's got plenty to learn, the fat swine."

Murmurs of approval again. I creep out of my bed.

"Gentlemen," I say, "excuse me if I have not behaved properly. I didn't wish to offend you. If I said nothing, it was because I thought some of you were asleep already."

A voice from an upper bunk calls out: "That's Zeese, he's deaf and dumb, he can't hear anything!"

I eagerly continue, "I'm not used to all this yet. I've only been a fortnight or so in remand prison. For the attempted murder of my wife . . ."

Murmurs of hearty approval. I have guessed rightly: "attempted murder" makes a much better impression here than "uttering menaces".

"My name is Erwin Sommer, I have a market-produce business, and I'm here for six weeks' observation . . ."

"You watch out it doesn't turn into six years," calls a laughing voice. "The medical officer loves us all so much, he doesn't like to lose any of us."

Laughter again, but the ice is broken, the bad impression is made good again. I go from bed to bed and hear the names: Bull, Meierhold, Brachowiak, Marquardt, Heine and Dräger. I shall not remember them, especially as it has become almost dark by now and I cannot recognise the individual faces in their box-beds. Then I creep back to my own bed.

A voice calls: "Hey, new fellow, tell us how it happened, that business with your wife."

Another calls heatedly: "Shut your trap, Dräger! What do you always want to be so nosey for? Leave it to the fellow to tell what he wants. You just want to go crawling to the chief in the glass box tomorrow."

A heated quarrel begins, about who is the head-nurse's "earwig". The occupants of other beds join in. Wild abuse is hurled to and fro. I am glad that, at least, they leave me in peace. I am tired, my nose hurts badly. The quarrel is just beginning to die down for lack of material when angry shouting is heard in the corridor, the sound of blows and howls. Our cell door flies open and a figure hurtles in.

A loud voice calls: "Will you get into your own bed instead of hanging round other people's cells, you damned queen, you!"

And a shrill complaining voice—I recognise it immediately, it is the fang-toothed man: "You've hurt me bad, keeper. Keeper, I shan't be able to work tomorrow!"

"You damned queen, you!" rumbles the voice outside once more. "Hurry up and roll into kip, or else you're for it!"

The fang-toothed one thrusts his face into my bed.

"Well, new fellow, so you're under me? I tell you straight, if you don't lie still in the night, if you wobble about, I'll come down and wobble you."

"I'll lie still all right," I tell him, and I think anxiously of my rattling and snoring.

The little man undresses with incredible speed and shoots his rags outside the door. Then with a disgusting lack of ceremony he uses the bucket.

"You could have done that outside, Lexer," calls an indignant voice.

"Are you too posh to breathe my stink?" cries the shrill insolent voice. "We're real posh in here now the new fellow's come! O.K. Now I'll shit more than ever!"

And he lets a thunderous one.

"In hell," I think. "I have landed in hell. However shall I be able to live here? And sleep? These are not human beings, these are animals. And am I supposed to live here for six weeks, perhaps longer? Perhaps very long? In this hell? This Lexer, or whatever he is called, is a devil!"

They try to question me further. But I do not want to hear or see anything more of them. I pretend to be asleep. And slowly they too become quieter, the shrill hateful voice falls silent. It becomes darker and darker, most of them are probably asleep already. I hear a clock strike three times. What would it be? A quarter to nine? A quarter to ten? I hope the clock strikes the hours as well. That would shorten the night. Above me Lexer tosses restlessly to and fro. My bed sways each time. And I am not supposed to move! I lie quite still, my face hidden in my arm. I am utterly alone with myself, I see clearly that from now on I shall always be utterly alone with myself. I am somewhere where neither love nor friendship can reach, I am in hell . . . I have sinned for a brief while and I am being punished for it, incredibly severely, for a long time! But one should have known, before one sinned, how severe the punishment would be. One should have been warned beforehand, then one would not have sinned . . . God, that bit of brandy-drinking, is it really so terrible? That squabble with Magda—well, all right, legally they could make out a case of uttering menaces, but do I have to spend a living death in hell on that account? If Magda knew how I am suffering—she would at least take pity on me, she would help me out of pity, even if she doesn't love me any more. There is just one hope, and that is the doctor. Dr Stiebing, the medical officer, had not made a bad impression on me during that car journey. He had joked and laughed with Dr Mansfeld like a real human being. Perhaps he is a real human being, not just part of a machine. I will speak to him as to a human being, I will fight for my soul with him, I will save my soul from this hell.

"Sir," I will say to him, "I take full responsibility for all I have done. I have never been so intoxicated that I did not know what I was doing. I want to be punished severely. I would gladly go to prison for a year, two years. I would do that gladly. But don't leave me in this place, in this hell, where a man doesn't know how he will come out again, and perhaps he will only come out feet first. Sir," I will continue, "you know our family doctor, Dr Mansfeld. You joked and chatted with him in the car. Ask Dr Mansfeld, he has known me for many years. He will confirm that I am a decent, respectable, sober man. That affair was just a sudden attack, I don't know how it happened myself"—No, I interrupted myself, I mustn't tell the medical officer that, or he'll certify me insane. "But Dr Mansfeld will confirm that I have always been decent. I put Magda into a private ward in hospital and paid the high cost of the operation without a murmur, and spared nothing for her comfort. I always was a decent man, sir, let me go back to live among decent men. Give me a chance. . . ."

The clock strikes, it strikes the hour, a quarter of the long night is past, it is now ten o'clock. And so I spend the first night in the asylum counting quarter-hour after quarter-hour, making speeches and writing letters, between sleeping and waking. Sometimes, exhausted, I have nearly fallen asleep, but then I start up again: Lexer above me has thrown himself about in his bed, or someone has gone over to the bucket. For a 'joke' I kept count this first night: from ten o'clock at night till a quarter to six in the morning seven men went to the bucket thirty-eight times. When I wanted to use it in the morning it was full to overflowing. And not a single man used paper—they were past that. Oh, I got to know a fine corner of hell that night.

38

I WAS clothed by the head-nurse. I got a brown jacket, striped cloth trousers, leather slippers, all new. The head-nurse treated me with discrimination. But perhaps it would have been better if he had given me old rags like the others. They could see I was wearing new things, and it strengthened their dislike of me.

"He wants to be something better than us, the fat swine," they said, throwing malicious glances at me.

Incidentally, I did something strange while the clothing was being issued. I was allowed to take soap and a toothbrush out of my case, and I was able, in an unwatched moment, to steal a razor-blade. I had done this once before, but then I had been weak and cowardly, I had no idea what was in store for me. Now I would behave differently, I would slash myself without fear of the pain. No, not just yet; what I had done, this secret taking of the razor-blade, was quite a surprise to myself. Not just yet—first I would fight with myself. But should the fight be unavailing . . . well, all right, when I had had my hearing and my permanent transfer to this institution was confirmed, then, yes, then. . . . I was not going to spend my life in this hell, that much was certain.

I have taken my first breakfast with my fellow-sufferers. At half past six in the morning, in the rays of the early sun their faces look absolutely disconsolate. Raw faces, animal faces, blunt faces. Over-developed chins or chins completely missing. Cross-eyed men, hunchbacked men, stunted men. As pale and sad as their worn-out clothes. The head-nurse has assigned to me a place at the last table, right back against the wall. That is good. I can see and observe everything and sit quite undisturbed. From the orderly I have got a mug of some hot chicory brew, and the head-nurse has given me three thick slices of bread. Two I spread with margarine and one with jam. I eat them slowly and with great appetite. I chew thoroughly. Who knows what there will be for lunch today? The cabbage-water has frightened me a great deal. Some get more bread, they also get something extra to put on it. The extras may be chives or onion or skim-milk cheese. These, I learn, are the outside workers. They are engaged on heavy work all day, which is why they get such precious titbits.

Shortly after breakfast, the order "Fall in!" is heard, and all those who are working, line up, and are let through the iron-barred door by a keeper, and all that remain behind are the orderlies, the sick, and myself. There are many sick. . . .

I stand at the window and watch how the people from every block line up in the yard. There are many, many people. Over to the left stands a line of women. Then the yard is emptied. A fat man in a white coat, the head-nurse, has detailed them off for work. Some have marched off with scythes, others with hoes, many have gone to the factory. Now I walk along the corridor with Hielscher, up and down, up and down. Hielscher is a little hunchback, who speaks careful German in a soft, very clear voice. Hielscher calls me "Herr Sommer", and that does me good. In his clear careful speech, he tells me many things about this place and its inmates. He usually peels potatoes. He has been peeling potatoes for six years. Altogether he has been eleven years in the asylum.

"I am a sexual offender," he says gently, choosing his words with care. "The medical officer has made his report about me. I got congenital mental deficiency coupled with lack of control and a drastically impaired sense of responsibility, and besides I have a hump, that is obvious of course, and also I limp. Is that bad, Herr Sommer?"

I am quite perplexed at this question.

"Bad?" I ask, embarrassed. "How do you mean, bad?"

"Well, is it a bad ailment or only a slight one, Herr Sommer?" And he looks at me with his lively but sad eyes.

"No, it's probably not too bad."

"That is what I think," says Hielscher. "I'm sure they'll soon release me. Have you by chance a little tobacco for me, Herr Sommer?"

I told Hielscher that I had a longing for tobacco myself, and that unfortunately I had none to give him. Thereupon Hielscher's interest in me faded rapidly, he left me, and I wandered alone up and down the corridor. That morning was interminable. I walked and walked, but the hands of the clock did not move on. Sometimes I glanced into one of the two day-rooms, but the torpid figures sitting there, the wrecks, repelled me. Only the orderlies were busy with bucket and broom, clean-looking, well set-up men, as in all prisons, skilful and unscrupulous, sucking up to the officials, informing on their fellow-prisoners about every trifle, corrupt, and rude to their comrades. I saw them going from cell to cell, pretending to tidy up, but mainly searching the beds for a hidden slice of bread or a plug of tobacco. It strengthened me in my antipathy when I saw that the hated Lexer was also a kind of orderly, an assistant-orderly, who spent the greater part of the day over in one of the workshops in the annexe, making brushes, but who always contrived also to make a job for himself in the block.

The staircase was being cleaned by a man in his middle years, with a face once clever but now confused and hopelessly sad; from time to time he broke off his cleaning, tore open a window and shouted filthy insults through the bars at some imaginary person outside. I watched Lexer creep up behind the yelling man, spring on him from the back and beat his head again and again against the iron bars.

He cried shrilly: "Will you get on with your work, you swine! What are you shouting about! You want to eat but you don't want to work for it! Just you wait!"

And he beat his head again. I would have liked to help the poor fellow, but the grill on to the staircase was locked and during the previous night I had firmly resolved not to interfere in any quarrels but to remain completely neutral. The more unobtrusively I lived, the more favourable would be the doctor's report. Besides, I was afraid of Lexer, and I had every reason to be. I long observed this scoundrel—or lout, rather; he was only in his middle twenties and of extremely backward development—with the watchful eyes of hatred. He was a born bloodhound. He took a delight in torturing his fellow-prisoners, he was always cuffing them here and pinching them there, hitting them, reporting them to the head-nurse. Nothing was too petty for him. If a prisoner brought in an onion he had secretly picked up, Lexer would either take it from him or else denounce him to the head-nurse as a thief. And since the onion really would be stolen, only from the institution garden of course, the thief would be bound to get fourteen days in the lock-up. The weaker ones Lexer would entice into some quiet corner and there he would beat them until they handed over their tobacco or whatever else of their possessions he coveted. The stronger ones he approached with cunning, deceiving them with promises of bread and never keeping his promise. But with the keepers, Lexer was not at all unpopular. He played the part of the court-jester; in his shrill insolent way, he always had some quick-witted joke at hand, usually at the expense of his fellow-prisoners. He would perform any service for the keepers quickly, skilfully, willingly, and if he was caught in any misdemeanour, he would take his thrashing with a comically lachrymose expression.

"You can't be angry with the swine," said the keepers and they tolerated him and his tyranny over the other prisoners. He was particularly useful to them; through him they got to know everything that happened in the place.

Lexer had been put into an orphanage at the age of six and from then on he had only spent a few weeks or months at liberty, and had always returned into the safe keeping of the State: in approved schools, reformatories, prisons. Eventually they had put him into this institution as incorrigible, and as he well knew, for life. But that did not upset him in the least. In this place, which seemed a hell to me, he was like a pig in clover. He felt in his element here. Here he could give rein to all his malevolence. He played the assistant-orderly, the assistant-keeper, the head devil. Here he was, beating the head of an imbecile, a schizophrene, against the bars and probably expecting praise for keeping the inmates so strictly to their tasks.

39

EVEN an interminable morning comes to an end. Lunch-time came, and the prisoners smiled: it was a good day, they got a good meal. Each man received in a string bag a pound and a half of potatoes in their jackets, and with it, in his aluminium bowl, a ladleful of sharply spiced gravy in which floated a few shreds of meat. Laboriously I peeled my potatoes with a spoon; knives and forks were too dangerous in this place of constant fighting. Watching the men as they ate, I noticed some who peeled their potatoes, put them in the gravy and waited until they finished peeling before they began to eat. But these were in the minority: most were so famished that they could not wait. The potatoes disappeared into their mouths just as they were peeled, only a few ever reached the gravy. Near me I saw a fat stocky man with iron-grey hair and the reddish-brown sunburnt face of a land-worker, who ate his peelings as he cut them off. I had hardly finished peeling my potatoes, when he threw a questioning glance at me, reached his calloused hand across the table, scooped up all my leavings and thrust them into his mouth.

"Hey!" I called. "There was a rotten potato among that lot!"

"Don't matter, mate," he said, chewing eagerly. "I've got to mow all day, I never get enough. Perhaps I can pinch some pig-spuds tonight. Hope so!"

He was not the only glutton, they were all hungry, always, even directly after a meal. I saw sick men going round, stealing tiny crumbs of potato off the table, while others scraped out

189

their already spotless bowls. I saw one in the corridor polishing the inside of the gravy cauldron with his finger which he licked again and again. All this was happening under the eyes of the keeper, who regarded it as a commonplace affair.

Here I am anticipating somewhat, but in this chapter I want to have done with my description of asylum meals, though it is not yet a closed chapter for me even today. We never got fresh meat to eat, just occasionally shreds—never lumps—of some old red salt meat floating in the gravy, and very rare shreds, at that! There was never butter, sausage or cheese, never an apple. And everything we had was quite inadequate, always watered-down, and badly prepared. Why it was so, I cannot imagine, even today. The prisoners maintained that the head-nurse was eating everything himself. But even the greediest head-nurse can't put away the food of a few hundred men. Perhaps the authorities wanted to take away our nature a bit, but I must confess that even on this starvation diet, the passions remained lively enough. However there were always folk among us who suffered no such hunger, who even lived fatly, within certain limits. First there were the orderlies, who had to cut, weigh and spread our bread for us. Officially a keeper stood by and watched, but let the telephone ring and the keeper would have to leave the kitchen and go into the glass box, and immediately a few slices would be thickly spread and disappear. Prisoners have sharp eyes, and hunger makes them sharper; it was inevitable that they should get to know that they were being robbed. One might see an orderly chewing a piece of bread in the lavatory, another might surprise him giving it to a "friend" or trading it for tobacco. But there was no point in informing on them. It was difficult to prove anything, almost impossible, for even if the bread was found (which hardly ever happened because no keeper could be bothered to look for it) the orderly could say "I saved it up from breakfast"; and then the orderlies were the keepers' blue-eyed boys, their tale-bearers; they would not hear a word against them. So practically nothing ever happened about it, but the envy and the hatred was kept awake all the time.

Even worse than this furtive way of procuring food was a quite legal way, condoned and even encouraged by the authorities. Such of the inmates as still had obliging relatives outside, were allowed to receive food parcels as often as they wished. One might expect that almost every one of the patients would have such relatives outside, who might at least send him a loaf now and then—even dry bread was a longed-for commodity there. But such was not the case. Apart from the fact that many of the inmates could neither read nor write (this dreadful place housed only the last dregs of humanity) or else were too insane or dull-witted to do so, the relatives of the majority did not wish to acknowledge them any more. They had caused grief and shame enough when they were outside, and now that they had been in this place for five, ten, even twenty years, they were done with and forgotten by those outside, to them they were dead and buried.

No, there were very few who got parcels; out of the fifty-six men in my block, perhaps only five or six. But these sat plump and well-fed at our common meal-table and lay beside the bowls full of watery soup, their thickly-spread bread, with sausage and cheese we never got a taste of; yes I even lived to see a fat peasant who had been put away on account of his ungovernable temper, devouring a roast duck at his ease in front of us, gnawing it bone by bone. He dripped with fat, and we sat by with our eyes growing bigger and bigger, our slavering mouths filling with water, our hands trembling, and our hearts full of envy and greed.

From all this, from our constant hunger, and our hatred of the thieving orderlies and our envy of the gluttons, arose an endless round of acrimony, quarrels, fights, punishments.

There was not a day's peace in the place, always something going on. One no longer even listened when two men insulted each other in the most obscene manner. One merely walked away when they blacked each other's eyes and bloodied each other's noses. One was thankful not to be involved oneself. One had to watch every word that was said, it would be immediately passed on, immediately turned against the speaker.

For my own part, I must confess that at first it was not only with envy that I regarded these parcel-hogs. It was so simple for me, I had only to write a letter to Magda and I could belong to this privileged class. Magda wouldn't be one to let her own husband starve! For a week I struggled with myself, and then hunger won, I decided to write. I had neither writing paper nor envelope, and nothing of the sort was provided by the institution; but I saved a slice of bread and got what I wanted. I wrote the letter, and then I waited. In bed of an evening I pictured to myself what would be in the parcel; when I thought of a slice of bread thickly spread with fat liver-sausage, I was nearly sick with hunger and craving. I had calculated the earliest day on which the parcel could arrive, but that day passed, and many days after it, and the parcel did not come. Then I heard that all communications had first to go through the censorship of the medical officer and then be passed over to the administrative offices for franking, and that letters were not sent off immediately, but only after a while, when a number had accumulated.

"They take their time," said the prisoners. "Do you think they'll start running just because you want 'em to? They sit all the firmer on their arses."

So I went on waiting and hoping.

Then one day the head-nurse casually said, "There's a letter of yours in the office, Sommer. They say it can't go, you've got no money for the postage."

"What," I cried. "Because of twelve pfennigs postage I

can't send a letter! I sent my wife four thousand marks from the remand prison!"

"You should have kept a few marks back," said the head-nurse, and tried to pass on.

"But sir," I cried, "It's not possible! Just for twelve pfennigs! They can ring up my wife, and she'll confirm . . ."

"A phone call costs ten pfennigs, and you haven't got it, Sommer," said the head-nurse coolly. "Keep calm, your letter will go off all right, next month when your first wages are credited to you."

I have no idea whether my letter to Magda was eventually sent off or whether it got lost in the meantime. Anyhow, I never got a food parcel, I always remained among the hungry ones, the greedy envious ones. For by the time I finally had some wages to my credit, I had long become too dispirited to write to Magda.

40

I HAVE hurried on far in advance of events. I am still on my first day in the asylum. I have eaten my potatoes very properly with no peel on them, and I am dog-tired after my sleepless night. I turn to the head-nurse and beg him to allow me to lie down on my bed for an hour, since I have not been able to sleep all night.

"That is forbidden," says the head-nurse sternly, but then in a milder tone: "All right, lie down. But get undressed and into bed properly."

I do so, and I have hardly lain down and shut my eyes before that hated yelling voice rises.

"Get out of bed this instant, you swine! You'd like that, wouldn't you, to loaf around while we do your work for you? Get up, get out of that bed!"

The ever-watchful bloodhound has tracked me down. But now I am in a fury, my hatred gives me strength to protest.

"Shut your mouth!" I shout furiously. "Do you think you're better than the head-nurse? He's given me permission and you, you swine . . ."

"He's given you permission, has he really?" he grinned and slobbered and showed his discoloured fangs. "Well, you must be pretty posh if the head-nurse makes an exception like that for you. Don't be angry, mate. I'm just here to keep order in the block, otherwise I get sat on by the head-nurse." Whereupon he disappears, and I lie back, quite content to think that I have got the better of him at last.

194

I have really fallen asleep but only for a few minutes, then something causes me to wake up. It is probably not a noise that awakens me, but an instinct by which I scent danger: in this place one develops the instincts of a hunted beast. I am lying on my side looking straight at the stool by my bed, where I put my clothes. I blink, and see something white, busying itself with my things. It is that Lexer again. Very carefully, infinitely quietly he takes up one article of clothing after another, searches the pockets and feels along the seams ... my first impulse is to spring up and rush at this devil, this indefatigable tormentor. But I hold myself back, I remain lying quietly, I watch what he does. Let him search. I grin. I have not the slightest thing in my pockets that he could conceivably want. Not the slightest thing?

My heart stops and again I would like to jump up, to snatch from him the razor-blade which he has now found, though I had carefully wrapped it in an old newspaper. He throws a glance at me. I shut my eyes, I am asleep. Then, when I peer again, I see that he is wrapping up the blade once more in the newspaper, and he puts it back in my pocket. Then he is gone. But I have realised the danger. With one bound I spring out of bed, take out the blade, and hurry with it to the lavatory. A pull of the plug, and the blade has disappeared, that precious blade that was to have opened the way to freedom for me if all else failed. A minute later I am in bed again. None too soon! For there stands the head-nurse by my bed and he puts his hand on my shoulder. "Wake up, Sommer!"

I wake up, just right I hope, not too easily, not too slowly.

"Get up, Sommer!"

I do so, and stand before him in my shirt.

"Sommer, have you got something forbidden in your pockets?"

"No, sir."

"You know that anything that cuts is strictly forbidden

here, for instance table-knives, razor-blades, nail-files. You know that?"

"Yes, sir, so I've been told."

"And you have nothing in your pockets that's forbidden?"

"No, sir."

A short pause.

Then: "Sommer, I'm warning you. Own up, and I'll shut one eye to it. Otherwise, on your first day I'll put you under punishment for four weeks."

"I've nothing to own up to, sir."

"All right, then turn out your pockets."

I do so, beginning with my jacket. I leave the trousers pocket till last.

"Undo this newspaper, Sommer."

I do so. Nothing, absolutely nothing. The head-nurse stands thoughtfully for a moment. Then he goes through my clothes himself, garment by garment, but again nothing.

"Get dressed, Sommer."

I do so.

"All right. Now send Lexer to me. You will stay in the day-room till the leisure-hour."

"Yes, sir."

I had set them a lovely task: under the supervision of the head-nurse, all the orderlies searched the whole cell, bit by bit. They found all manner of things, but no razor-blade. In the end, they abused Lexer, they imagined it was some idiotic roguish trick of his. But Lexer at least knew that I had really had a razor-blade. I had got the better of him. And strangely enough, though they all abused him, from the head-nurse down, he bore me no grudge. I had got the better of him, that impressed him. From that time, he never picked on me directly, though he could never quite leave off nagging.

41

THE afternoon was endless. The only slight diversion was that, for our "leisure hour" we were taken outside for two hours from two to four. "Outside" was a small garden within the high prison walls, perhaps four hundred square yards in extent, in which a single narrow path, just wide enough for two people, ran round a grass plot. The sun was shining, it was a fine summer day. But what the sun shone upon was not so fine. I am not speaking now of the surroundings, high walls, red and naked or clothed with dead grey cement, decked with barbed-wire, the bars at the windows, the blind window-panes —this alone is enough to rob the most beautiful summer day of its brilliance.

But I do not mean all this. I mean my comrades, my fellow-sufferers, who lean against the wall in their discoloured rags squat on a bench, or scuffle along the sandy path, in wooden shoes or barefoot. How revealing is the pitiless sunlight on these faces, which seem merely like distant lost memories. Grief, sadness, bestiality and mad despair. I shut my eyes and see them standing, squatting, scuffling there, as I have seen them a hundred times, and shall perhaps see them a thousand times more. There is a tall shaky man whose close-cropped iron-grey head is covered with blood-red or festering "pig-boils" as they call furuncles here, his face hard and angular and his dark deep set eyes entirely devoid of brightness. Ceaselessly, this fellow, a Rhinelander who was once probably a street-trader, murmurs: "Two hundredweight Kanalstrasse 20, one hundredweight Meier, Triftstrasse 10, market police, market police...."

He raises his voice as he looks up to the blind barred windows, waiting for buyers. "Seed potatoes! Seed potatoes! Buy my seed potatoes!"

No buyers come. Despairingly he shakes his hideous head and begins again: "Two hundredweight Kanalstrasse 20, one hundredweight...."

Yet if you ask him what time it is, he looks up at the sun and gives you quite a sensible and approximately correct answer, but no sooner has he done so than he resumes his eternal litany once more: "Seed potatoes! Seed potatoes! Buy my seed potatoes!"

How it still rings in my ears!

And then there is that other whom I have already mentioned, the schizophrene who hears voices, whose poor sad head Lexer had so mercilessly beaten against the iron bars—he shuffles round and round in slippers whose entire back part is missing. Suddenly he stops, he lifts his arm and makes a threatening gesture towards sky, walls and bars, but he does not see sky, walls and bars, he sees some invisible enemy whom he now threatens in a most obscene way. He is the only Saxon amongst us, and his abuse is uttered in such a pure Saxon dialect that the few among us who have their senses, smile. But it is really nothing to smile at when this lost man, the son of a good family, abuses the unseen enemy who prevents him from explaining everything to his parents. Why does he always thrust himself in the way, what is he after, this eternal trouble-maker? Isn't the son the one best qualified to explain things to his parents?

Apparently this poor fellow had once committed some offence which had separated him from his parents. Perhaps it was only some indiscretion; in any case he was weak—he had wanted to hurry to his parents to explain everything to them; but he had been arrested straight away. And the years went by, one after another, and the iron bars were still between him and his parents, between his guilt and the family discussion that would have set his heart free. He threw himself against the bars, he cared nothing that some swine beat his face till the blood came, he fought day after day with an enemy invisible to us, and day after day he took up the fight anew. In between times, one could exchange a sensible word with him too, about the primitive things of life, how the soup had tasted and where the handbrush was. He even managed a little work; as I have already said, he swept the staircase. Incidentally this Saxon, Lachs, was the one who got most food parcels from home; but unfortunately he no longer noticed what he ate, it was all the same to him whatever the head-nurse put in his hand.

A third man, who talked a great deal, was a wiry patient with sharp features and a narrow aquiline nose: he looked like a white-skinned Arab. He laboured under the delusion that he was a high-ranking politician of a neighbouring country who had a bad reputation for recklessness, even for murderous tendencies. This patient always walked round in a circle or leaned against the fence which shut off our little grass patch from the main building. When he was thus leaning, he gave the impression that he had been there for ever; his bleached discoloured clothes seemed to melt away in the sunlight, leaving visible only his once-bold Arab face. Most of what he cunningly babbled to himself, with a sardonic giggle, is unrepeatable; he indulged in long fantasies in which he cut off the sex organs of his enemies, male or female, and ate them. Sometimes he indulged in such rigmaroles as this: "It is logical that you should have first to pass the examination at Landsberg, if you want to be a Field-Marshal in England. Otherwise of course it can't happen. You wear a red-boot on the right foot, a blue one on the left. . . ."

He turned and sniggered at me, highly amused, and then

immediately in full swing, he mowed down the French with a machine gun and in the same breath he remarked on the unbridled lasciviousness of Tungus virgins. His brain was constantly busy associating the most incompatible things, it was as if he were threading necklaces in which an old shoe-polish tin dangled next to an ostrich-feather fan. With this man, one could have no sensible conversation; if he was addressed, he never listened, but either calmly went on talking or else fell silent. A fellow-prisoner told me that this "Arab", Schniemann by name, used formerly to be more sensible, and even capable of proper work. He used to go with an outside working party to a factory in the town. There he had made an attempt to escape, but had been recaptured. As he resisted his new arrest with almost animal desperation, a violent commotion broke out around him; in the course of it, somebody had trodden on his arm, and broken it. When he returned from hospital, he was as insane as he is now; his arm, which had mended badly, was no further use to him, and he always kept his hand in his pocket. This added a characteristic and unforgettable touch to his melancholy figure.

42

BEFORE I finally return to my own experiences, I must mention one man, a scintillating figure who made his appearance among us for a few brief days at the beginning of my stay here, only to disappear for ever, transferred to another asylum. On my very first day I had heard of a prisoner who because of a fight had already been eight weeks in the punishment cells on dry bread and water. If I thought of this man at all—with a shudder at the seemingly unbearable length of his solitary confinement—I pictured to myself a fellow like Liesmann, a fellow about thirty years old, with a brutal angular face, who wore a black patch over one eye, and went about the block mute and sullen. Everyone avoided him, even the most quarrelsome did not dare to start anything with Liesmann, who had a reputation for suddenly lashing out at the merest hint of an insult, and for not giving over until the other man was battered into submission.

And then Hans Hagen made his appearance in our block, a handsome healthy-looking young man of thirty, with the figure of a trained athlete, jet-black slightly wavy hair, and an ivory-coloured face of pure classical line. He had obtained from the head-nurse an entirely new outfit instead of the rags which the others were obliged to wear, and he wore his brown corduroy trousers and rush-coloured jacket as elegantly as if the best tailor had made them to measure. His every movement was swift, purposeful, beautiful. The way he spoke, and his dark eyes lit up as he did so, the manner in which he was able to impart charm and amiability to the most casual utterance was sheer delight in this place of misery.

"How can a young god like this come to be in such a hell?" I asked myself, and aloud, "A newcomer?"

"No," they answered. "That's the prisoner who was eight weeks in the punishment-cells for fighting."

I could hardly believe my ears.

Later I often walked with Hans Hagen for a few minutes along the corridor or out in the yard, and I always listened to his chatter with new delight, whether he was talking of his youthful escapades in Rochester—he had been educated for some years in England—or of his bold sailing voyages to the North Cape. By what he told me, this passion for sailing had been his downfall. He had gone on buying bigger and more beautiful yachts and apparently he had committed some insurance fraud over the last yacht, which brought him into conflict with the law. As I have said, this was the version which he quite lightly and casually told me. As I later found out, he had been rather more frank and honest with other prisoners. He was one of three sons of a merchant in Rostock, who had a very flourishing sports outfitter's business, a wealthy man who was able to give his sons a good education. But with the youngest, this same Hans, simply nothing would go right. In his schooldays certain things had happened which necessitated his hasty removal from Germany and his trip to England. There, too, he seems not to have led a particularly respectable and industrious life. He told me of his secret nocturnal trips from Rochester to the London suburbs, and when he was in a good mood he would sing me softly in a pleasant tenor voice, little songs he had picked up in bars and dance-halls there. In English of course—but still I found it delightful what pains he took to amuse me and cheer me up. Back home at Rostock, he officially devoted himself to the study of medicine, but in reality he was discovering his passion for the sea and sailing.

He bought himself his first yacht, and I doubt if it was his father who financed the purchase. Even a prosperous sports outfitters' concern cannot afford tens of thousands of marks for one of three sons, particularly as Hans Hagen merely wanted to live well on it, to make long expensive trips with his girl-friends, and never worry about money. At this time he found out how easily a good-looking and well-connected young man can do business even if he hasn't a pennyworth of working capital. He dealt in houses, sold stocks and bonds, acted as car agent and insurance broker and picked up commissions right and left. His quick, brilliant, resourceful brain enabled him readily to perceive any good business opportunity and to step in quickly. He used his power over women unscrupulously, and there were not many men who could resist his charm either.

But as the money flowed in, so his requirements increased also. They were always a step ahead of his income, and his pocket-book was always empty. But he knew only one thing: at all costs he wanted to keep on with his life of pleasure, the only life that suited him. He became more and more unscrupulous about his choice of the means by which he obtained money: he stole cars off the streets, he even stole the handbags of women as they danced with him—in short, he became a swindler and a thief. That could not go on successfully for long.

His first case was hushed up because he was the son of an influential father; the second landed him in prison, and from prison into this sad place in which he had already been living for six years.

43

Six years—I could hardly believe my ears—this young man had been living for six years in these wretched surroundings, and had retained all the flexibility and charm of youth, he still bore about him the brightness of the outside world! It was a puzzle to me, after being there only a few days I was already worn down and crushed. Since then I have thought a great deal about Hans Hagen and I believe I have discovered how he managed to remain so unalterably strong.

First, nothing penetrated him very deeply. So nothing could deeply hurt him. He lived so much on the surface, his brilliant gifts enticed him here and there, he was always busy yet he never did anything seriously. He could do everything about the place, he cut the keepers' hair in an unusually bold and elegant style, he laid bricks better than a bricklayer, he gave lessons in shorthand, English, French, Russian, he worked hard in the factory, he did carpentry, he had been looking after the pigs—he could do everything, but he did it in a brilliant offhand way, he was irresponsibility itself, nothing was durable. But the main reason for his immutability, his unconquerable youth, was that here in this death-house he lived hardly differently from outside. True, his surroundings had changed, but not Hans Hagen. If he had charmed women outside, here he charmed sick men. He did not overlook even the dullest one among them, he would not rest till a ray of his charm had touched him. He was the real king of this place, was Hans Hagen, and the authorities knew it too.

And like a king he collected his tribute—exactly as he did outside. I never saw Hans Hagen ask for anything, beg for anything. That was not necessary, to such an extent did his followers look after him. A keeper told me that while Hagen was in the punishment cell, there was a constant coming and going, every unguarded moment was taken advantage of to pass him something on the sly. There was an endless whispering at the spy-hole, whose glass had been broken so that the most precious commodity in the institution, matches, could be handed in to him. If another comrade was in the punishment cells he was forgotten, nobody thought any more about him. His reappearance was received as indifferently as his disappearance. Not so Hans Hagen. I have seen myself, often and often, how they came to him, these poorest of the poor, with hunger gnawing at their bowels. One outside-worker brought him a cucumber, another a pocketful of potatoes, here a piece of bread, there an onion, a few sprigs of parsley, carrots, windfall apples, salt, a handful of picked-up cigarette ends. In this place, these are all most precious valuables, difficult to obtain, there is none who can give out of an over-abundance, all are sacrificing what is most essential. And Hagen took everything, everything. He laughed, he thanked them, he made a joke. He could say "Thank you" so charmingly. And then he would turn his back and the giver was forgotten.

Hans Hagen had sometimes given me some of his surplus, in that swift spontaneous way that was peculiar to him. I was sitting disconsolately over my water soup, and Hagen cried: "Here, Sommer, catch!" and from the next table a piece of bread flew across to me, and he laughed heartily as I clumsily caught it; even as he laughed he had already forgotten that he had given me something precious for which I was obliged to be grateful to him. That is how he was: without memory. That is how he stands before me: without past or future, only living for today, abandoned to the moment. But it worried me that I allowed him to give me presents, that I accepted his company and his amiable chatter, without having anything to offer in exchange. For who was I, after all? A mediocre little businessman gone astray!

44

It was one of the inconceivable things about our administration that among this gang of fifty-six decrepit, bestial and criminal men, they should allow two youngsters to live, one of seventeen, the other eighteen years of age. One would have thought that this place, whose walls were constantly echoing with obscenities, curses and brawls, whose atmosphere was saturated with hatred and baseness, was anything but a suitable place for the education of youngsters, before whom a whole life lay. But they were among us, not transiently, but for good. They shared our dormitory, our table and our work. I do not doubt that they also shared our way of thinking and feeling, and if they differed somewhat from us older ones, it was that their wickedness was perhaps transfigured by the glitter of youth, but was more deliberate and calculating than ours. They were both handsome youths; the one, Kolzer by name, I shall mention later in another connection. The other, the eighteen-year-old Schmeidler, belonged to Hagen's closest circle. Also belonging to this circle were Liesmann, the gloomy taciturn fighter with the black leather patch over his right eye, and a tall, strange, somewhat Don-Quixoteish figure of twenty-nine years old, Brachowiak by name. In contrast to Hans Hagen, all these three had been in state institutions since their sixth year. They had been in orphanages and reformatories, they had been put in prison and eventually they had landed up in this place. Though they always resisted its discipline and complained about it, they felt at home in such a place, its poisonous atmosphere was their life-breath. All three had been repeatedly released on probation and all three had failed to pass the test: within five or six weeks they were back again in the hands of the law, for they shied away from any form of work and preferred to live only by stealing.

I heard with astonishment and at first disbelief that Liesmann, whom I constantly saw in the company of the scintillating Hagen, who was his most faithful friend with whom everything was shared, that Liesmann was the very one with whom Hagen had fought so savagely that he had been given eight weeks in the punishment cells. But I had to believe it, for I heard from the head-nurse himself that apart from minor brawls, Hagen had successfully fought Liesmann three times: once he had dislocated his jaw, once he had stabbed him through the hand, and this last time he had so damaged his eye that Liesmann had almost entirely lost the sight of it. And Hagen himself once pulled the black patch off Liesmann's brow, showed me the fixed and sullen-looking eye and said, "That's where I hit Hein—can you see a bit again, Heini?" with a note of touching solicitude.

"Well, it's as if I'd been looking too long at the sun," answered Liesmann placidly.

Yes, they were the best of friends, they looked after each other. Liesmann bled the weaker ones without scruple, man-handling them until they parted with their treasured scraps. They looked after each other and they fought, not just brawling but as if they were fighting to the death, impelled by a blind and furious jealousy. For the handsome little eighteen-year-old Schmeidler, the male whore, was shared by the two of them, quite peacefully as a rule; but if young George—he was nick-named "Otsche" Schmeidler—happened to favour one of them a bit more than the other, the fighting broke out. It was just like outside, it would not have been Hans Hagen if he hadn't been able to procure for himself the pleasures of love, even in this house of the dead, a dark corrupt love, but still love, with all its voluptuousness and its dangers.

This youngster with the fair wavy hair, the blue eyes, the almost Grecian profile with its straight nose and round chin, scampered about among these men of a morning in the wash-room. He would whisper in his short shirt, his slender white limbs as yet unspotted by any boils, and they turned their heads towards him, a light came into their eyes, their hearts beat faster, and in this comfortless place the day would seem not quite without comfort after all. The place was deranged by love, a flower on a muckheap; other men moved lasciviously about the fringe of this circle and dare not come nearer for fear of Liesmann's brutal strength and Hagen's cunning ju-jitsu holds. But the boy Schmeidler, the whore, did not ignore these distant mute admirers. He "kept them on the boil," he took their last bit of tobacco, for a smile he got bread, for a swift tender caress he got the best morsel from a newly-arrived food parcel. Oh, he looked after the interests of their common household, did Otsche Schmeidler, he did not allow himself merely to be kept, he contributed also. And his two friends were generous, they were men of the world, they shut one eye; in short, even the charming Hans Hagen was a pimp, nothing more nor less. He let his boy-whore run around provided that it brought something in. Have I not said that we lived in hell? Nothing was lacking in this hell, not even love, but even love was corrupt, it stank to high heaven!

45

I would never have got to know as much about these various entanglements, had I not daily sat at table beside Emil Brachowiak. I have often noticed that people prefer to make quiet silent men their confidants, and during the first week after my arrival in the asylum, I hardly spoke at all. So Brachowiak made me his confidant, he poured all his amorous troubles into my ear, he even tried to make me a sort of cupid's messenger. Many an hour we walked side by side up and down the long corridor while he talked indefatigably. I have seen him cry and I have seen him laugh with happiness.

Outside it was getting dark already, the patients leaned forlornly against the walls; when they drew on their pipes the glow burned red; in one cell, Hagen, Liesmann and Schmeidler were at their secret business; and the outcast went on talking more and more feverishly to me, whether he should disclose the whole filthy affair to the medical officer, whether he should split on them or better still write a letter to Otsche.

" 'Otsche', I'll put, 'I've done so much for you. I've given you two and a half packets of tobacco and a little gold ring I found in the factory. I know full well you gave the ring straight to Hagen, and he swapped it with one of the orderlies for a pound and a half of bacon stolen from the kitchen. But I won't complain about that if you'll be nice to me again. Since yesterday morning you've not as much as said "Good day," you don't even look at me any more. You'd better be nice to me or I'll go and split to the doctor. I'll tell the doctor everything you told me about those filthy tricks Liesmann and Hagen get up to with you.' That's what I'll put."

"If I were you, I wouldn't split," I answered. "You'll only get the worst of it."

"All right, then will you take the letter to Otsche this evening?"

But no, I didn't want to do that. I didn't want to take any active part in this affair. It didn't matter at all, for Brachowiak easily found another messenger, and next morning, he reported in a voice trembling with indignation, that Otsche Schmeidler had sent him an answer. . . .

"What sort of answer?" I asked. "Is he going to be nice again?"

"I can lick his arse," cried Brachowiak furiously. "That's the message I get from that snotty-nosed little whore. But you wait, my boy. I'm finished with you now for good and all. You're not getting anything else out of me, not another pipeful of tobacco!"

Oh, it was all right for Brachowiak to talk, I knew full well he hadn't a shred of tobacco left, Otsche had cleaned him out, and Otsche knew it too.

But what had Hagen, our king, to say to all this, that charming and amiable young man who always kept up the appearance of cleanliness at least? Emil Brachowiak was utterly without shame in his amorous troubles, he knew Hagen's relationship to Schmeidler, he constantly saw the youngster in the closest proximity to the king, Otsche himself had told him of the filthy tricks they practised with each other—but despite that Brachowiak went running to Hagen and poured out all his troubles to him, as he had to me. And Hagen listened and was kind and friendly, he spoke comfortingly and promised to act as a mediator with Schmeidler. And behind Brachowiak's back they laughed at the useless fool—oh, what a truly hellish atmosphere of baseness and deceit!

Brachowiak was a clever and industrious worker, he had to some extent a position of trust in the factory, also he often came in contact with civilian workers and knew how to flatter and to beg, in a short time he once more had tobacco.

"This time I'm not giving in, this time he won't get anything, not a pipeful!"

And Brachowiak went up and down the corridor with his long-stemmed pipe, and blew smoke into Schmeidler's face without even looking at him. Brachowiak had reported sick and was not going to work. He spent his leisure-hour with me and, lo and behold, this time Schmeidler appeared in the prison yard, Schmeidler, quite alone, without Hagen and Liesmann. A rare sight.

"I won't even look at him!" Brachowiak assured me, as we passed Schmeidler, who was sitting on the steps in the sunshine. The light summer wind moved his fair hair, he looked young, he looked fresh, he looked uncorrupted.

As we passed for the second time, Brachowiak said, "Otsche smiled at me just now."

"Hang on to yourself," I warned him. "The young lout is only after your tobacco—by the way, can you give me a bit of tobacco for a cigarette?"

"I haven't got any tobacco down here," said Brachowiak quickly. "No, he's not going to get a bit of it. He only wants to clean me out again."

But at the third time round, Schmeidler said quite amiably to us: "Shall we have a game of cards?"

And he took out of his pocket a filthy pack on which one could hardly distinguish the pips. Brachowiak was willing enough, so I did not say no either, but I nudged him and he nodded reassuringly, as if his mind was firmly made up. So we played our game of cards, Schmeidler with extraordinary luck, Brachowiak with equally remarkable ill-fortune. Schmeidler was the winner, I came second.

The youngster cried: "That'll cost you a bit of tobacco, Emil," and laughed at him, and Brachowiak took out his tobacco (which he hadn't got with him!) and generously filled the youngster's tin, while I, when I held my hand out, got barely enough for a cigarette. Then the two went round the yard, arm in arm, pressing closely together. I was forgotten. That evening, Emil Brachowiak was in tears again: Schmeidler had cleaned him right out and would have nothing more to do with him. And next day, Brachowiak really split on them, not to the medical officer, but to the head-nurse. But nothing happened, nothing at all. Why not, I do not know. The authorities had everything in their power, they could have punished the offenders, they could have separated them, they could have put the youngsters, that constant source of trouble, into other institutions. They did nothing, just as they did nothing about our hunger. I suppose it was immaterial to them how we lived and in what filth we rotted away. Of fifty-six, there were not six who would ever see freedom again. All, or nearly all, were sentenced to live in this place for ever. It was quite unimportant how they did so, that didn't matter. They had to work as long as a bit of productivity could be squeezed out of their emaciated bodies. Let them put up with it or perish, life was outside, and this was the house of the dead!

46

I RETURN now to my own experiences. It is still the day of my arrival, the leisure-hour is just over, I have formed my first impressions and made my first acquaintances, and now I stand in the long dim corridor that remains gloomy even on the brightest day. Hour after hour I wander to and fro, idle, tormented and yet dulled. I am glad when the head-nurse or a warder comes by with a patient taking washing to the store or carrying a pile of old documents. At least something is happening! What is happening does not concern me, and really nothing is happening at all, but I am diverted from myself and my uncertain fate; I may not, I cannot bear myself any longer.

Sometimes I stand by the one window that is accessible to me—the other is obstructed by the glass box—and stare out over the barb-wired walls, into freedom, which lies glittering in the sun "outside". They must be limes; they shade a highway along which cars are speeding by, I see girls in bright dresses riding on their bicycles—but I turn my head away and walk on in the gloomy corridor. Life outside tortures me, it does not belong to me any more, I am severed from it, I want to know no more about it. Drive on, all of you. May the trees wither, the sand blow over meadows and fields, there should be desert about such a death-house as this, dry dead desert.

Sometimes I go into one of the two day-rooms, either the big one or the small one, and sit there for five or ten minutes with my fellow-sufferers. Fellow-sufferers? They cannot suffer as I do, their fate has been decided already, it is the uncertainty that torments me so much.

Some sleep with their head on the table (for it is forbidden to sleep in bed), others stare dully ahead, a small youngish man, completely crooked, with a squint in both eyes (but each in a different way), and a pear-shaped head, has an incredibly dirty pack of cards in front of him, and very slowly he lays one card on the other and grins stupidly at it. One has a newspaper in front of him, but he is staring over the top of it, and one has even taken his trousers off and with a face distorted by pain he examines the suppurating and bleeding furuncles on his leg—at our meal-table!

I retire in disgust and stand in the corridor again. I read the name-plates on the cells; I read: Gothar, Gramatzki, Deutschmann, Brandt, Westfal, Burmester, Röhrig, Klinger. And as I go on I repeat them to myself, repeat them like the vocabularies I used to learn as a child: Gothar, Gramatzki, Deutschmann, Brandt . . . I go on repeating the list, till it sticks. Then I pass on to the next name-plate . . . So I learn, I pass the time, this endless time, two and a half endless hours! What are two and a half hours outside? And what are they here? Then at last the inside working parties march back to their cells, the mat-weavers and brush-makers; doors are slammed, shouts are heard, water runs in the wash-room, pipes are lit. Life, thank God, a bit of life!

And already the cry is heard: "Here comes the factory party!" And immediately after, another cry: "Food servers fall in!"

A little later we are sitting in the day-room which is now fully occupied; those who have been in the factory are asked for news, and they tell how this time they had to carry boxes weighing a hundredweight and a half, whereas yesterday the boxes only weighed one hundredweight twenty pounds. At once a furious quarrel breaks out, concerning how this difference in weight is to be explained. We do not need to worry about our food, it just eats itself, it is water with a few morsels of kohlrabi. I am still so finicky that I put these morsels, which are completely woody, beside my bowl. A great toil-worn hand reaches across the table, takes hold of the morsels and stuffs them into a wide-open mouth. Immediately a furious voice calls to me from the other side of the table.

"Why the hell do you give Jahnke your kohlrabi? The bastard stuffs everything into him that he sets eyes on!"

And Jahnke roars back furiously: "What's it to do with you what I eat, snotnose? If the new fellow gives me his kohlrabi, that's his business. Are you his keeper? Every young snotnose round here wants to act the keeper . . . !"

Fortunately, in this new quarrel in which of course others immediately join ("Shut that row, God damn you! Can't you keep quiet!"—"What's up with you?"—"He's right! We want some peace!"—"I'll shout as much as I want to!"), fortunately, in all the uproar which now arises, I am completely forgotten. But the keeper in the glass box, which has a window on to our day room, does not even lift his head at the din, he goes on calmly reading his newspaper.

The meal is over, I have managed what yesterday I had thought impossible; I have ladled into myself a whole quart of warm water. At the moment I feel satisfied. But in the night the rumbling of my stomach will teach me that I am utterly and absolutely unsatisfied. From now on, I too am to be among those who constantly visit the bucket. The head-nurse collects together all the men who are supposed to or want to see the doctor, the latter only if he approves of their intentions. From our section alone, about twenty men fall in, I am not among them.

Outside the bars which separate one corridor from the staircase, other sick men from the two buildings opposite have gathered. I count over thirty. And now "the women" march in, mostly girls, led by their wardress. They are put quite close to the wall, and the wardress keeps a sharp look-out so that none of us can exchange a word with them. But that is over seventy patients—and already it is past seven in the evening! Is the doctor going to hold his consultations till well past midnight? The outlook for me is bad. "Are there always so many?" I ask another patient.

"So many?" he answers indignantly. "It's only a few today. In this cursed place every single one is ill. But I don't report sick any more, there's no point in it."

The doctor came while I was at the other end of the corridor. I did not notice him. But that does not matter, I am not seeing him today, in any case. It is better that way, with more than seventy patients he would not have proper time for me. It is better for me to wait till some other day when things are quieter. I have to tell him my story in full detail.

The head-nurse calls: "Foot-patients first, shoes off!"

And now it starts, at a breath-taking speed. Six men at a time are ushered into the consulting room, and at the latest after one minute the first man is out, doctored and treated!

The head-nurse calls: "Shirts off, you others! Fall in, one behind the other."

The girls watch how the men slip out of their shirts. This arouses the anger of the wardress, a robust elderly person with a red face. She rushes up to one girl who has a few curls hanging at her temples, under her kerchief.

"What's this?" she cries angrily. "All you think of is men, eh? Wait, I'll show you to make yourself pretty here!" and she tears the scarf off the girl's head.

"What!" she cries indignantly. "You've been pinning curls up, have you? Haven't I told you a thousand times you've got to wear just a simple parting? I'll show you!"

And she tugged at the girl's hair, she tugged the few poor curls apart. Without a sign of protest or pain the girl patiently moved her head this way and that as her tormentor pulled her hair. But I had no time to follow this shocking incident (which I seemed to be the only one to find shocking) any further.

The head-nurse came towards me. "Quickly, Sommer, pack up your bedding and your things. You're being transferred!"

My bedding and belongings were packed into a bundle quickly enough, and I followed the keeper, who opened a cell door near the glass box. The cell was smaller than my former one, but there were only four beds in it. Fortunately one did not sleep in two tiers here. The cell was lighter and more airy too, it did not smell bad. I had decidedly bettered myself; I rightly attributed it to the doctor's influence. "Thank God, he's favourably inclined towards me," I thought. "Everything's all right." Meanwhile the head-nurse had chased an old man out of bed.

"Come on, come on, out of it, Meier," he cried. "Be a bit quick about it. You're going in Wing 2."

"Oh God!" wailed the old man; "Have I really got to move, sir? I get pushed around all the time! I've only had this bed a few weeks! And it was so peaceful in here, and such nice air...."

But the head-nurse was not inclined to listen to an old man's jeremiads.

"Out of it, Meier!" he shouted and he gave the old man a violent push. "Stop your nattering!"

With his bundle of bedding, the old man staggered out of his cell on his thin sticks of legs; his short shirt barely covering his behind.

"You can make your bed later!" said the head-nurse. "Now come with me to the doctor. He's waiting."

47

THE doctor really was waiting for me—hardly an hour had gone by and a good seventy patients had already been treated.

Dr Stiebing, in a white coat, smiled at me amiably, invited me to sit down, and even offered his hand. The head-nurse stood in the background, with watchful eyes, waiting; not a word, not a movement, did he miss. I was pleased that he saw with what discrimination the doctor treated me, this friendly greeting now, beforehand, the transfer to a better cell—he would be careful about dealing too hard with me.

"Well," said the doctor, smiling, "Now you've landed up with me, Herr Sommer. A fortnight ago we could have put you in somewhat more comfortable surroundings, my colleague Mansfeld and I. Well, well, you'll be able to bear it here. It is a well-disciplined place, you'll get your rights here. A little discipline is good for everybody, isn't it?"

He was really amiability itself. Rather touched, I thanked him for the better sleeping quarters allotted to me.

"Oh, that's all right," said the doctor. "We'll do what we can to make your stay here easier. Of course there are certain unchangeable house-rules. . . . "

He looked at me with a friendly expression of regret.

Then: "And you'll do everything you can to lighten our task, too, won't you, Herr Sommer?"

I assured the doctor of this, and asked whether he had to make a report on me.

"No, not yet," he said quickly. "I suppose they will ask me for one, but for the time being you have just been assigned here for a stay, Herr Sommer."

"But then everything will take so long!" I wailed. "Why can't you make out your report immediately? It's quite a clear affair. It's only a slight case of uttering threats, and I'm convinced that Magda, that my wife will testify that she had not really felt herself menaced by me at all. For such a small matter as that, they can't keep me here for weeks!"

I had been speaking more and more seriously and emphatically. I wanted to make it clear right away what an enormous disparity existed between my slip and my stay here.

"But, but," cried the doctor, and laid a soothing hand on my arm. "Why are you in such a hurry! First you must have a thorough rest and get quite well again . . . "

"But I am quite well," I assured him.

"No dizziness?" asked the doctor. "No sweating? No loss of appetite and then sudden hunger? No longing for alcohol?"

"I simply never think of alcohol!" I cried, shocked at such a dangerous suspicion. "I feel absolutely well!"

"Really no symptoms of de-alcoholisation then?" asked the doctor doubtfully. "Well, how is it, head-nurse? Have you noticed anything?"

I looked expectantly into the hard dark face of the head-nurse. He could not have noticed the slightest thing, of that I was sure.

"Yesterday evening," he reported, "Sommer felt an urgent hunger and demanded supper, but he only ate four or five spoonfuls of it. Lexer swore today that Sommer had a razor-blade in his pocket; we couldn't find it, but still—as a rule Lexer's information has been reliable up to now. Then, too, Sommer is very restless, he can't stay in one place for five minutes, can't occupy himself with anything, hasn't touched a newspaper . . . "

"But," I cried, indignant and shocked at such misleading information, "there's quite other reasons for all that. That has nothing to do with alcohol or the symptoms of de-alcoholisation either. Really, doctor, I never think of schnaps . . . "

The doctor and the head-nurse both smiled thinly.

"But really," I cried still more emphatically. "I have had such a shock, with my arrest and all its consequences; I'll never touch another drop of alcohol as long as I live!"

"That sounds better," said Dr Stiebing amiably, and he nodded.

"And if I only ate a little of my cabbage soup yesterday, it's merely because I'm not used to this kind of food. Certainly," I added hastily, "the cabbage soup was very good, but at home I just eat different things . . . "

They both looked at me watchfully.

"And if I've been walking up and down a bit and haven't been able to rest, it is quite explicable, in my position. Anyone who is uncertain about his whole future is bound to be restless. Anyway, everybody paces about if they have to wait a long time, you can see that in any dentist's waiting-room or police-court corridor . . . "

"All right, all right," the doctor interrupted, but I had the feeling that I had not convinced him, and that he did not find it "all right" in the least.

"And what about the razor-blade? You've quite omitted that!"

I tried not to blush—and yet. . . . No, perhaps I did not blush at all, I only imagined it. In any case I said with great firmness, "I didn't omit the razor-blade. I just didn't think any more of it. I've never had a razor-blade here. Why should I? I've got no razor. . . . "

Perhaps I pretended to be too simple, perhaps the doctor had it in mind that an accused person always protests most vigorously against a false charge. In any event, I found this preliminary discussion, in which my case was not even mentioned, full of snares and subterfuges.

I could not guess what the doctor thought of my words. Quite kindly, he said:

"In any case, I hear that it's not long ago since you first started to drink, so the effects of de-alcoholisation shouldn't be so drastic. You were previously in remand prison too . . . "

"Yes," I said, "and I worked every day in the wood-yard there—I volunteered for it—and you can ask any warder whether I didn't do as much work as anyone else, though I'm not really used to this kind of work."

"You drank quite heavily then?" asked the doctor, and he seemed disinclined to pursue enquiries about the quality of my wood-cutting. "One might say, very heavily?"

"Never more than I could stand!" I assured him. "I never staggered, sir, and I never fell about."

For a moment I was obliged to recall that scene when I tried again and again to pull myself up on to the roof-edge below Elinor's window, and kept falling back into the bushes. And immediately another scene came to mind, a scene which the medical officer himself had witnessed, when more than half-seas over, I had sat at the inn table kicking up a din with a villager just as drunk as myself, and I had nearly fallen over as I went out, and Dr Mansfeld had to help me to the car. . . .

"I shouldn't have said that," I thought desperately. "That was wrong. It detracts from my other absolutely true remarks."

I wanted to prevent the health officer from turning this over in his mind, so I continued quickly: "In any case, in that scene with my wife which they first put down as attempted murder, I was in full possession of my mental faculties. I knew perfectly well what I was doing, and I did not do a bit more than I intended. And I had had comparatively little to drink before it."

"Yes, my dear fellow," said the doctor, suddenly smiling almost sarcastically, "our two views of what constitutes a little to drink seem somewhat far removed from each other. Reckon up for me how much you had to drink every day, on an average, as far as you can remember."

I thought of Mordhorst and how he had reproved me for my foolish truthfulness in giving the magistrate such a detailed account of my consumption of liquor. I reflected whether the doctor would already have received these documents for perusal and decided that was hardly likely, since he had not yet been asked for a report. Nevertheless I decided to be very careful, not to deceive him too much, and to try to make as good an impression as possible. Till now, I had had little success with my statements, that much was clear. But everything depended on making a good impression on the doctor at the outset; once you've won a man over, it is difficult for any subsequent reports, even if quite unfavourable, to shake this good first impression. So I reflected, and arranged my testimony accordingly. I had hardly ever drunk more than a bottle a day, and mostly less. . . . What I had had to drink in the inn, I really couldn't say for sure, because I had been drinking out of small glasses, and had mixed my drinks, and also I had paid for other people, I declared. The doctor listened to my rather rambling discourse with his head in his hand, almost in silence, just occasionally throwing in a question. Finally, when I had no more to say, he said: "As I told you, no report about you has been asked for yet. We've just had this little preliminary chat, so as to get to know each other. But get the idea out of your head, Sommer (Sommer! no more 'Herr' Sommer), that your account of things can decisively influence your stay in this place. The only thing that can influence your future is your will to be strong and to resist the sort of temptations you had before. . . ."

He looked at me seriously. I am not very quick-witted, in-

223

deed I am a rather slow thinker, so I nodded eagerly in token of my will to be better. (Only ten minutes later, when I was in bed, did it become clear to me that with this phrase, the doctor had branded my statements as lies—of course he had already been handed the documents and had seen there how I had accounted for my consumption of alcohol for pretty well every day, and had put the amount much higher than I had tonight. So it was already definitely too late to make that "good first impression".)

Anyway, the doctor kindly offered me his hand and said: "Well, we'll have another talk. I'll send for you. Goodnight, Herr Sommer."

I was just about to go when the head-nurse asked: "Is Sommer to work, doctor?"

"Of course he'll work!" cried the medical officer. "Then time won't pass so slowly for him, and he won't brood. You want to work, don't you, you busy wood-cutter?"

I assured him that I had no keener wish. I had seen a lovely big garden outside the wall, perhaps I could be put to work in the nursery? I always liked gardening so much.

The doctor and his right-hand man looked at each other and then at me. They smiled rather thinly.

"No, in this early period we had better not let you work outside," said the doctor gently. "We'll have to get a bit better acquainted first . . . "

"Do you think I'd run away?" I cried indignantly. "But doctor, where could I run to, in these clothes, with no money, I wouldn't get ten miles . . . "

"Ten miles would already be too much," the doctor interrupted. "Well, nurse?"

"I think I'll put him on to brush-making, we need a man there. Lexer can instruct him."

"Lexer?" I interrupted the head-nurse, terrified. "I beg you, anyone but Lexer! If ever I hated a man, it is that disgusting yelling little beast! Everything inside me turns over with disgust, just at the sound of his voice. . . . Anything you like but, please, not Lexer!"

"Did you suffer from such violent antipathies outside, Sommer?" asked the medical officer softly. "You've hardly been twenty-four hours in the place and already you've conceived such a hatred of this harmless feeble-minded youngster."

I was embarrassed, nonplussed, I had made a mistake again.

"There are such sudden antipathies, doctor," I said. "You see a man, you just hear a voice and . . ."

"Yes, yes," he interrupted me, and suddenly he looked tired and sad. "We'll talk about all that later. Now, goodnight, Sommer!"

48

It was a defeat, an ignominious defeat, and nothing could gloss over the extent of the defeat in my mind. I was unmasked as a liar, I had symptoms of de-alcoholisation and suffered from sudden morbid antipathies. Perhaps I thought of escape. Powerless and despairing, I lay on my bed, I could have wept for shame and regret. So much thought out, so many precautions taken, and I fall into every trap like a stupid brainless youngster! And it's not at all true, what they think of me, I cry desperately to myself. I really don't think of escaping, I really have had no symptoms of de-alcoholisation, or only in the very first two or three days, and then only very slightly, and if I had lied a bit about my consumption of alcohol, it was not with the intention of deceiving the doctor. He came here with a preconceived and bad opinion of me, an opinion which did not accord with the facts, and it was a duty, an act of self-defence, for me to destroy this preconceived opinion by any means at my disposal.

But I could tell myself what I liked, the fact remained that I had suffered a heavy defeat, that in the eyes of doctor and head-keeper I was just a flighty little criminal who tried to wriggle out of the consequences of his guilt by hook or by crook.

"Guilt?" I thought. "What is this great guilt of mine? That little threat—Mordhorst told me that for uttering menaces one got three months at most! That's nothing, one couldn't count that! But they make a gigantic affair of it, they shove one in prison and in this asylum, they take the 'Herr' off my name Sommer, they give me cabbage-water for food, and they third-degree me as if I'd murdered my mother and was the lowest of human beings; I'm sure, if I could only be allowed to talk to Magda for five minutes, I could convince her; together we could confront that ridiculous prosecutor with the jutting underlip and staring eyes, and the fellow would have to stop proceedings against me immediately. But," I suddenly, painfully thought, "but it's Magda's fault as well! If she had had a little love and loyalty, as partners in marriage should for each other, she would have applied for permission to visit me long ago, she would have moved heaven and hell to get me out of this death-house! Nothing of the kind! Not even a letter has she written me. But I know how it is: she's hand in glove with the doctors. They tell her I'm well looked after here and have nothing hard to put up with, and that is enough for her, she doesn't give me another thought. She has got what she wanted, she can do what she likes with my property— that's the most important thing for her! But just wait, one of these days I'll get out of this place by hook or by crook, and then you'll see what I'm going to do...." And in a wild rage I submerged myself in fantasies of revenge. I sold the business behind her back and I gloatingly imagined to myself how one morning she would arrive at the office and in her— in my place at the boss's desk, the young proprietor of the rival concern is sitting, smiling at her ironically: "Well, Frau Sommer, come to buy a little something from me? Ten kilos of yellow Victoria peas, perhaps? A kilo of blue poppy-seeds for the Sunday cake?"

She would go red with shame and anger and desperation, and I, hidden in the big filing-cabinet, would see it all, with an exultant heart. Or I imagined how, after my release from this death-house, I would wander out into the wide world, how I would roam through foreign countries as a beggar and a tramp, and only eventually, unrecognisable to anyone, I would return to my native town.

There I would beg for a piece of bread at the door of my own house, but she would sternly refuse me. Then in the night I would hang myself from the plum tree in front of her window, with a note in my pocket to say who I was, and that I forgave her all the wrongs she had done me.... Tears of emotion at my unhappy lot came into my eyes, and these fantasies, childish as they were, did something to comfort my heart.

My companions had chatted together until it grew dark, two of them, that is—the third, an elderly man with a handsome sad face and a wonderfully-modelled high forehead, had pulled the blanket over his head immediately. Now they had all long since fallen asleep. I congratulated myself on such quiet, decent sleeping-companions. I observed that night that they had got each other to use the bucket only for the lesser business, they reserved the other function for the daytime. I felt a mild rush of gratitude towards the artful doctor who had transferred me to such improved sleeping-quarters. I was convinced that I had been put in among the most irreproachable and sanest men in the whole place. A few days passed before I found that the elderly man with the beautiful forehead and melancholy face, who bore the unusual name of *Qual*,* was a killer who had murdered his cousin for money in a most bestial way. Now, through all the torments he had undergone, first during long years in prison and then in this place, his mind was utterly confused. With him, in any case, his name was his fate, you could see that in his face.

For days on end he would remain silent and then from time to time he would talk in a high cheerful voice (yet almost toneless, and quite without resonance) of many things; of the parching Sun-god, of the glass house on Mont Blanc where the

* *Qual*, in German, means Torment.

next Ice Age would be spent, and of horse-chestnuts and acorns which were becoming edible because of some fancied reversal of sap. By this means, the authorities would be in a position to give better food, at no cost at all (as with all of us, Qual's thoughts, though confused, circled incessantly round the subject of food). At other times, Qual would fall silent again, irritable and quarrelsome, and then everybody kept out of his way. He had the reputation—probably quite unfounded—of being a cold-blooded murderer who would kill a man for a single word. I think this reputation was entirely unjustified.

I liked the murderer Qual. It made me sad when they took him off to the annexe one day, to the death-cell where most of us will end our lives. He died of tuberculosis, the deadly scourge of this death-house.

My second cell-mate was the orderly Herbst. At first I struck up a kind of friendship with him, but it soon went to pieces when he found there wasn't the slightest thing to be got out of me. Herbst, a young fellow of twenty-five, who had already been in this place five years and formerly had served a two-year sentence in a reformatory, was really a butcher by trade. He was a big sturdy fellow with a long fat face, almost dead staring eyes, and sandy hair which he brushed and combed for at least a quarter of an hour every morning, to the keen, but prudently suppressed, anger of the rest of us, because he was always standing in our way in the narrow cell. Herbst's beard was a flaming red, before it came under the clippers of a Saturday (the clippers were a shaving machine used in place of the forbidden razor-blades). This gave rise to many un-flattering remarks about the character of our mess-room orderly, remarks that unfortunately were only too just. Herbst was utterly unscrupulous in the way he allowed him-self to take tobacco, food, soap, fruit, on the sly from all sides —without ever a thought of giving anything in return. The

229

man who gave him a whole handful of tobacco one day, would the next day be refused a few crumbs to chew on.

I soon learned to watch keenly whose plate the orderly filled most amply. In a place where hunger rules pitilessly, the man who serves the food enjoys an easy superiority. Of course it was strictly forbidden, by rights, for the orderly to serve out the food himself, that was part of the keeper's duties. But the keepers had to do a great deal of running about, and in any case they did not care. In this place an angel from heaven could come down and dish out the food and there would still be complaints. So everything went its old way, and all the time orderly Herbst got fatter on it. His best business was done with cutting and spreading bread. I have already said that a keeper was supposed to supervise this, but Herbst availed himself of the keeper's every momentary absence to steal bread, margarine, jam. Since all these articles were carefully weighed out so much per head, he was obliged to shorten our rations accordingly. But if he only took ten grammes from each of fifty-six men, that meant he had already acquired more than a pound of bread, and on a pound of bread a man can eat his fill! The bread he thus obtained, the fat man either ate, or exchanged for tobacco when he needed some badly, but generally it found its way to his "friend" Kolzer, whom I have already briefly mentioned as being one of the two youngsters who trailed a whiff of corrupt love among us older men. Kolzer was not a whore like young Schmeidler, who sold himself to anybody, he was faithful to his friend Herbst. Herbst ruled him with a rod of iron, often beat him whenever he had, in Herbst's opinion, committed some stupidity or other, but he fed him to bursting point and kept a watchful eye on him. Kolzer, a big strong youngster with ash-blond hair, had a not unhandsome face, which however gave an impression of stupidity and lifelessness. He was very feeble-minded, and could neither read nor write, but under the tireless efforts of his friend, he had at least learned to play Lotto. Yet, however undeveloped Kolzer's mind might be, the youngster knew very well how to assert himself in our block, and in particular, how to avoid work for long periods. He always had small unpainful injuries or slight temperatures that made it impossible for him to work. On this account, a perpetual ill-humour prevailed among the patients, and they felt just the same towards Schmeidler.

"Those hefty young louts sit around the place while the worn-out old men have to do the work."

That was indeed true, but Kolzer had a powerful mediator in the person of his friend Herbst who was constantly in and out of the glass box, and was the head-nurse's trusted news-carrier. So Kolzer was fed on bread and jam, and as no man can ever isolate himself in this place, he was often surprised by other patients in the act of stuffing himself with stolen food.

"Kolzer was eating bread in the closet again today, that thick with butter!" (In this place, margarine is always called "butter".) Then Herbst would be in a fury with the informer. Called to account by the head-nurse, he would declare that he had only given Kolzer the crumbs from the bread-cutting, perhaps there had been a broken-off corner of a slice among them, and Kolzer had scraped the margarine off the wrapping-paper. . . . Moreover, if these complaints went on, he would chuck the job up and go back to the factory. Let others see if they could fill his job better. He had—and here his voice took on a wailing, whining tone—he had always been decent and honest. But in this bandit-ridden place that was just what a man couldn't be! No, he'd had enough of it, now he was going back to the factory. . . .

Then the keepers would speak soothingly to him, and he would graciously stay. He had his advantages: he looked after himself, he was clean, and he was quite unscrupulous about informing the keepers of everything. But to his comrades Herbst did not whine when he was informed on. In his rage against such accusations, he lost all self-control, he would scream at the others, white in the face, and he never forgave such insults to his "honesty". He was devilish careful of getting into fights. Previously he had often been in the punishment cells on account of his brutal pugnacity, but the medical officer had made it clear to him that he could never reckon on release if he could not learn to control himself. And Herbst wanted his release at all costs. He had spent the seven most decisive years of his short life behind bars. Release was his great hope. For this release he had made the greatest sacrifice: he had voluntarily been castrated. Herbst had been sentenced for sexual offences against young boys, and he had been made to understand that he could never count on freedom unless he agreed to be castrated. For a year and a half the young man had wrestled with himself and finally he had consented. At the time when I was admitted, it was barely half a year, perhaps only three months since his castration. Already he was getting fat, his face looked puffy and unhealthily pale. His eyes seemed disconsolate. But he hoped for his release from day to day, the medical officer had endorsed his application, they all told him. He had steeled himself to this terrible expedient, this castration, and still he was not free. He waited from day to day, from week to week, but the longed-for decision from the Attorney-General did not come. Sometimes Herbst would rage: they'd properly done him, the doctor and the head-keeper, they'd fooled him all right! Now he'd got his testicles off, and for what? For nothing, except so that the high-ups could laugh at him!

Meanwhile, strangely enough, this castration had not altered his feelings for Kolzer in the least. Kolzer remained his friend as before, his only associate, his sugar-baby. He lived for him, he thought only of him. If the youngster had a slight temperature in the evening, Herbst would not take part in our bed-time conversations by so much as a word; he would pull the blanket over his head, but he did not sleep. Well, perhaps Kolzer noticed that in some ways Herbst's feelings for him had changed, but we could see none of it.

Of everybody in the place, Herbst most hated a prisoner named Buck, a cobbler, a vain, stupid, conspiratorial fellow who had the same tendencies as Herbst. And when the cobbler had informed on young Kolzer one evening for illicit bread-eating, Herbst, probably driven off his head by his long, vain wait for release, fell on this Buck and beat him to pulp.

At the medical officer's next visit, he was summoned before the doctor and informed that his release, which had already been granted by the Attorney-General, could not now take place, since by fighting in this way he had shown himself to be completely lacking in self-control. Along with the rest of the inmates, I doubt whether Herbst would really have been released, or whether this was not a pretext of the doctor's to wriggle out of a promise, whose fulfilment had become very difficult owing to the Attorney-General's attitude. In any case, instead of his longed-for freedom, Herbst first got fourteen days in the punishment cells, and then returned to his old job of orderly. He was a bad character and yet I had to admire the way in which he took this dreadful disappointment. He never said another word about release, he did his work as quickly, cleanly, and dishonestly as before, he lived only for the institution and its routine.

49

OF MY third cell-mate, Holz by name, I have little enough to report. He was a strong young man of about thirty—looking younger than his years, and one might have thought the little fair moustache under his nose coquettish, had it not been that his immeasurably sad face forbade any thought of coquetry. He had only been some six months in the institution, but he had come straight from a convict prison, where he had spent six years.

As Qual was either silent or else talked nonsense, and as Herbst could only talk about himself, his friend, or his hated fellow-prisoners, Holz was the one I chatted with for the two hours between half-past seven and half-past nine when we usually kept ourselves awake in order not to wake up too early in the morning. Mostly it was I who talked, often of my former life, for it was essential to me to impress on one man, at least, the fact that in my own circle, I had once been an important and respected man. Or I told him of the worries and anxieties which now obsessed me, and it would have been better if I had paid more attention to Holz's simple advice: "You want to crawl to your wife, Sommer," he often warned me. "Don't rely on your brains and some legal tricks, the others are better than you at that. I know how they can play about with simple people—and you're only a simple fellow too, Sommer. The doctor will always get you tied up—and then it'll be the Public Prosecutor's turn! Agree to any conditions your wife makes, give up your property even, what's the odds, only see that you get out of this hole! You don't know yet what it's like to be shut away for a long period. Write to her, Sommer, write to her immediately, tomorrow afternoon!"

So said Holz in his quiet even and toneless voice. Occasionally he would talk of himself. But never of his past life at liberty, of this I only found out that he was born and brought up in Hamburg. What his parents were, what he had learnt, what crimes (and they must have been serious crimes!) had earned him such a long gaol sentence, I do not know. I believe a warder once told me that Holz had formerly been a celebrated burglar. I can hardly believe it. He was so quiet, so simple, without any initiative or protest, I simply cannot credit him with sufficient energy for this dangerous calling, requiring as it does considerable presence of mind and an ability for making quick decisions. But of course it is always possible that his long stay in prison had completely changed him.

"I was six years in gaol without once being punished," he told me on one occasion.

Simply as he said it, the words had a ring of pride. He liked best to talk of his time in prison. He told me about his work, he recounted in full detail how he had begun by weaving material for mattresses, and had progressed to shirt-material. Then he had been put on to knitting stockings on the "flat machine"—I could hardly imagine what a flat machine was, even after I discovered that there was also a "round machine" for knitting stockings.

Then came Holz's best time in gaol; he became a washer-up in the kitchen. Here he had as much to eat as he wanted, was in the company of his comrades, and even got to see women at least once a day. These women came from the nearby women's prison to fetch food. Despite all precautions, glances and notes were exchanged and they even managed to pass bread, sausage and margarine to the women. Holz assured me that he only did what all his companions among the kitchen-staff did, but when the affair came to light they put the entire blame on him, and he was taken out of the kitchen. Only his good conduct saved him from the punishment cells. A horrible year ensued: Holz had to pick oakum in a solitary cell—and at the mention of this task how very clearly I recalled Magda's arrangement with the prison administration, and my journey to Hamburg. Eventually Holz, being considered not liable to escape, was put on to outside work, and the prison cell only saw him at bed-time, he worked outside the whole day through, in the open fields, or in the sawmill in winter-time. Holz liked to talk of all these simple things. He still knew every task that had been allotted to him; strands which had given him trouble in picking he could still describe with the same fresh anger he must have felt in his solitary cell.

But Holz's speciality was his disquisitions on food. Since everybody was always hungry, they constantly talked about food, probably it was all they thought of. Talking of food was a kind of mania, it only made the pangs of our hunger worse, but we could never leave off. In this Holz was an absolute master. Not that he thought up any refined meals to make our mouths water, no, his descriptions were of a biblical plainness. The meals he described were simply the same as those a com-mon labourer eats, they were the meals he got in the convict prison. His head, never used for deep thinking, was sufficiently clear for him to tell me of any slight change in the usually constant prison menu; he still knew the ups and downs of the bread ration; the number of potatoes a prisoner under punish-ment is entitled to at midday instead of bread, and the extra allocation of bread, sausage and cheese for overtime and land-workers. He still knew all the Christmas extras, and he was most eloquent when he described how a farmer, pleased at a good piece of mowing, had given the convict-party pieces of bread spread thick with "good butter" or dripping, and five cigarettes per man as well. Each experience of this kind had engraved itself deep in his memory, and even today his voice trembled as he described how his stomach had not been able to stand the unwonted rich food, and he had brought it all up again. Holz's accounts of food were as simple as that, yet I always liked to hear them over and over again, they were so moving! But each time, it struck us that a convict got about twice as much to eat as an institution inmate.

"There, you can see," Holz would say, "how they rob us! But what can you do? A donkey is there to carry turnips and get beaten, and we're worse off than a donkey, because he is worth a few marks whereas with us, they're glad when we're dead."

Holz would say such things without any reproach, without bitterness even. For him, they were the matter-of-fact evidences of the unalterable way of the world.

In the asylum, Holz enjoyed a good reputation, both among the keepers and the prisoners. Here too he had immediately been put on to outside work without any probationary period, he worked in a gravel pit, for a building contractor. There he came into contact with many "civilians," and had all kinds of things given him. He always had a couple of matches to spare for a friend, or a little onion, and he was the much-envied possessor of a glass containing salt, and of nutmeg and pepper. With these, he beautified his water-soup. From an old sardine tin which he found, he made a grater by punching holes in the bottom with a nail, and with this he would grate parsley-roots, celery-roots, carrots, raw potatoes even, if his hunger was very keen. With all these trifles, which a man "outside" would take entirely for granted, he garnished his plain life, and brought a little joy into it, and always had something to look forward to. He never joined in any game, either because he could not play or did not want to. He never read a newspaper, and only listened to the lightest dance-music on the radio.

237

"That cheers me up!" he would say then. A little light would come into his eyes, and he would smile, a rare and touching smile. All in all, a modest courageous man—I am glad that I never seriously tried to find out about his crime, I do not want to blacken this picture.

50

THESE were the three companions with whom I shared the cell that first night, to whose heavy breathing I listened, while shame, remorse and anger shook my heart. Outside the window stood the night, sometimes I raised my head and saw a few stars twinkling; I read a poem about them once, how they have been looking down for thousands of years, with the same cool glitter, on human joy and human sorrow. At the time, it had not touched me, but now it did, and I wondered whether the stars had ever witnessed such a desperate, so foolishly-occasioned sorrow as that which had overtaken me. It seemed almost impossible. And as the night-hours slowly dragged on, one after the other, from chime to chime, towards the new morning, I thought more leniently of Magda and the cunning doctor, and I swore to myself once again that next time I would be shrewder and more truthful. I convinced myself that nothing was lost yet, and I imagined long conversations with the doctor, in which I displayed a rare wit and a charming candour.

Eventually—an hour or so before unlocking-time—I really fell asleep. In my dream I was in my home town, I went through its streets and alleys, I saw many friends and acquaintances but they did not see me and passed by me without a greeting. Eventually I saw Magda sitting on that bench that is associated with our earliest schoolday friendship. I went towards her and sat down beside her. But she did not notice me. I wanted to touch her dress, I reached out my hand, but I could not grasp her dress. I tried to speak to her, and I did speak too, but my voice made no sound, I could not hear it, and Magda could not hear it either. Then I realised with a sharp terror that I was only a shadow wandering among the living, that I was dead. I was so terrified that I awoke—the head-nurse's key was rattling in the lock and his voice cried "Get up!"

Yes, a new morning was beginning and now I was no longer a guest in the death-house, instead I was enrolled in the ranks with the others, like all of them I whiled my gloomy hours away here. They made no more fuss of me, they spoke to me, and then they began to quarrel with me, in the washroom they shoved me away from the basins, and sneered at me when I tried to keep my fingernails clean with a sharpened stick.

"Look at him! What's he doing that for? He's as deep in the mud as we are!" And I made my little deals like them. I saved a slice of bread from my roaring hunger and traded it for a few crumbs of tobacco, and the first time I was cheated, there was very little tobacco, and a great deal of dried rose-leaves mixed in it. Once, too—I will confess—I stole from our orderly Herbst two slices of bread thickly spread with butter, which he had hidden under his bolster. But I was so excited, that I neither enjoyed them, nor did they agree with me. That is the only thing I ever directly stole. I am a weak man, I know that now, but I am no thief. My fear is always greater than my appetite, and in that I am weak too.

And on this first day, when the order to "Fall in" sounded, I lined up with the others, enrolled among them, I had no advantage now over any of them. A keeper came and took me to a single cell in which there was no bed, only a table, a stool, and a number of different working materials, at which I stared with anxious and wondering eyes, convinced that such a clumsy man as I would never in my life be able to learn such strange work. I saw the ready-cut brush- and broom-holders, and hair bristles, the rice-straw and millet and fibre for the various kinds of brushes and brooms, which I was to learn to make. I saw rolls of thick and thin wire, and a knife—no, I would never learn it! Nobody came, I was shut in my cell— now that I had so urgently begged the doctor to deliver me from Lexer, was I to make brushes without my instructor? I tried it, I seized a few bristles and tried to fasten them in the holes which were already bored. But they were too few, and they fell out again. The next time I took more, but now it was too many and when I tried to force them into the holes, some broke and the others fell to the floor. I bent down and quickly tried to tidy up the mess, the key rattled again, and in sprang little Lexer with his discoloured fangs, and seized me by the breast and cried shrilly: "What did you do with that razor-blade? You're not going to shit on me, Sommer!"

I tore myself away furiously and cried: "Keep your hands off me, I tell you! What have your lying tales got to do with me?"

The little scoundrel looked at me for a moment, astonished and silenced, then he laughed again in an ugly way and said: "All right, just as you like. But one day, I'm going to shit on you!" (However he has mostly let me alone since then, as I have said.) And suddenly changing, he asked: "Haven't you got a chew of tobacco for me, Sommer, just a little one?"

I had none, and I told him so, and he said angrily: "There is nothing to be done with you. What did they want to shove a fellow like you in here for? Hang the wire up on the stand. No, not the thick wire, you ox, you're supposed to make hand-brushes first, out of good bristle, they're the easiest. Take the fine wire. Two hundred holes a day is your task for the first week, the work inspector will tell you, and if you don't do it they put you in the cooler with the hard bed and make you get a move on! I can do a thousand holes a day, two thousand when I want to, but I don't. Why should I? So the fat boys can make more out of us? We'd still have to go hungry! Look, first you pull the wire through the hole like this, so it makes a loop, and then you stick the bristles in, just as many as you can pick up with two fingers, that's just right. And now you pull the loop tight, and there's your bristles already fixed! That's the whole knack, a kid could learn it in five minutes, and now you do it and show you can do as much as a kid!"

And while Lexer had been breathlessly declaiming all this in his shrill voice so that the spittle stood on his lips, I had been watching with astonishment how his dirty fingers with their bitten nails had drawn the fine wire through the hole with incredible dexterity, had seized just enough bristles to fit exactly into the hole without any space between, and finally had gently and quickly pulled the loop tight. As he did it, it really seemed childishly simple to me too. But what happened when I tried this simple thing myself? My wire would not go into the hole, it buckled instead of making a loop, and I picked up too few or too many bristles, and scattered them on the floor. Meantime Lexer was abusing me ceaselessly and he pushed me and nudged me and splashed me with his spittle, till I threw the brush down and cried again furiously: "Leave me alone, I tell you!"

So we worked the whole morning, I absolutely desperate over my clumsiness, and convinced I would never learn, and he all the time getting shriller, more triumphant, more over-bearing. At the end of the morning we had finished only one single brush, of eighty holes, and it did not look right, as even I could see.

"Stick this on the rubbish-heap yourself, Sommer!" yelled Lexer. "Pull the plug on it before the work inspector gets to see it, or he'll put you under punishment for wasting material!

I'm not coming back into this stinking hole this afternoon. You know now how it's supposed to be done, and if you don't do it, that's your look-out, you'll have to answer for it. I'm not going to have anything to do with it!"

So after five hours I was free of my disgusting instructor and I could have saved myself that sudden outburst of antipathy that had been so ill-received by the doctor. But I was absolutely in despair over my brush-making that afternoon, and by evening I had not finished more than thirty-seven holes, and those badly done. That night for once I did not brood over myself and my adverse fate and Magda and the medical officer, but only about brush-making. But this must have been far more welcome to my head, for I fell asleep over it, and for the first time I had a fairly good night.

51

THE days went by, one after another, and one day, before I had expected, I was a tolerable brush-maker. I had learned it, I made nail-brushes and hand-brushes and hair-brushes and dairy-brushes and windowsill-brushes. I could make brooms too, millet brooms and fine hair brooms. Eventually I learnt to make shaving-brushes and dusting-brushes and all kinds of paint-brushes. My fingers were now as skilled as Lexer's, they took up just as many bristles as were necessary, neither more nor less, and the wire gave me no more trouble. Now when I met Lexer in the leisure-hour and he shouted at me in his shrill voice: "Well, Sommer, how many have you done?" I would answer: "Eight hundred holes," or: "a thousand," or even: "eleven hundred."

Then Lexer would pull an angry face and yell: "Are you trying to suck up to the bosses? You won't get any better grub than the rest of us, you arse-creeper!"

But I did not work so hard in order to curry favour, I worked for my own satisfaction. Work passed the time for me; before I expected it, the key would rattle and the keeper's voice cried: "Lunch-time!"

The days, long as they sometimes seemed to be individually, went quickly enough: a week, a month had passed, I said to myself: "Now I've been here a month already, now two, now nearly three. . . ."

Now that my hands did the work of their own accord, now that I no longer had to think and worry about it all the time, my mind was free to reflect and brood on my own fate. But work imparted quite a different tone even to this brooding. Sometimes I stood for a while by the window and looked out over the country, in which they were already cutting the corn, then bringing it in, then ploughing the stubble, then mowing the hay. I had a good bright cell which, so they told me, kept warm even in winter. I looked out, and when my heart plagued and urged me to get out into freedom again, it was probably the work which made me say to myself: "Patience, it'll all come right. For the time being, let's get on with finishing this lot of washing-up brushes!"

Yes, I enjoyed my work. It was humble work that, sure enough, any child and almost any of my feeble-minded companions could have done, but there is always consolation in a job well done, however insignificant it may be.

I had no fear of the punishment-cells now, nor of the work inspector; he occasionally came into my cell to take the finished work away, and he never said a hard word to me, but often: "Good, good, Sommer." Or perhaps: "You needn't do more than your quota, Sommer, it's not necessary."

And once he gave me a crust with jam on. When my first month's work was finished, I lined up with the other workers outside the glass box and drew the tobacco which had been bought out of my "wages" (four pfennigs a day, one mark a month), namely, one packet of fine-cut and one packet of shag. Half the shag I swapped for a little pipe, for I did not want to roll cigarettes in newspaper like the others, it always either blazed up or else it charred and tasted horrible. The bowl of my pipe was quite small, it only held enough tobacco for ten or twelve pulls; that was fine, I could have five smokes a day and still last the whole month. Not that first month though, for I was still foolish and let myself be talked out of some of it, and lent some which I never saw again. I learnt, too, the dread which all property-owners have of thieves; nothing in the cells was safe from them, however cleverly it might be hidden. Constantly the agonised cry echoed through the building: "They've pinched my tobacco!"

So we were obliged to carry all our belongings about with us in our pockets, even the spoon which was our only eating utensil, much to the annoyance of the head-keeper, who complained of all the bulges in our clothes. I got myself a small box in which I kept all my possessions, a little salt, perhaps a saved-up piece of bread, my pipe and tobacco. I always had this by me, in the mess-room and the lavatory, in bed, and even on my visits to the doctor. Later, the kindly Qual who was working in the carpenter's shop, made me a little wooden box with a sliding lid and a handle of string, and would take nothing for it. Yes, now I was really enrolled, I belonged, and to tell the truth, after those first few weeks of getting used to the place, I did not feel too bad about it. I became accustomed to starvation, constant quarrels, bad air and boils, and many of my companions who were unresponsive and dull I just did not notice any more. I belonged; and yet I did not quite belong, I was only "provisionally admitted", and later I was merely "pending report". One day, my hearing would be held, I would serve my sentence for uttering threats, and then—I hope, I hope!—I would be able to return to freedom. What I was going to do there, I did not know. It seemed fairly certain to me that I would not go home to Magda, nor did I want to work in my old business again.

The time I spent in my cell, this constant isolation, had made me rather shy of my fellow-men, I preferred to be in the narrow room among my brushes, and I thought with aversion of the noisy crowded streets of my home town. I had the notion of going to some quiet village and spending the evening of my life there as an unknown, rapidly-ageing man, in a quiet room in which I could go on making brushes. . . .

246

I imagined something of the sort. Yes, a little joy had come back to me, an almost cosy contentment filled me—this time is best compared with the time I spent in the wood-yard of the remand prison. True, Mordhorst was lacking here but I did not really miss him. Mordhorst had always been driving on, complaining and agitating—and now I was all for peace. This place was horrible, with its filth and meanness and envy, but that was how it was, and what was the use of rebelling against it? We prisoners, we patients, were not worth it.

At the end of the second month I swapped my whole packet of fine-cut tobacco for a rimmed magnifying glass and now I could always light my pipe, even in my work-cell, provided the sun was shining. I imagined myself richer and happier than ever before when I leaned by my window and smoked my little pipe. I felt I had never enjoyed my life so deeply or been so happy as here in my warm cell. Perhaps the contentment of my cell-mate Holz, his gift for extracting pleasure from the slightest things, had already affected me.

52

In the quiet peacefulness of those days, my interviews with the doctor were the only disturbing thing, and their effect lasted but a few days at most, before I had become completely at ease again and returned to my calm and agreeable condition. On the whole the interviews did not go favourably for me, though none were as bad as that first one. Unfortunately it was quite impossible for me to behave naturally with him, in my dealings with him I never achieved that freedom and self-assurance which, outside, would have been so much a matter of course for me. I was always oppressed by a dark sense of guilt, as if I had at all costs to hide something from him. I was never quite free of my fear of his hidden cunning and trickery; at the most innocent question I was hunted by one thought: "What's he trying to trip me with now?"

I never thought of him as the helpful doctor, only as the ally of the Public Prosecutor who in a confused and difficult moment had charged me with the attempted murder of my wife, and who would do anything to keep me inside these walls.

Whenever I really managed to overcome my feelings, and to tell the doctor what moved my heart, it unfailingly ended in disappointment. For instance, one day I told him quite freely about my changed plans for the future, how I was going to retire to some quiet village and just live by brush-making. I had expected to get the doctor's approval of this plan, his praise even, and I was astonished and disappointed beyond measure when he vigorously shook his head and said: "Those are just fantasies, you're pulling the wool over your own eyes. You can't live like that, and you don't want to. You need your fellow-men, and above all, Sommer, you need a helping and guiding hand. No, that only comes from that quite unwarranted aversion of yours to your wife. Get the idea out of your head that your wife wants to harm you. You are the one who has wronged her and if your wife weren't such a decent sort she would have every reason for being a bit spiteful towards you. But she hasn't given a single unfavourable word of evidence against you, she tries to excuse you all the time! And here you tell me you don't want to live and work with her any longer! What a fellow you are, Sommer! Can't you see anything as it really is? Must you always invent some rigmarole?"

Naturally I was bewildered and indignant at this unwarranted attack; as Magda had not written me a line and never made any attempt to see me, I quite justifiably assumed that I was irksome to her, that she considered me dead and buried. And, as is the custom, she spoke no ill of the dead. But it was decent of me to keep quietly out of her way, to make no trouble for her, to leave her in full possession of my property. That the doctor refused to acknowledge my generosity, and instead assailed me with hard spiteful words, proved to me how prejudiced he was against me, and that made me keep my mouth shut all the tighter in future, made me still more reticent and shy. Really he was nothing but my enemy, a pitiless enemy who tried by all the means at his disposal to outwit me and who unscrupulously used his weight as head of the institution against me. The other prisoners had been right when they constantly warned me of him.

"Don't trust that Stiebing! He's friendly to your face, but behind your back he makes a report about you so you never get out of this hole alive!"

They were right.

During these few weeks, the doctor did not often send for me, and his demands on me did not become more frequent after he informed me that he had now been asked to prepare my report. Quite the reverse, in fact, another proof that he had a preconceived opinion about me, and did not want to find out anything further. In general, unless there was something specially urgent, the medical officer visited the institution twice a week, every Tuesday and Thursday evening. But I was sent for much more rarely, hardly once a week. Of course I rather welcomed this, since every visit was, as I have said, a torture that took me days to recover from. But these rare summonses showed me, too, how lightly he took this report on which the fate of my whole life depended. Yet in itself, my case was a particularly interesting one for a psychiatrist. In education, I was head and shoulders above the other inmates, I had achieved something in my lifetime, I was a respected man—and now I was in this death-house. The medical officer must have been able to see there was more in me than in the others, I had more to lose, I was more sensitive, too, and more prone to suffering than these utterly dull, stupid fellows. But no, he treated me like any Tom, Dick or Harry, he was often quite rude to me, called me an incorrigible liar and romancer! I had every reason to mistrust him and to be on my guard. When he upbraided me for my lack of frankness, that was just one of his baseless charges, to which I remained completely silent.

53

A CHANGE in my relations to the doctor only came when he visited me in my cell one day at an unusual hour—early in the afternoon, in fact. I had just been smoking, which is forbidden in the work-cells, but he made no comment on the tobacco-laden atmosphere, even although he usually insisted on a strict observance of the regulations. That day, he was not wearing his light doctor's overall, and was without his eternal shadow, the head-nurse. For a moment Dr Stiebing looked at my work and then asked absently: "Well, how are you getting on with the brush-making, Sommer?"

"Quite well, doctor," I answered. "I think the work-inspector is pleased with me."

He nodded, still rather absently, my good work did not seem to interest him much. He reached in his pocket, took out a silver cigarette case, and then he did something that completely astonished me, that almost bowled me over: he offered me the case.

I looked at him disbelievingly, and a thin smile lay on his face as he said: "You can quite safely take one, Sommer, if your doctor offers it to you."

He even gave me a light first, and then stood for a moment calmly smoking under the high-set cell-window, in silence.

Then he said: "I had a long talk about you yesterday with your wife, Herr Sommer. I had asked her to come in and see me some time, and yesterday she came."

I did not answer, I only looked at him, my heart hammered;

it moved me, it shook me that this man had been with Magda just yesterday. I could not speak, I think I was trembling in every limb.

"Yes," said the doctor thoughtfully. "I got your wife to go over everything again, from the very beginning of your marriage, up to that unfortunate evening. A psychiatrist hears much more from relatives than they themselves would guess."

A wave of furious indignation began to rise in me. "So you've been trying to trick Magda too, and very likely have tricked her," I thought. "Magda is so innocent, she has no notion what sort of man you are!"

But the wave ebbed away again.

He said: "On the whole, I have a not unfavourable impression from this account of your wife's. I really think it is possible we may be able to do something with you, Sommer. You have a very brave and efficient wife. . . ."

Again I felt on the defensive: I would have preferred that the doctor had used some other word than "efficient" in connection with Magda.

"Yes, Sommer, of course I can't say anything definite just yet, I'll have to keep you here under observation for a few weeks more. But if you go on behaving quietly and working hard, and if nothing special happens . . ."

"Nothing special will happen, doctor," I cried excitedly, "I'll go on behaving quietly and working hard . . ."

The doctor smiled again, and in that very moment when he was being so kind to me, I did not like his superior smile at all.

"Well," he said, "we keep all temptations away from you here, Sommer! To behave yourself here means nothing much. You have to be sure that you can resist every temptation outside, particularly alcohol . . ."

"I'll never touch alcohol again," I assured him. "I decided that long ago. Not even a glass of beer. I'm going to be a total abstainer, I give you my firm promise on that, doctor."

"Oh Sommer," he said sadly, "you'd better not promise me anything, what sort of promises do you think I get to hear, when people want to get out of this place? And three months outside, one month even, and one man's stealing again, the other drinking. No, I don't think anything of promises—I've been disappointed too often."

"But I really have changed," I said and for the first time I could speak quite frankly to the doctor. "I would never have believed that it could happen to me. I thought I could do anything I liked, and Magda spoilt me, too, in that respect. But now that I've seen what has come from my drinking, this is going to be a lesson to me for ever. When I am tempted, and I look back on the weeks and months in this place . . ."

I shuddered. The medical officer watched me attentively.

"That was honestly spoken, Sommer," he said at last. "If this experience has given you such a shock that it has quite cured you of drinking, then we really can take a chance on it. But now you'll have to try to put your attitude towards your wife in order as well. You're an easily-offended man, Herr Sommer, but I must tell you quite frankly that in your marriage, your wife is the guiding hand, the superior partner. She's your good angel, Sommer, and when you drifted away from her, you fell. So get used to the idea that your wife only has the best intentions towards you, subordinate yourself to her a little. . . . There's nothing to be ashamed of in that, it doesn't make a henpecked husband of you. It's a good thing when the weaker one lets himself be sheltered and guided by the stronger. . . ."

So the doctor went on talking to me for a long time. It was not easy for me to hear him out without contradiction. It really was not quite as he imagined. Certainly Magda was efficient, but ever since we owned the house, I had managed the business perfectly well without her. True, lately things had not gone so well as before, but that was due to other causes, a few unfortunate accidents, not to my bad management. But anyway, once I got out of this accursed place, I would find my feet again. Let Magda be the guiding hand, I wouldn't make any trouble for her. So I kept silent and I was reconciled to my new position *vis à vis* Magda by the thought that she had spoken so well of me to the doctor. So she still loved me!

"So," said the doctor finally, "I don't promise you anything definite, I can't do so. In let's say three or four weeks' time I shall present my report, then the court will arrange your hearing, you will get a light sentence, perhaps four weeks, perhaps only fourteen days. . . . "

"So little?" I cried in astonishment.

"Well, you had better ask a lawyer about that, I don't want to raise any false hopes. I'm only a doctor. And then when you are at liberty again. . . . "

"I shall always think of this place, doctor, I promise you!" I concluded.

54

This visit altered at one stroke my thoughts, my feelings, my whole life. Suddenly I saw the most recent past through quite different eyes: I had not been living in an almost comfortable calm and self-sufficiency, but in a paralysis of the will, in almost complete hopelessness, in apathy. Now I understood for the first time how slight my hopes had been of getting out of this dreadful place, how near I had been to renouncing life. Holz's joy in the little things of life seemed cheap and stupid to me and of an evening I bored the patient fellow with long harangues about all the things I was going to do after my release. For I intended to be very active. Though the doctor had asked my pardon for his frankness, I could not forgive his remarks about Magda's superior efficiency. The more I thought about it, the falser it seemed. The moment I was out, I would show him and Magda and the whole world how efficient I could be. And I pestered the good-natured Holz with long descriptions of the opportunities offered by the market produce business, opportunities which I, of course, was going to seize on and exploit as quick as lightning. In vain he warned me out of his long experience.

"Sommer, you're not out yet! Don't make too many plans! You never know what might happen yet!"

I cried: "What could happen now? It's up to me entirely, and I'm sure of myself."

In my work at brush-making I had changed, too. It wasn't that my work was bad, my hands couldn't do that now, they could manage without any conscious guidance, and my productivity hardly fell off, either. But I worked now by fits and starts. I would stand half the day at my cell-window, looking for hours on end at the quickly scudding clouds in the sky, enjoying the meadows, the cattle, the woods, and smiling after the girls who raced by on their bicycles. Soon I would belong to all this again, I would be part of the world, no more kept away from it and already a living corpse. Then again I would apply myself to my brush-making with a burning zeal. The work simply flew through my hands, every gesture was just right, in two hours I had finished the finest nail-brush. Sometimes as I worked, I thought with longing of Magda and I heartily wished she could see me at work for once. I could be efficient too, extraordinarily efficient! Even my attitude to my workmates had considerably changed since this interview. If I had avoided them up to now, and never interfered in their quarrels, and left them all to go their own way however disgusting it might be, my present good mood made it possible for me to take part in their conversations, and even on one occasion to call out to a disagreeable fellow: "Thiede, don't lick the table with your tongue! If the gravy's been spilt, use your spoon!"

I can't say that my fellow-sufferers took very kindly to this lively change in my bearing. My witty remarks were mostly received in deep gloomy silence, and my exhortations to good manners brought down vile insults on my head. But all this had little effect on my good-humour.

I only thought to myself: "You poor idiots! In a few weeks I'll be out, while you'll have to spend all your lives inside these walls. What do I care about your insults? You just don't exist for me!"

The change in my way of thinking showed not only in my attitude to things inside the asylum, but also in relations to matters outside. After I had wrestled with myself for two nights, and had talked the matter over thoroughly with Holz, who advised me strongly against it, I got old Herr Holsten to come, a somewhat old-fashioned lawyer, who enjoyed the greatest respect among the respectable citizens of my native town, and who had occasionally advised my firm in odd legal questions that cropped up. With him I drew up a document conferring authority on Magda by power of attorney, and I made a will in which I named Magda as my sole beneficiary. I charged the old gentleman to place the power of attorney in my wife's hands the very next day, but to deposit the will in court. This was my thanks to Magda for the beautiful way in which she had spoken of me to the medical officer. I was delighted that I could thank her in such an impressive fashion. To be sure, Holz, who at this time did not like to go about with me, groaned: "You'll regret that in a few days' time, Sommer. A moment's thought ought to tell you that you shouldn't put yourself right into another person's hands. And what for, anyway? Nobody asked you to, so why do it?"

"I've always been a generous man, Holz," I replied. "I've always had a passion for giving."

I must say that the old lawyer was very far from happy about drawing up these two documents for me. Not that he didn't agree with their content, quite the contrary.

"It's always a good thing when a man puts his house in order, Herr Sommer," he said, "and your wife is of course your nearest relative. You are facing an uncertain future. Have you already selected an advocate for your hearing, or would you like me to defend you?"

"Thank you, thank you," I said lightly. "I intend to defend myself. In any case the whole affair is just a trifle which my dear fellow townsmen have blown up far too much."

The lawyer was shocked at my "frivolity" as he called it.

"It's never a trifle," cried the old man indignantly, "when a respectable citizen has to go to prison, not just for his own sake, but particularly for the bad example it affords! Let me take on your defence, Herr Sommer, perhaps, almost certainly, I can get you bound over. Then you will avoid the dishonour of going to prison."

"My honour is my own affair," I said proudly. "Other people can't take it from me."

Smiling sadly, the old man shook his head.

"In any case this is a matter of *crime passionel*, and the consequences of such an offence are never dishonourable."

Again the old man sadly shook his head. "That kind of talk," he said, "I have heard quite frequently within such walls as these, but I would have preferred not to hear it from you. How is the district psychiatrist's report proceeding? Do you know anything about it?"

I assured him that it was all most favourable, and that the medical officer did not consider it necessary to keep me in the asylum.

"I do hope so, I hope so with all my heart," cried Herr Holsten. "Well, Herr Sommer, I must go now. And if, despite your present intentions, you need me after all, you can call me at any time. For all my years, I'm not afraid of the long journey from town to this asylum, if only I can help you."

Rather touched, I thanked him, but I was convinced that I would never require his advice, and that if I were in real need I would undoubtedly go to a younger and cleverer lawyer than he.

55

So THE next few weeks passed in relative peace and quiet, a different peace from that which I had felt before the doctor's interview, a more active peace, full of hopes and plans. I did not sleep well again, but that failed to affect my good mood: I was only a guest in this death-house. Daily I expected the indictment and the date of the hearing, and when it did not arrive, I hoped it would come the next day. In mankind, hope is indestructible, I believe the last thing that runs through the brain of a dying man is hope. The doctor never sent for me any more, I did not see him again after that interview, a sign that he had finished his report and forwarded it to the Public Prosecutor. My comrades tried in vain to make me uneasy.

"What, trust that dirty dog? He says one thing to your face and another thing on paper."

I gave a superior smile. The doctor might do something of the sort with the likes of them, but to me he had expressed himself so positively that there was no doubt whatever about a favourable result. In any case, the man was judged quite wrongly—I too had misjudged him at first. That was the fault of his overbearing and sarcastic manner, which rather repelled one. But he was a man of knowledge and insight, where he could give anyone a chance. Of course, where it was quite impossible. . . .

Just one thing had a disturbing effect about this time. The consequences of malnutrition made themselves apparent on me too, I also broke out in distressing boils. So long as

these boils—usually they were blind boils, under the skin—
appeared only on the arms and legs, it was not too bad, but
when they appeared on the nape of my neck and my back, I
suffered considerably. Particularly as I now had to lie on my
stomach of a night-time, a position in which I have never been
able to sleep. Now I joined the long file which lined up each
morning outside the medical room and was salved and lanced
and finally bandaged by the head-nurse. But even these pesti-
lential "pig-boils" could hardly damp my present high spirits.

"Once I'm out of here . . . " was the thought that occurred
to me a hundred times a day. I now began to pay more attention to my appearance, since I was to be released in such a short
time. I began to take care of my hands again, especially my
nails, which had suffered from my work. I had my hair cut and
washed my feet two or three times a week. I was particularly
concerned about my face. The bandages had come off some
time ago and my nose had healed. I had always been afraid to
look at my face, and it had been made easy for me not to, since
there was no official mirror in the asylum and shaving was done
by Lexer with the clippers. But now it was different. I knew that
Herbst, the orderly, possessed a little mirror which he constantly
used when parting his hair. Now I borrowed it from him
sometimes.

Of course he sneered: "What do you want a mirror for?
Want to look at your conk? Leave it alone, it's handsome
enough without looking at it!"

He had hit on the right reason, quite by chance, but he didn't
have to know that. I murmured something about my boils.

When I saw my nose in the mirror, I got a shock. It was
completely deformed by that bite, just before the tip there
was a deep hollow, out of which the tip rose crookedly,
marked with a flaming red scar. It looked really horrible, I
was completely disfigured. ("That damned Lobedanz. He's
the real cause of all my misfortune!")

Neither did a further examination of my face make me any happier. The consequences of starvation had marked it deeply. It was almost ash-coloured, the eyes sunken deep in their sockets. A five-day's growth of stubble covered the lower part of my face. The mirror only betrayed that in this sense too I was enrolled in the death-house: I really looked no better than its poorest ghost! No better? Worse, perhaps! and I used to be a tolerably good-looking man, accustomed to wearing a good suit from our best tailor, with style. "What have they made of you?" I said sadly to my image.

With a deep sigh I handed the mirror back to Herbst.

"What, not good-looking enough?" he asked with feigned astonishment.

"These damned boils," I complained. "If only we got something decent to eat! The carrots we had for lunch today were just plain water again! Nobody can keep healthy on that!"

With that, I had brought him round to the inexhaustible topic of this place: food, and nothing more was said of my personal appearance. Subsequently I often borrowed the orderly's mirror, but always in his absence and without asking him. At the third or fourth time, I found I had judged my appearance too unfavourably. After I had inspected myself in the mirror a few times, I found that I really looked quite tolerable. In any case, one would quickly get used to this slight disfigurement. I had got used to it, Magda would get used to it, so would my fellow townsmen, so would everybody. There were people who had been much worse disfigured in the World War, and still had married pretty women, and lived happily with them. I was absolutely convinced that this scarred nose would not interfere with my happiness with Magda.

56

I WAS soon to have the opportunity of putting this to the test. One afternoon the head-warder Fritsch entered my cell and said briefly: "Come on!"

Fritsch, a fleshy man with a rubicund face, was one of those officials to whom a man might put a question. He did not look on us merely as criminals.

"What's the matter," I asked. "Is it the doctor?"

"No," he replied. "Visit. Your wife. The medical officer's given permission for you to put civilian clothes on. Get a move on, Sommer, your wife's waiting, and I haven't much time."

He conducted me to the clothing store, where my suitcase lay on a shelf, rather lonely. Most of the patients were put in here for life and never needed civilian clothes again. Sitting on a table, the head-warder watched me as I first undressed, then dressed again. All the time he was urging me to hurry. But I couldn't go so fast. My hands trembled so much, my heart was thumping. A visit from Magda in this death-house, life had come to visit me, soon I would be with her again. . . . And a deep emotion, a boundless love for my wife filled my breast. She had come to me at last, the long time of trial was over. Love had come back to me again, and I firmly determined, at this very first meeting, to show her how deeply I loved her, that the time of our estrangement was over, and that I put myself entirely into her hands, unreservedly and with complete confidence. Suddenly something dreadful occurred to me! It was Friday and we didn't get shaved till Saturday: my stubble was in the worst possible condition!

"Sir," I cried imploringly. "Could I shave myself quickly? My shaving things are in the suitcase here. I really would be very quick. Please let me."

"Out of the question, Sommer," said Fritsch coldly. "How much time do you think I've got? Besides, you can't keep your wife waiting that long."

"But it's so important for me to make a fairly decent impression at this first meeting! Whatever will my wife think of me?"

"As far as that goes, Sommer," said Fritsch, "I don't think shaving would improve your beauty much. If your wife can put up with your nose, she should be able to stand a few bristles."

"But she's never seen my nose yet!" I cried, still more desperately. "That only happened in remand prison!"

But it was no use, Fritsch remained implacable, and I had to go with him, the saddest figure in the world, even the civilian clothes the doctor graciously allowed me, could not help much. Besides, they were completely crumpled through being in the suitcase so long.

With the warder, I enter the administration building. The corridor before me is long, gloomy and dark, my knees are shaking and I would like to lean against the wall for a minute, to rest and compose myself. But the head-warder's voice sounds peremptorily behind me: "Come on, come on, Sommer! Third door on the right!"

If only he wouldn't shout so loud and in such military fashion, Magda can hear him by now!

A hand on the knob, and the door opens! Useless to hesitate, in this life you are driven forward pitilessly.

There is no rest, no remission.

I see Magda. She has been sitting by the window, now she gets up and looks towards me. Momentarily I notice the expression of puzzled astonishment in her face. But already I hurry over to her, my arms wide open, I cry, "Magda, Magda, so you've come! I'm so thankful. . . ."

I fold her in my arms, I try to kiss her on the mouth, as in the old days, the old days that are going to come again—and I notice an expression of shuddering resistance in her face.

"Please don't," she whispers, still in my arms, suddenly almost breathless. "Not here, please!"

I have let her go, all my joy is extinguished, a cold ominous silence overtakes me. She looks at me, the expression of confused astonishment still in her face.

"I hardly recognised you," she whispers, still breathless, "what's happened to you? What's the matter with your—" she dare not say the word. . . . "What has changed you so much?"

Head-warder Fritsch is sitting on a chair behind us, and now he loudly clears his throat. I know that it is not permissible for us to stand here whispering by the window. With a pretence at light-heartedness, I say "Shan't we sit at the table here, Magda?"

We do so. Then: "You find I've changed? You don't like my looks? Well, to tell you the truth, I didn't like them either, when I saw myself quite recently in the mirror for the first time again." (I shouldn't have said that. Head-warder Fritsch may ask me later where I got the mirror from, and then I'll have got Herbst into trouble. Mirrors are forbidden in the wards. You can't be careful enough in this place!) I quickly laugh: "But one gets used to it, Magda, I don't look so bad as you think; I've got better rather than worse. . . ." At these last words, into which I put deep meaning, I have noticeably lowered my voice. But Magda takes no notice.

"What's the matter with your—nose?"

At last she manages to utter the word, even if only after a brief hesitation.

"It looks really bad, Erwin."

"A fellow-prisoner tried to bite it off, while we were still in the remand prison," I explain. "It was that Lobedanz who stole your silverware, you know, Magda."

She only looks at me, with a slight twitch of the mouth. Perhaps I shouldn't have said that, either; perhaps Magda thinks it was I who stole her silverware in the first place. But no, she can't think anything so stupid and unjust, the silver was bought out of my own money, so it was my silver, one can't speak of theft in such a case.

"I tried to get it back for you, but unfortunately without success. You haven't heard any more about it, Magda?"

She shakes her head as if it were all quite unimportant.

"You're changed in other ways, Erwin," she maintains. "Your voice sounds quite different, much louder. . . ."

"There's fifty-six of us in one block, Magda," I explain. "Over thirty men eat in the one room with me, so you have to strain your voice a bit if you want to make yourself understood."

"I see."

She smiles weakly, defensively.

"You lead a very changed life, don't you, considering you were always so much for keeping to yourself."

But again, with irritating obstinacy, she returns to my appearance, she can't get over it.

"But you really look bad, Erwin. Is anything the matter?"

"Nothing," I say deliberately. "Practically nothing. A few boils, look, I've got some on my neck here, and on my back . . . but one gets used to them, everyone in this place has them . . ." (Head-warder Fritsch clears his throat warningly. Perhaps this is unseemly criticism of the institution. But I would not dream of taking any notice of that.)

I continue, "And if I look thin and rather grey, well, Magda, we don't get roast goose and red cabbage here every day. Generally we're fed on good hot water...."

Now my rage has run away with me, rage over the rejection of my love, over Magda's horror of me: I speak with a voice trembling with scorn, I want to wound her to the heart, since I cannot move it. Head-warder Fritsch says threateningly: "One more remark like that, Sommer, and I'll break this visit up and report you."

Magda turns to him: "Oh, please don't be cross with him! You can't imagine how changed he is. He must have been having a terrible time!"

Her voice trembles, I listen to this weakening feminine voice with greedy delight.

"A little while ago he was a fine good-looking man—and now I wouldn't have known him in the street!"

A few tears well up from the depths of her eyes and run slowly down her cheeks. I note them with delight. No, they do not move me. Nothing can soften my heart now, she has offended me too deeply! But I enjoy seeing her suffer too: she ought to be made to feel, and at last she does feel, what she has done to me, how seriously she has harmed me with her spying and her talk, what a fate she has brought down on my head. Magda continues, in almost feverish agitation, half turned to the head-warder, half to me: "But I can send you what you need, Erwin! If only I had known! May I send him a parcel of things to eat, Herr——?"

"That's quite in order, Frau Sommer," says Fritsch graciously. "Tobacco is allowed too. A great many things are allowed here—But," he continues and looks at Magda, blinking out of his fat face, "you must remember many of these patients really don't know when they've had enough. They eat and eat—a whole parcel, two loaves in one day! And then they're ill and we have trouble with them. You mustn't believe everything the patients tell you."

And I have to sit quiet and listen to this common liar. The fat Fritsch is my superior, I dare not contradict him. I think of the figures of starvation back there, who eat potato peelings and lick off the table every drop of spilt gravy, and my rage rises within me again. But I control myself, I quickly say with a smile: "Thank you very much for your good intentions, Magda, but I really don't need anything. Head-warder Fritsch is quite right: the patients don't know when to stop. But thank the Lord I don't belong among them. Please God I'll soon be out of here. . . . "

Magda looks at me in confusion.

"But you yourself just spoke about getting water, Erwin . . . " she said.

"I spoke about roast goose," I laughed, "and I only mentioned water as a contrast. No, no, Magda, think no more of it, we get quite sufficient to eat, as Herr Fritsch has explained. After all, I'm not doing any heavy work, I make brushes, Magda, I've become a real brush-maker. Can you imagine that, Magda? You're sitting in my chair in the office, and your husband is making brushes in the meantime. Isn't there a song about the happy brush-maker? Oh, no, it's a happy soap-boiler. But I'm happy and cheerful, brush-making in my cell. I whistle and sing all day, well, no, I don't really, of course, because in this place where such a great many things are allowed, that is forbidden. But inwardly I whistle and sing. . . . "

I have been speaking faster and more sarcastically all the time, I am carried away with anger, but I manage to control myself. Outwardly, everything looks calm and peaceful. I notice the growing perplexity in Magda's face; during my words she has occasionally used her handkerchief and wiped her eyes. Fritsch has been leaning back in his chair, with a bored expression, counting the flies on the ceiling. He is much too coarse-witted to detect the ironical undertone in my words. Incidentally, Magda is wearing a costume which I do not recognise: a very smart dark-grey costume with a light pin-stripe. I reflect bitterly how my very own wife, while I am suffering beyond measure, has time and leisure to think of a new costume, to go to the dressmaker, to have fittings. . . . So unjustly is fortune shared out, so thoughtless are even the best of wives! By the way, Magda is looking very well, during the period of our separation she has considerably improved, she looks decidedly pretty. While I, during this time. . . .

57

AFTER my swift ironical words, a deep silence ensues. I am in no hurry to break it. Magda fidgets rather uneasily in her chair, I am waiting for what she will say next. But when she begins to speak it is only to thank me for the power of attorney.

"I don't really need it. Neither the post office nor the bank have made the slightest trouble about my signature. But I understand what you meant, Erwin, and I want to thank you for your good opinion of me." She reaches her hand to me across the table, and I take it coolly and cautiously, being careful not to press it warmly. The hand returns somewhat disappointed to its owner.

"And how's business?" I ask, just for something to say.

But Magda livens up.

"I'm happy to be able to tell you, Erwin, that business is going well. Yes, remarkably well. The harvest turned out quite satisfactorily, and we did well out of it. Particularly with peas and beans, I had unbelievable luck. I bought just before the price suddenly went up. . . . "

For a while we go on quietly talking about the business. Really, quite incontestably, an efficient woman. How her eyes light up, how lively her voice becomes, as she speaks of it! Her eyes did not light up before, when it concerned her husband. But it was always like that with her: the business, the garden, the house, everything was more important than her husband. I might have been jealous of these inanimate things,

had it not been somewhat ridiculous. But perhaps not so ridiculous as this efficiency which the doctor found so praiseworthy,
too. If only she could think a bit more rationally, she wouldn't
go to all that trouble, she would lease the business for a small
income and live comfortably on our property. But of course
such a thing wouldn't occur to a woman of her kind.

So my thoughts ran on, while I listened absent-mindedly to
Magda's eager chatter, which awakened memories of old
clients, of drives through off-the-track villages, of lucky deals.
. . . But suddenly I prick my ears up, for Magda has mentioned
our rival, the young beginner who had set up in my native
town in defiance of myself, and had already given me some
trouble on two or three occasions. Am I mistaken, or does a
special undertone creep into Magda's voice, something warmer
than hitherto? I listen very attentively to what Magda is saying.
"Yes, just think, Erwin, I've got to know Herr Heinze personally. One day I got so angry about our constantly undercutting each other just for the sake of snatching a few customers, and we were both losing by it. So I simply went to
his office and said: 'Herr Heinze, I'm Frau Sommer, can't we
try to come to some sensible arrangement? There's a living for
both our firms in this town, but if we go on undercutting
each other, we'll both end up bankrupt!' That's what I
told him."
Magda looks at me triumphantly.
"And what did he say?" I ask eagerly.
"Well," she says, and again I detect the warm undertone in
her voice, "Herr Heinze is not only an educated man, he is
intelligent as well. In five minutes we had come to an understanding. Every morning, midday and evening, we inform
each other of the prices we're paying, neither offers a
groschen more or less, and poaching customers is completely
abolished!"

"Oh, you innocent!" I cry, "he'll land you properly in the cart. That Heinze is just a cunning double-dyed rogue. Naturally he'd say nothing to your face, but behind your back he's pinching your customers one after the other. Eventually he'll have the whole business in his hands, and you'll be left with nothing!"

"Poor Erwin," says Magda, "still so full of suspicions. No, I've got to know Herr Heinze really well. I meet him socially sometimes. . . ."

I wondered what lay behind that "socially sometimes" but Magda did not blush. She continued: "I know enough about human nature to be able to say: Herr Heinze is a thoroughly upright, decent man, whom I would trust blindly. And if you think me too trusting, Erwin, perhaps our books would be sufficient proof. We've increased our turnover by half as much again this autumn. That would hardly be the case if Herr Heinze had been snapping up our customers!"

She looked at me triumphantly, her eyes shining with joy. I said icily, "The figures on their own prove nothing. You say the harvest was good and the weather particularly favourable for early crops, so the turnover might well improve for a short time and you could still be losing customers. . . . By the way I can't remember, wasn't this Heinze married?"

"Certainly," Magda nodded. "But he was divorced a year ago."

"Is that so?" I answered, as indifferently as possible. "Divorced—of course, she divorced him?"

"How can you say such a thing," cried Magda, almost furiously. "I told you just now he's a highly respectable man. Of course the blame was on the other side!"

"Of course . . . " I repeated, rather sarcastically. "Pardon me, but you seem quite thrilled about this fellow, Magda!"

For a moment she hesitated, then she answered in a firm voice: "Yes, I am, Erwin!"

We looked at each other for a long time in silence. Many unsaid things were in the air. Even head-warder Fritsch had noticed something, he had leaned forward on his chair, his elbows propped on his knees, and watched us both expectantly. Incidentally, the usual visiting-time was over long ago.

58

"HAVE you already started divorce proceedings?" I finally asked, in a low voice.

"Yes," she answered just as softly.

Again a deep silence fell between us. Suddenly we both looked round at head-warder Fritsch, who got up from his chair with a jerk and rattled his keys.

"Well," he said, almost embarrassed, "visiting-time is up by rights, but as far as I'm concerned, you can have ten minutes more." And he went over to the window where he ostentatiously turned his back on us.

"Erwin," whispered Magda hastily, "I had a long struggle with myself, it seemed so wrong to leave you in such a position; but then when I heard from the medical officer that your case was going all right, and that you would probably be let out in a short time. . . ."

She looked at me imploringly, but I was silent. I did not help her with a single word. I was possessed by a wild and furious rage.

"We can arrange everything as you like, Erwin," Magda continued still more hastily. "If you want to take over the business, all right. We're ready to move away from here, too. Heinrich, I mean Heinze, will make over his business to you, too. Don't look at me like that, Erwin, it won't help! Inside ourselves we've been quite estranged for a long time, think of that horrible time when we were always quarrelling! It's better if we part. . . . "

I was still silent; so that was the reason for the new costume, the fresh colours, the warm trembling undertone in her voice. A new man—and already the amorous little pigeon starts to coo. The husband is clapped into gaol, and along comes the other one, the upright one, the highly respectable one, whom she blindly trusts. I looked intently at her white neck, already becoming a little fat. Her throat moved, touched by her own words, the good woman swallowed her tears, as they say. I would so much have liked to span that throat with my two hands, and I swear I would not have let go again, for all the Fritsches! But I kept a tight hold of myself, only a few days separated me from freedom. It wasn't only her I meant to get, there was the other one, the highly respectable one, who had the effrontery to steal the wife of a sick man! She still went on looking at me, and now when she began to speak, the tone of her voice had grown colder, she was no longer imploring. A line of determination, of hardness even, was about her mouth.

"You're looking at me all the time and not saying a word," she resumed. "I can see a threat of something dreadful in your eyes. But that won't deter me, nothing can deter me. For once in my life I want to know happiness. I've sacrificed so many years for you, for your meanness, your obstinacy, your stupid conceit and misanthropy, and above all what you call your love. A funny kind of love, that I only get to feel when you have demands to make—but I never dare to make any! No, I've had enough of it. . . . "

She would probably have gone on talking but I had had enough of it too, of her tirade, I mean. After failing to lure me with sweetness, she was going to crush me with hatred. I leaned far over the table and spat right into her face.

"Adultress!" I cried.

At this loud exclamation, head-warder Fritsch turned from

the window and stared in utter amazement for a moment at the scene confronting him: I, leaning across the table gazing at Magda contemptuously, threateningly, and my former wife, who made no move to wipe away the spittle that ran down her deadly pale cheek, returning my gaze steadfastly from the very depths of her brown eyes. And as we stared at each other in this way, it seemed to me as if I penetrated deeply into this woman with my gaze, sank right into her for a fraction of a second, and encountered a being I had never known. . . .

Then it was all over, for head-warder Fritsch had seized me by the shoulder and began to shake me furiously.

"You insolent swine!" he shouted. "What do you think you're doing? I'll report you to the medical officer! That's a respectable woman, d'you understand?"

And he shook me again with all his strength, so that my head rolled loosely from side to side.

"Let the man go, warder," said Magda, in a deep, utterly exhausted voice. "He's perfectly right: I am an adultress."

She paused for a moment as if in thought, then she turned to me, her eyes lit up again, her voice was ringing once more.

"And I'm glad I did it!" she said in my face.

Then she went slowly out of the visiting room wiping her face at last, though only mechanically.

59

How I got through the night after that dreadful meeting, I cannot say. I did not sleep for a minute, of that I am sure. That night I was utterly crushed and would have put an end to all my misery, had not the thought of revenge sustained me. And I intended to have my revenge down to the smallest detail, not merely after my release but immediately, by tomorrow I would set my plans in motion. I would engage a smart young lawyer and I would cross-petition in the divorce case, Sommer versus Sommer, and I would name Magda as the guilty party. Hadn't I a witness, head-warder Fritsch, before whom she herself had admitted her adultery? Oh, I would give Magda every reason to regret that rash confession, and I had good grounds for hoping that that highly respectable and successful business-man Herr Heinrich Heinze would not be sparing of his reproaches about it either. Furthermore, I would lodge an application that the divorce court judge should forbid the two adulterous parties ever to marry each other. Oh, she would get to know the sort of happiness she longed for, under my whip. I would sell up the business and follow on their heels all the time, a constant avenging angel. I would never weary of it. If I was a bad partner in love, as Magda had suddenly discovered, I'd be so much the worse in hatred. And I pictured to myself how, on my travels, I would sleep in the next hotel room to theirs, and disturb their sleep with furtive knocking. I saw myself, unrecognisably disguised, getting into the same railway compartment, and watching everything they did from behind my dark glasses; I was driving a car immediately behind them, and only put my brakes on at the very last moment so as to gloat over their fear of death, and, the most beautiful of all my images of revenge, I saw her dying, murdered by me, but undetectably, and he was kneeling at her side, abandoned to utter despair, and I stood behind him and whispered in his ear what I had done, but of course it was undetectable—I raved, the images chased each other through my brain, I was feverish. My companions had long since fallen asleep and I still stood at the cell-window, spinning the web of my revenge ever tighter and more tangled, in the cold glitter of the stars.

Morning came, and found me empty and almost completely apathetic. I must have eaten my breakfast with the others, but I remember nothing of it. Before the working-parties fell in, I availed myself of an unguarded moment to slip over into my work-cell. The sight of my fellow-sufferers disgusted me. I seized a few bristles between two fingers and tried to insert them into the hole, but I had taken too many, as I had when I was first beginning. I let them fall carelessly to the ground and went over to the cupboard. By now I had writing-paper and envelopes in it, I ought to write the letter to the lawyer. But however urgent it had appeared to me in the night, I could not bring myself to it now. I stared at the paper for a while, then went to the window. Outside autumn was drawing on already—swaths of grey mist drifted across the countryside, I saw the first early potato-pickers among the rows. "Autumn is coming," I said to myself. "That's bad." I did not know myself what I meant. I only knew that I was in a bad way, very bad. Two lines from a poem I once read, ran through my head: "This is the autumn, it will break your heart."

Obstinately, they returned, they kept returning with a desperate obstinacy.

"This is the autumn, it will break your heart." Two words tacked themselves on: "Fly away! Fly away!"

Yes, to be able to fly away from this soiled world, from this unclean "I"! And again and again: "This is the autumn, it will break your heart," and again the echoing warning: "Fly away! Fly away!"

I looked across at the stout knife with which I levelled-off the bristles. It would be such an easy matter to cut my arm so that I bled to death. But I knew I would never have the courage to do it. For I was cowardly, at this moment I confessed to myself without reserve, that I was a coward; when Magda was enumerating my faults, she had forgotten that one.

"Fly away!" And still too cowardly....

So the head-nurse found me. He had missed me from among those who came to be bandaged. He spoke sharply to me: my boils would never get better unless I took care to have them dressed regularly! Completely indifferent, I followed him to the medical room. The stream of patients had gone away, I was the last. The head-nurse tore off my dressings, applied ointment and iodine, and lanced a boil which seemed to him to be ripe. Sensitive as I usually am to pain, this morning I took no notice at all. I was completely dulled. Then the telephone rang in the glass box. The head-nurse went away, leaving the door wide open. For a moment I stood motionless, then my gaze sought the medicine-chest, whose door stood open also. I took a quick step towards it. There lay many hours of oblivion, release from the unbearable torture in which I was living now, the means to good peace-giving sleep for days on end. My hand was grasping a small glass tube, when my glance fell on a row of bottles that stood on the lowest shelf. Right in front stood a half-filled bottle with the label: Alcohol 95%. I had made no decision, I acted quite mechanically. I did not bother at all about the open door, or the head-nurse who was bound to return at any moment. I took the bottle and went to the wash-basin that was let into the wall. I took a tumbler and poured out two-thirds of a glass of alcohol, then very carefully I filled it up with water. My hand did not shake. I put the potent mixture to my mouth and drank it down in three or four gulps. For a moment I stood as if stunned, an immense brightness spread rapidly within me. I smiled, ah, that happiness, again that wonderful boundless happiness. My Elinor, my *reine d'alcool*! How I love you! How —I—love—you! Senseless, I fell forward to the floor, flat on my disfigured face.

60

My case was never heard. The proceedings against me were suspended under Paragraph 51 and my permanent detention in an asylum was ordered. The divorce case was heard, however, but it was not necessary for me to be present, for by now I was certified. One of the chief secretaries, over in the asylum administration, has been made my guardian. Incidentally, both Magda and I were decreed guilty, but Magda was allowed to marry her Heinrich Heinze, my petition never came up for consideration. I am only a lunatic. I saw the announcement of their wedding in the newspaper. They have two children now, a boy and a girl; they have merged the two businesses—but what has that to do with me? What has the outside world to do with me? I don't care about anything. I'm just an ageing, repulsive-looking brush-maker, of moderate proficiency, insane. The initial period of raging desperation is over. I gave up long ago the notion of putting my arm under the knife and trying whether I might, just for one minute of my life, be courageous. I know that every single second of my life I have been a coward, I am a coward, I shall go on being a coward. Useless to expect anything else.

I enjoy a certain degree of trust in this place, I cause no trouble, I make no work, I keep myself apart from the others. I can move about the place fairly freely. Only I am never allowed to enter the medical room unless the head-nurse is there, under pain of eight weeks in the punishment cells. I would often like to, I could do so occasionally, but I dare not. I am just a coward.

I am quite comfortably off, I always have enough to smoke and never suffer from hunger. Twice a week my guardian does my shopping, out of the money which my former wife regularly pays in on my behalf. He buys me whatever I want that is permissible. I can never use up all the money that is paid in, I shall die a wealthy man. I have no idea to whom the money will go, and I am not interested. The will I had previously drawn up was made invalid by the divorce, and I cannot make a new one, I am insane of course. But I am not so insane, and have not grown so apathetic, that I haven't still a plan and a little hope. Of course, I have had to give up all thoughts of the knife, but I can endure, I am able to bear whatever may befall me. I am, if I may say so without presumption, a great sufferer.

I have not previously mentioned the fact that on the ground floor of the annexe we have five or six tubercular patients, who are isolated from us. They get rather better and richer food and need do no more work until they die. These patients have little flasks in which to expectorate, and their isolation is not so strict that I, who am allowed to move about the place quite freely, cannot sometimes get hold of these flasks. I just drink them. I have already drunk three of these little flasks, and I shall drink more of them.

No, I do not intend to grow very old in this place and slowly rot away, I want to die a kind of death which anyone outside might die—a death of my own choosing.

I am certain that I already have tuberculosis. I have constant stabbing pains in my chest, and I cough a great deal, but I do not report this to the doctor, I conceal my illness; I want to become so ill first, that I cannot be saved in any circumstances. And then, once I am lying in the annexe and my last hour is near, I will have the doctor come to me and I will say to him, "Doctor, I have caused you much pain and anger, and you have never been able to forgive me, that on my account the report you had prepared was annulled, by reason of which your reputation as a psychiatrist suffered in the eyes of the court. But now that my end is near, forgive me, and do me one last favour," and he will make his peace with me, because I am a dying man and one does not refuse anything to a dying man, and he will ask what that favour is.

And I shall say to him: "Doctor, go to the medical room and mix me with your own hands a drink of alcohol and water, just a tumblerful. Not of a kind which will make me unconscious immediately so that I have no benefit from it, as before, but one that will make me really happy again."

And he will accede to my wish and return to my bedside with the glass, and I will drink, at last after so many years of privation I will drink, gulp by gulp, at long intervals, savouring my endless happiness to the full. And I will become young again, and I will see the world blossoming, all the springtimes and the roses and the young girls from time past. But one will approach me and lean her pale face over me, who have fallen on my knees before her, and she will enshroud me with her dark hair. Her perfume will be about me and her lips laid on mine and I will no longer be old and disfigured, but young and beautiful, and my *reine d'alcool* will draw me up to her and we will soar into intoxication and forgetfulness from which there is never any awakening!

And if it happens thus in the hour of my death, I shall bless my life, and I shall not have suffered in vain.

STRELITZ,
6.9.44—21.9.44.